The Magnolia Triangle

DOGWOOD
PRESS

The
Magnolia
Triangle

BY
JOE LEE

*FOR NANCY—
BEST WISHES,
JOE LEE*

DOGWOOD
PRESS

Library of Congress Control Number
2009933445

Printed in the United States of America

Jacket design by Bill Wilson
Author photo of Joe Lee by Leslie Lee
First Dogwood Press edition: October, 2009

DOGWOOD PRESS
P.O. Box 5958 • Brandon, MS 39047
www.dogwoodpress.com

For Leslie and John. And for Rose.

Acknowledgments

My wife Leslie and son John continue to be wonderful sources of support and encouragement. Leslie again answered my countless legal questions and never once threw me out of the house. Sam Williford, also an attorney, painted a vivid picture of the practice of law in a very small town. Jason Roberts did the same thing regarding small-town law enforcement. Their contributions, because of the crimes involved in this novel, cannot be overstated.

In addition, my old TV chum Wayne Carter advised me on how a local story involving a professional athlete could quickly gain traction and become national news. Dr. Steven Zackow patiently answered my questions about the devastating effects when alcohol and anti-depressants are mixed. And Joseph and Marilyn Lee, my father and stepmother, were my real estate consultants and helped me construct a key background element of this novel.

My sincere thanks to Cindy McCraw-Dircks, Duke Denton, Andy Smith, Bruce Coleman, Barbara Coats, Melissa Williams, Cindy Raper, Jeanie Ables, David and Leigh Wright, Donna Biggert, and fellow authors Louisa Dixon and John Floyd for reading early drafts of this novel and providing me with honest, detailed feedback. All of you are worth your weight in gold. The same is true of my friend Bill Wilson, a good guy and a fantastic graphic designer.

My mother, Rose Reynolds Finley, passed away in 2000 and did not live to see the publication of my first novel, *On The Record.* But given that I actually began writing *The Magnolia Triangle* nearly 20 years ago, she is also among those who read a very early draft—back when it was certainly a manuscript "only a mother could love." Remembering Mom in this way is the next best thing to presenting her with a copy of this book.

The Magnolia Triangle

James Bryan drove north on Route 505 and passed the crumbling Victorian home where the crazy Oakdale cop murdered that nice old couple last winter. The house stood empty, the for-sale sign still in the front yard after the busy buying season had come and gone. He wondered if Sherry Rutledge or whoever listed the property even showed it any more. It could be fixed up, then converted into an apartment building and would seem the ideal rental investment with the university ten minutes away and loads of grad students who longed for quiet places to live and study. He was financially able to take the risk and might consider doing so if he wasn't contemplating suicide.

One mistake. For which he would apparently pay the rest of his life.

He cruised along in his Toyota pickup and watched his speed after spotting a sheriff's deputy between Oakdale and Hampton Falls. He knew the roads would be packed with law enforcement on Independence Day weekend and figured he'd see a million cops and highway patrolmen before he got where he was going. But was he in such a hurry to die after all if he was worried about getting a ticket? Thoughts of City Park, though, swiftly reinforced his almost maniacal need to split town. Like nearly every other Oakdale family, the Bryans went to the park each July fourth for the annual patriotic concert from the Oakdale symphony and the spectacular fireworks display. Melanie and the kids would naturally assume they were going tonight, but James would be long gone by then.

He pulled into a rest stop just before the ramp to the interstate. It was empty, thankfully, and he parked and climbed out. He grimaced at the stifling July humidity and felt his back pop when he stretched. Cicadas sang high in the towering pines, the way they did in his backyard on Peachtree Street. A bobwhite called out in the distance. He inspected a pair of cement picnic tables and a ragged pavilion that looked as weather-beaten as the poor Victorian back up the road. Then he moped to the closest table, heaved himself onto it, and stared out at the lonesome two-lane highway. He removed his cell phone from his belt and punched buttons until it was off. He was tempted to hurl it into the woods, but he wasn't going to do that out here. Nor was he going to blow his head off anywhere in Smart County.

His clothing store on the town square was closed for the holiday. He'd told Melanie at breakfast that he needed to run up there and do some last-minute paperwork, make sure everything was red-tagged correctly for the after-the-fourth blowout sale this weekend. The preparation was already taken care of, of course, and he simply booted up his computer and e-mailed a reminder to his managers that he and Melanie and Keller and Holly were headed to Chicago for vacation. He'd planted the seed yesterday and was assured by his team that everything would run smoothly in his absence. He didn't doubt it would.

He'd returned home an hour ago and was prepared to lie right to Melanie's face about the phony trip, but she wasn't there: A note on the kitchen counter explained that she had taken Holly to breakfast at McDonald's and would drop by the bookstore afterward to work on inventory. Their son Keller had his own place after starting college a year ago, which allowed James to make his decision in the quiet of the empty house. He grabbed clothes, toiletries and his Colt .45 and threw them in a duffle bag. He scribbled his own note, describing a fictitious e-mail from a rep with a major clothing line based in Chicago: The man, James said, planned to pull their distribution from small stores all over the region, and the only way to save this crucial account, James felt, was a face-to-face meeting. He left the note in the kitchen, apologized for being away from his family on the holiday, and promised to call soon.

He wiped sweat from his forehead and looked up when a log truck rolled past. Jack Rutledge had taken this path to the interstate six years ago before slamming into a granite restraining wall in a construction zone north of Memphis. Jack was survived by Sherry and their daughters Nancy and Caitlyn, and Sherry still lived three houses away. Although the death was officially ruled an accident, James and everybody else knew better. Had Jack stopped at this very spot and taken one last look around, or did he motor as fast as he could to his death? And had Jack spotted the wall on a business trip and made a mental note of where he wanted to die, or was he speeding away from his shambles of a life—as James was about to do now—and made his own life-ending decision in a split-second?

James wasn't sure he would ever see these old woods again, let alone hunt and fish in them. The same was true of his many Oakdale friends as well as Melanie and his beloved children. He knew all too well how cowardly and selfish the decision to take his life would be, if he actually went through with it. Although Keller was a mature young man of nineteen, eight-year-old Holly would grow up without a father. Melanie's life would be turned upside down, too. How would she survive as a single parent, let alone run an independently-owned bookstore?

But he just couldn't live with the pressure any more, not one more day. And being confronted in front of everyone at City Park tonight was more than his mind could handle. He climbed off the bench and trudged back to his truck.

It was time to go.

TWO

McCullough Boulevard in Tupelo was hardly Beale Street in Memphis, but the city's major thoroughfare was packed with cars, sport utilities, and four-by-four pickups. Keller Bryan sat in the passenger seat of his girlfriend's Jeep Cherokee and watched the traffic as Caitlyn Rutledge inched along. The Jeep was filled with frosty air and the sound of a brokenhearted female on the area country station. It was absolutely blistering outside, with humidity that would linger well after sunset. They'd gone to City Park last night for the fireworks, and the mosquitoes and heat were so bad that he and Caitlyn and his little sister Holly and their mother Melanie stayed in the Jeep and enjoyed the air-conditioning. Keller's father James would have insisted on being outdoors after spraying a cloud of insect repellent on all of them, but he was on the road.

"Oh, that's just great," Caitlyn said. "I left my cell phone at Mother's."

"Thought I saw it on your coffee table…"

"No, I went and snooped while she and Nancy were at Joan's funeral. Had it with me, and I know I left it there." Caitlyn turned to him with a raised eyebrow. "Have I even told you about the will?"

"Joan's?"

"Yes. You know she died Tuesday. But Mike told me

that last weekend he was going through her file cabinet for an insurance policy or something, and found a *revision*," Caitlyn said, almost spitting the word. "You won't believe this."

They eased past the apparent source of the logjam. Two police cars were flanking a ratty pickup, and Keller saw a pair of officers giving the business to three greasy-looking, shirtless men sitting atop the tailgate. The flashing strobes were powerful even in the bright sunlight. Wanting to avoid an instant headache, he turned away from the cops and the would-be criminals and saw that traffic was now moving smoothly. They would be at the pizzeria before long.

"Joan inherited a lot of money when her folks died," Caitlyn continued. "She's divorced, and everything was to be split evenly between Mike and his brother. They're on good terms."

"He's in, like, St. Louis, right?" Keller said. "Shouldn't Mike get a little extra, seeing how he and Nancy moved her in and he was basically her caretaker the last few months?"

"That part's none of my business. But they divorced years ago, and Mike said everything was in order. He could tell someone had been rooting around in the file cabinet, though, and he didn't see how it was his mother—she was too weak to even get out of bed by then and had round-the-clock sitters from hospice. He said they would have told him if she'd been on her feet."

"One of them do it?"

"What I thought. But Mike said no. He discovered a new heir in the will."

There was something in Caitlyn's tone, and Keller turned to her. She was watching the road as she talked and eased around a laboring old car as she picked up speed.

"Nancy," she said.

"*What?*"

"Way it reads now, she and Mike split the money and

property, and the brother is completely out in the cold. No way in hell they'll get away with it—when I say *they*, I mean she and Mother, because you know she's in on it. But the new will has phony signatures from all parties including Joan, and now Mike and his brother will have to fight in court. Mike said he decided to wait until after the funeral to tell his brother, because his brother never liked Nancy and would be angry enough to put out a hit on her. Didn't want a huge scene when they were burying Joan."

"Then has Mike even talked to Nancy about this?"

"Not yet," Caitlyn said. "He wanted to throw her off their balcony. But he decided, with his mother just having a few days left, to lay her to rest, *then* talk to his brother and get their ducks in a row. They both stand to inherit four hundred grand, so we're not talking about pocket change."

Keller shook his head slowly. Caitlyn's brother-in-law, Mike Morgan, was a broadcast meteorologist and did the weather each morning on the station in Tupelo. Keller had met Mike and found him as down-to-earth a celebrity as one could hope to meet. Caitlyn had tremendous respect for him after the way he'd cared for his dying mother in recent months.

"Nancy'll probably tell everyone she played Florence Nightingale while Mike advanced his career, and nothing could be further from the truth—you could almost feel Nancy waiting for that sweet old lady to die so she'd have her house back," Cailtyn said. "More I thought about it, madder I got. Going over to Mother's with them down in Jackson at the funeral was a nifty idea, but I spent two fruitless hours trying to get on Mother's computer and find a paper trail."

"And you left your phone there," Keller said.

"Which means I have to go back. That won't be fun. But I'd give anything for some evidence they designed and planted this bogus will, and ditto for that crap I'm certain she and

Doug Cockrell are pulling on Angie. She told me about it over breakfast. Talk about a web of corruption."

Angie Bartman was the assistant basketball coach at the university and had recruited Caitlyn, now an all-SEC power forward, at Oakdale High School. Angie was about thirty and played briefly in the WNBA before going into coaching. She and Caitlyn were all business on the basketball court but like sisters away from the sport, and nobody, Keller knew, was more loyal to those she cared about than Caitlyn. But if you got on her bad side, look out below.

"See, Ang bought her house three years ago and listed it when she decided to buy a condo," Caitlyn said. "Doug Cockrell, who appraised it back then, did it this time, too—Oakdale only has one home appraiser, which is a racket in itself. And somehow, despite a new roof, and new construction in the neighborhood, the appraisal price fell. Didn't just drop, babe, it *plummeted*. And because Angie's realtor told her that Doug's second appraisal would be a formality—which it should have been—they ended up signing a contract with the buyer before they had the appraisal. And it was late and turned out to be real low. By law, the buyer can buy the home for the appraised price, and it ended up costing Angie fifteen grand."

"How could that happen?" Keller said. "The low appraisal, I'm talking about."

"What we all want to know. Not only will Doug not talk, he won't even show Angie's realtor the report. Just said he missed some things the first time."

"Like what? What do you miss when you're appraising a house?"

Caitlyn stopped behind a carload of teens at a traffic light. Keller counted six kids packed inside an Oldsmobile and would have bet everything he owned they were drinking.

"Nobody knows," she said with a sigh. "Angie's fit to be

tied, but all she can do is pay through the nose to hire another appraiser, probably somebody from here in Tupelo, who'd drive to Oakdale and do his own survey and all that. Assuming that one turns out like it should, it would be averaged with Doug's. And Angie would still take a bath because the buyer can buy at the *averaged* appraisal price. But that's not the half of it. The buyer's realtor is—ready for this?—Mother."

Keller felt his shoulders slump. Sherry Rutledge, the mother of the girl he knew in his heart he would marry one day, was a despicable person. Her desire for money, status, and power was apparently hard-wired into older daughter Nancy, who babysat Keller long ago. Nancy, it sounded like, had attended the funeral of her mother-in-law this afternoon while preparing to steal nearly half a million dollars from the Morgan estate. If true, it was one of the most nakedly brazen displays of greed he'd ever heard of. And to think he'd once been in love with Nancy from afar in his early teens.

"That was another reason to snoop," Caitlyn said. "I mean, with Vince Cockrell as their attorney and his lame-brained son Doug as the home appraiser, Mother and Nancy, being the realtors that they are, are probably up to their necks in ill-gotten gains from Kickback City, USA. But this time, my darling, they picked the wrong dog to mess with."

Keller wasn't sure if Caitlyn was referring to Angie, herself, Mike Morgan, or all three of them. He frowned when she hit her blinker and pulled into the parking lot of the Hampton Inn.

"What are we doing here?"

Caitlyn didn't reply as she steered past the front lobby. She wound to the back side of the three-story hotel and seemed to survey the scene. They'd passed the pool, which was on the south side of the structure, and Keller saw a young mom and dad with a trio of little kids in bathing suits with towels and little plastic face masks and snorkels. The sight brought a smile to his face and reminded him of Holly, who was eight. At the other end was a dumpster, and beyond that, a dilapidated wood fence that shielded the motel from a convenience store. Keller watched as Caitlyn backed the Jeep into a parking spot and cut the engine.

"Now then," she said as she slapped his thigh. "What's happening in Oakdale this weekend?"

"Nothing, now that the Fourth is done."

"Nancy and Brad's tenth high-school reunion."

"That's right—"

"Remember Roger Conrad, year behind us in high school?"

"Sure," Keller said. "What about him?"

"Works in sports information at the school, and there's no bigger Brad Valentine fan, babe. He told Angie today that Brad promised to get him an internship with the Atlanta Braves in exchange for a quiet place to stay when Brad comes home and doesn't want to get mobbed by his adoring hometown fans. And Roger, turns out, has a contact at this very hotel."

There was a little grin on Caitlyn's pretty face. Keller smiled back stupidly, knowing he wasn't seeing something right in front of him.

"Ang and I had breakfast this morning," she said. "I told her about the reunion after she filled me in on the crap with her house. Then I told her about Nancy and the Morgan estate. We both pretty much hated Nancy and Mother's guts by the time we walked out of McDonald's. And we both had a hunch that Brad, even though the Braves are in St. Louis this weekend, would be coming to town."

"For the reunion."

"In a manner of speaking," Caitlyn said. Her grin broadened. "I told Ang she oughta go butter up the hard-working little sports information guy, see what fell when she shook the tree." Caitlyn shielded her eyes from the sun and pointed back toward the pool.

"See that black Navigator way down there? That would be Brad."

"Whoa," Keller said quietly. "You know the room number?"

"Angie felt she'd be pushing her luck and didn't ask. But since that's Nancy's Beamer next to it, bet they're in one of those rooms down there." Caitlyn reached into the backseat for her purse. Her digital camera was in hand a second later. "The vigil begins."

THREE

Eddie Ray Chester stood on the patio of his mother's home and drank beer as he gazed at the pink, twilit sky. Beads of condensation from the outside of the bottle dripped between his fingers while droplets of sweat trickled from his temples. He thought about what a rotten joke life was at times and wanted to heave the bottle as far as he could, see how high up in the pines he could throw it.

Daphne was pregnant.

His father Blake was a dry-wall specialist and a tobacco-chewing, foulmouthed man who eked out a living for his family and proudly hung the Mississippi Confederate flag in the front window of their trailer. His mother Monica, a grocery cashier with an eighth grade education, was a kind person but from the same side of the tracks—she belched and broke wind right along with her husband and couldn't care less when people laughed at her hick ways and ragtag wardrobe. Eddie Ray had a smattering of friends growing up, but he was painfully aware at school that REDNECK LOSER was pretty much stamped on his forehead for all to see.

Blake was killed in a construction accident the day Eddie Ray turned twenty-three. Monica sued the contractor, alleging that his cost-cutting ways led to an unsafe work environment and the resulting roof collapse, and the jury awarded her a seven-figure settlement when a former partner of the contractor verified the shoddiness in court. With more money than she ever needed safely in the bank, Monica sold the trailer and bought a sizable home on a tree-lined street in one of Oakdale's classy, older neighborhoods. She upgraded from her ancient Pinto to a Lexus and bought new clothes. She quit the grocery store and told Eddie Ray it was absolutely fine if he punted his route with the bottling company and continued to live at home. He worked a few hours a week as a towel boy at the Smart County Hospital wellness center to earn spending money, although it was understood that Monica would buy him whatever he wanted within reason.

Even though the accident was four years ago, and even though Monica paid a lawn service to maintain the property and avoided hosting poker parties so their trailer park friends wouldn't line the street with junky cars and pickups, the snooty women in the neighborhood never stopped reminding Monica that she and her long-haired son would always be *little* people. The worst was Sherry Rutledge, the widowed realtor who lived around the corner and drove a pink Cadillac. Eddie Ray had graduated high school with Sherry's daughter Nancy, a gorgeous little brunette on whom he'd had a secret crush for years. Nancy, of course, wouldn't pee on him if he was on fire.

But that sure wasn't the end of the world. Eddie Ray was shooting pool at the sports bar six weeks ago and couldn't keep his eyes off a curvy, familiar blonde who looked and was dressed a lot like his dream date Britney Spears. He got up his courage, went over to speak, and was stunned to find out that it was Daphne Kendall, a neighbor from the old trailer park: The skinny young thing with the runny nose and dirty feet was all grown up and wasn't shy about telling a man what she wanted. He'd seen her every day since, and the routine was to sneak Daphne into the guest room after Monica ambled off to bed. He'd taken her to City Park last night to watch the fireworks before they got high on pot and nearly set the guest bed ablaze with their own Independence Day spectacular. Life was good.

Until now.

After roaring up tonight in her broken-down car and announcing her news at the top of her lungs, Daphne immediately asked if she could move in. She pointed out that Monica's clean house, dependable transportation, and unlimited financial resources would be better for their unborn child than the mangy trailer she shared with her half-sane, poverty-stricken mother. Given Daphne's easy reputation, Eddie Ray wondered for an instant about a DNA test, the kind they were always talking about on *Law & Order* and would prove whether the baby was his. But Daphne had sworn she was on the pill. She also had a point about the house being healthier for the baby than the nasty old trailer. A week ago Eddie Ray would have gone right to his mother and talked her into it. But Monica had just returned from a cruise to the Bahamas with a new husband.

Arnold Webber had grown up in Oakdale. At sixty-four, he was sixteen years older than Monica, and Eddie Ray gathered that something happened between them before she met Blake Chester, back when she was *very* young. That wasn't important, though. The problem was that Monica, after running into Webber on the cruise after all those years, fell so hard that she insisted on marrying him before a justice of the peace as soon as they returned to Oakdale. Just like that, Webber moved in with them, and Eddie Ray knew it would only be a matter of time before he was asked to get a place of his own. And while that was understandable, seeing how his mother would want to enjoy her privacy, Eddie Ray didn't like what he heard today at the sports bar.

His new stepfather, it seemed, was a con man.

The bartender said Webber was run from town twenty years ago after ruining several Oakdale families that invested in his risky schemes, and that Monica Chester better guard her wallet with both hands. Although Eddie Ray knew she would have a hissy fit if her son immediately accused her new husband of being a crook, Eddie Ray felt obligated to at least warn her. He was trying to work out in his mind how to start such a discussion when Daphne came driving up. He'd been in no mood to discuss a baby, and they had their first quarrel. She'd marched right back to her Toyota and—

"...*you can do your own damn dirty work!*"

Eddie Ray whirled at the hissed voice. It was young and female and came from a nearby yard.

"*What did you say to me, little girl?*"

"*You heard me. I'm NOT doing it!*"

Eddie Ray forgot about Webber and Daphne for the moment and started to move toward the noise. Then he held up, afraid the women would hush if they heard footsteps. The breeze, thankfully, was still, although it was difficult to make everything out over all the crickets. Then a car went past. He kicked at the ground, knowing he'd missed something crucial, and strained to hear.

"*...ruin you in a heartbeat. Nobody messes with Sherry Rutledge, not even you.*"

Eddie Ray nodded. It was Sherry, all right, and it sounded like she'd been in the sauce. She was about his mother's age and looked pretty good for an older woman, but she wore a ton of makeup. He'd wondered over the years if she looked half-dead without all the rouge and eye shadow and lipstick. For that matter, maybe a bunch of red alcoholic splotches were under the war paint. It was funny how Sherry and Monica, who couldn't be any more different, actually had things in common: Both had money, and both had lost their husbands. Jack Rutledge, whom Eddie Ray remembered as quiet but friendly, died in a car crash a few years ago. At least Jack no longer had to put up with—

Eddie Ray jumped when a bottle exploded.

"Oh, go to hell, Mom. Go straight to hell. You don't mess with me."

So Sherry was fighting with one of her daughters. But was it Nancy or Caitlyn? Nancy left for Jackson after college but returned home. Like her mother, she was also a realtor and drove a fancy car. She was married to the weatherman on the Tupelo station, and God, she was hot—the ravishing little thing modeled formal wear in TV ads for a dress shop on the town square. Caitlyn, on the other hand, was a basketball star at the college. She was a younger, much bigger girl who was headed for fame and fortune, if the write-ups in the paper counted for much. Caitlyn wasn't nearly as sexy as her older sister but seemed like a genuinely nice person.

"You best get out of my face—"

Eddie Ray wondered if lights were coming on around the block and people were stepping outside for a ringside seat. Someone might even be calling the cops. Then he heard a splash and wondered if someone had jumped—or been pushed—into Sherry's pool. He stood completely still, trying to block out the chorus of birds and bugs and pick up the voices. But he didn't hear anything else, not even water being splashed about.

This was getting spooky.

He waited a few seconds, then put down his beer and stole through his mother's backyard. He slipped around the corner of the house and peered at the Rutledge property. He saw the pair of large oaks in the fading sunlight. One of them shouldered a tree house which looked sturdier than the trailer in which he grew up. He stepped forward and paused. He now had a clear view of the Rutledge pool.

He didn't see a soul.

Could someone have gotten in and out of the pool and gone into the house in the time it took him to get over here and look? It was possible, but wouldn't he have heard something, especially with a second person involved? He looked at Sherry's house and saw lights on inside. He peered at the concrete around the pool and thought he saw shards of broken glass but couldn't be sure. He was tempted to walk up to the pool and look in the water, then knock on the sliding glass door of the house and see if everyone was all right.

But Sherry wasn't pleasant while sober, and Eddie Ray sure didn't want to meet up with her when drunk. Nancy, if that had been her, was liable to spit on him. She wasn't about to dignify a loser classmate in front of her high-society mama even if the women were fighting.

Eddie Ray turned around and started back to his mother's house.

FOUR

Keller's eyes popped open. He smelled Caitlyn's clean scent, felt her warm body nestled against his, and heard her slow, deep breathing. He opened his eyes and squinted at the light from the lamp and then at the TV. They'd dozed off on her couch while watching the Braves game, and what looked like an adventure flick was now on. He felt the sensation again and realized it was his cell phone. It was in the pocket of his cargo shorts and set to vibrate, rather than play his Kid Rock ring tones.

The trick would be to get out from under Caitlyn without disturbing her and answer the phone before the caller hung up or left a message. He moved his free leg, causing Caitlyn to murmur in her sleep and adjust her position. That gave him an opening, and he jumped to his feet. He reached into his shorts and grabbed his phone as Caitlyn became still. The phone rang a third time as he looked at the screen.

James and Melanie Bryan.

His father was on a business trip to Chicago, he understood, so this would be his mother. He wondered if something was wrong with Holly. He backed away from the couch and crept toward the front door, knowing exactly where the scuffed, stained hardwood squeaked in the living room of Caitlyn's duplex. He turned the knob and opened it enough to squeeze through. He eased open the screen, pulled the door closed behind him, and answered as he tiptoed across the porch and out into the driveway. The humidity, even at night, made it feel like he was walking into an oven.

"Mom?"

"Hey. Are you in town?"

He frowned at what he considered an odd question. Caitlyn roomed with a teammate from Finland who was gone for the summer, and since his roommate had so many girls over, Keller spent more time here than he did at the townhouse he and Patrick rented. His parents certainly knew that he and Caitlyn spent their nights together, although the subject had never come up.

"I'm at Caitlyn's. What's the matter?"

"Are you...can she hear you?"

"No, I came outside. What is it?"

"Oh, God, what a mess," Melanie said. Keller thought he heard ice cubes clinking in a glass, as if his mother was having a drink. "Sherry's dead. Nancy found her in the pool."

FIVE

Keller felt his heart somersault. "What did you just say, Mom?"

"Oh, Jesus. The sitter just left, Holly was up late—"

"Sherry's *dead*?"

"Yes," Melanie said firmly.

Keller had lost interest in Caitlyn's stakeout at the Hampton Inn after forty-five minutes and was starving and irritable by the time Nancy, wearing a slinky little black dress, emerged from a first-floor room not ten steps from the Navigator. Brad appeared an instant later, clutching what looked like a joint between his index finger and forefinger. They passed it back and forth and pawed at each other, and Keller, having forgotten his appetite, stared open-mouthed while Caitlyn snapped pictures as fast as her fingers could operate the camera. They raced back to Oakdale so Caitlyn could upload the shots and burn them to a CD for Mike Morgan. She grabbed her purse and keys, told him to turn on the Braves game and make himself at home, and raced off in the Jeep. She'd returned with her temporarily-misplaced cell phone, a Fed-Ex receipt, and a carryout pizza from a place near the duplex.

"What happened?" he heard himself say to his mother.

"Well, I had dinner with…with a friend," Melanie said. Keller frowned at an odd titter in his mother's voice. If what she'd just reported was accurate, though, he didn't doubt she was shaken up. Even though his parents didn't drink, maybe she'd bought some alcohol and poured herself something good and strong nonetheless. "Had a sitter for Holly. Got home from dinner and the sitter said she heard sirens and saw a fire truck, and an ambulance came past our house and stopped down the street—"

"Slow down, Mom. Please slow down." He felt the stirrings of a headache as he tried to get his mind around the fact that Sherry was *dead*. "Who saw all this, you or the sitter?"

"The sitter. Really frightened your sister. You know how scared she is of fire trucks."

No, she isn't. "Okay, a fire truck and ambulance went by. You sure they stopped at Sherry's?"

"Yes. Now, I didn't know that right then. The sitter's boyfriend had come by and Holly was still up. Had to get rid of them and Holly to bed and then the phone rang. One damn thing after another."

Caitlyn's pad was exactly a mile from the football stadium and coveted because of its proximity to the academic buildings. Apartments, townhouses and duplexes like hers were packed into every available square inch of space on University Drive, and students were everywhere on Friday nights during the fall and spring. Nobody wanted to hang around the sleepy little place on a holiday weekend when cities like Memphis, Jackson and Birmingham were within reasonable driving distance and offered entertainment aplenty, though, and Keller was thankful at the moment that Oakdale was a ghost town. Even the married couple next door was away, which afforded him the freedom to talk in the driveway without clumps of people overhearing as they cooked out, strolled by, or threw Frisbees.

"I still don't understand," he said. "Nancy called you herself, or what?"

"No, baby. Priscilla Hall called, across the street from Sherry," Melanie said. There was that titter again. Keller wondered if his mother had declared it Ladies Night Out with her husband away and was tipsy, instead of pouring herself something after getting in. His mind jumped to Holly, but it sounded like she was in bed.

"Nancy's with Priscilla? She's over there now?"

"Well, I know she was," Melanie said. "Priscilla said Nancy went running over there after she called emergency."

Keller squeezed his eyes shut and tried his best to concentrate, wanting to learn everything he could before waking Caitlyn from her peaceful slumber and dropping this bomb on her. Before mailing the CD, Caitlyn said she arrived to find Sherry's Cadillac in the open garage and was prepared for trouble when she went inside. But the sliding glass door in the living room was open, and Caitlyn heard her mother having an animated conversation out back—Sherry was apparently on the phone, since the cordless base was lit up. Caitlyn said she went straight for her old bedroom, found her cell, and escaped without attracting her mother's attention. If Sherry was found in the pool, Keller figured, she'd gone out there at some point during the evening and taken her cordless and possibly an adult beverage with her. It was troubling, though, that Nancy, who found her mother, got there so quickly after he and Caitlyn spotted her and Brad at the hotel room in Tupelo.

Maybe she saw us and ran to tell Sherry. But what happened after that?

"You're absolutely sure about this?" Keller asked, lowering his voice as he kept his eye on the duplex. As hard as this would be to explain, he didn't want Caitlyn walking out here and staring after she picked up on the fact that something was wrong. "Before I wake Caitlyn up and tell her."

"Yes. Nancy found Sherry in the pool. She called emergency, then ran across the street and woke up Priscilla and her husband. Priscilla called me, and I'm calling you."

"When did all this happen? And why did Priscilla call you, anyway?"

"Look, I just got here twenty minutes ago, and I had to get Holly to bed after I got the sitter and her boyfriend out of the house, and I was changing clothes when Priscilla called, okay?" Now Melanie sounded frustrated at having to repeat herself. "I remember Priscilla saying that Nancy thought *you* would know how to find Caitlyn."

Keller felt fear zip through him. It would be just like Nancy to have spotted her hated sister and little boyfriend and let them sit there, thinking they *hadn't* been seen, rather than race over right then and give them the third degree. Even in the face of her own mother's death, Nancy might still set them in her sights and plot the perfect revenge. And although Keller hadn't said so aloud, he'd been uneasy all night about the photo shoot and thought that sending the CD to Mike Morgan was a bad idea.

Maybe he felt that way because Angie Bartman had put herself way out on a limb to help Caitlyn—it would be one thing for one of Caitlyn's girlfriends to aid and abet, but the *assistant basketball coach*?

"That's fine, Mom," he said reassuringly. "But how long ago was the ambulance called?"

"I don't know!"

"Could you guess? Please?"

Melanie sighed. "In the last little while, but I'm not sure."

"What time is it now?"

"Ten-thirty."

He realized he'd been asleep about an hour. "All right," he said. "Should I take Caitlyn to the hospital, or what?"

"That's where Sherry'd be, I'm sure," Melanie said. Now it sounded like she was about to cry. "You know how much I love those girls. Hug Caitlyn for me, sweetie."

Keller looked again at the duplex. He'd never admitted everything he knew about Nancy to his mother, and it would take hours if he started at the beginning. That presentation would be for both parents, not just Melanie, and could be made when his dad returned home from Chicago—what a time for him to be gone. But because Holly was so young and vulnerable, Melanie needed to know that Nancy was unstable and couldn't be used as a sitter in the future. Tonight's sitter, whoever it was, invited her boyfriend and probably didn't keep a good eye on Holly. But now wasn't the time to make an issue of it and put his mother on the defensive. Especially if she might be a little looped.

"Need me to come over?" he asked. "I'm sure Caitlyn will want to talk to you. You can give her that hug yourself."

"No. Bring Caitlyn in the morning, or whenever she's up to it."

"You sure? I can swing by for a minute, put an arm around you. I know you got your hands full with Dad out of town."

"Don't get me started on that. I just need to lay down," Melanie said with that same, odd titter. "Quicker I can get this crazy day overwith, the better."

"And Holly's okay?"

"She and her stuffed animals are all huddled under the covers."

This made Keller smile. He and Caitlyn took Holly to McDonald's every few days, as well as the park and the occasional G-rated movie at the theater. The age difference of eleven years was so substantial that there'd never been a hint of sibling rivalry with Holly—he had tacit permission from his parents to turn disciplinarian when he judged it necessary, and his parents backed him whenever she acted up in his charge. When that happened, she usually went to bed early and lost dessert and TV for the night.

"Then get some rest, and I'll take care of Caitlyn," he said. "I'll check on you tomorrow."

He told his mother he loved her and said goodbye. He returned the phone to his shorts and felt tightness in his chest. Caitlyn, over time, had found a winning formula to survive her cataclysmic childhood: Daily medication, strenuous exercise, weekly therapy, no alcohol, and plenty of rest kept her on an even keel. But she and Sherry barely spoke, and the news he was about to deliver would send her little brain into orbit. All he could do was hold her, be there for her in the coming hours and days as she processed the information and dealt with the death of her mother. He could only imagine what Sherry's final moments were like. Then a chill went down his spine.

Could Caitlyn have left a couple of things out? Like Sherry was drunk as usual and started some crap, and Caitlyn—

He tried to shove aside the little voice in his head and started for the duplex.

SIX

Eddie Ray killed an hour riding around town after leaving the Rutledge property. He muttered obscenities as he returned home and opened his mother's garage with the remote, having forgotten that Webber's Ford Ranger now occupied the space where he'd always parked his Grand Am. He couldn't help but think it was one more *this-is-my-house-now* dig from the stupid creep as he left the car in the driveway. He entered the kitchen after making sure the garage door was down. The fluorescent kitchen light was on and cast a milky, shadowy glow into the otherwise dark living room. He figured Monica and Webber to be in front of the television, but only his mother was there. He smelled peanut butter.

"Eddie Ray, you missed it," she said, her mouth full as she ran the channels. She leaned over and switched on the end table lamp and blinked several times as she tossed graying bangs from her eyes. He saw a huge jar of Jif in her lap with a spoon plunged in the middle of it. A plastic bottle of Coca Cola was on the end table, an empty one at her feet. Monica snacked constantly and exercised about as often as Halley's Comet came around, yet she'd maintained her figure over the years without diet pills and boasted recently that she was no heavier than she'd been at twenty-one. Even her closest friends, all of whom had gained at least a few pounds over time, griped about her bumblebee-like metabolism.

"Missed what, Mother?"

"All them sirens at Sherry's house," she said. "Walked over to see what the fuss was about, but couldn't get close enough to ask no questions. People all up in the yard, police and fire folks yelling."

"What, someone broke in?"

"Not with a fire truck and ambulance. Wonder if someone got hurt."

Eddie Ray's eyes widened as he finally remembered the odd splash in the pool, which came during that shouting match between Sherry and one of her daughters. He tried to replay the younger voice in his head and determine whether it was Nancy or Caitlyn. He couldn't be sure, although there was something about dirty work, wasn't there?

"What?" Monica said. "You looked like you was about to say something."

"Nothing. Where's your little friend?"

"In bed, snoring his fool head off. Wine knocked him slap out." Monica sipped her soft drink. "I know you think I don't love you no more, Eddie Ray, but we'll be one big, happy family. No reason to think y'all are competitors or nothing."

Eddie Ray shrugged, trying to convey to his mother that he just didn't believe her. Webber probably told her to say it, probably had a list of talking points and a schedule of when she was to use them. First he'd clear Eddie Ray out, then worm his way into Monica's investments. Eddie Ray wondered if he should alert Monica's financial guy that Webber was trouble and ask him to speak to her about it. But the financial guy, Eddie Ray knew, wouldn't get near that. He wasn't about to open his mouth and risk Monica taking her portfolio or whatever they called it elsewhere.

"I got an idea," she said. "How 'bout you get Daphne and Patricia to join us for supper this weekend? Cook some steaks, drink some beer. I know they'd like to meet Arnie. Sound like fun?"

They'd done just that on Memorial Day, which was before the arrival of Prince Charming and seemed like a lifetime ago. Monica and Daphne's mother were old trailer park buddies, and the routine was for them to start talking about old times and drink until they were three sheets to the wind. Once both women had passed out that afternoon, Eddie Ray and Daphne, feeling just fine after guzzling beer and sharing a joint, staggered to the guest room and knocked themselves out as well. In addition to Daphne expecting, though, Patricia Kendall was going downhill at a scary clip: She was forgetting names and faces and didn't know what day it was a lot of the time. Eddie Ray had seen that for himself, and Monica, who hadn't been around her friend in several weeks, would certainly notice the difference.

"I guess I can call in the morning and see what they're up to," he replied, trying to feign enthusiasm he didn't feel. He sure didn't want to talk about Daphne being pregnant and started down the hall. "Going to bed. Night."

"Love you, Eddie Ray. Good night, baby."

He entered his room and closed the door. He stood at the window in the dark and gazed into the backyard. He thought about Sherry Rutledge, and how that bottle shattered loudly enough to be heard crystal clear on his mother's patio. If it weren't so late, he'd try to find out what happened, seeing how emergency personnel was called to the scene.

But he could do that tomorrow.

SEVEN

Oakdale police chief Henry Blair was on the treadmill in his garage when he heard the emergency call for an ambulance over the scanner. Blair, who was ordered by his doctor after the heart attack to start taking care of himself, had dropped sixty pounds and kept his weight around 200. He finished his daily half hour of exercise, then slipped a towel around his neck and called the dispatcher to see what was up. He was told that a woman had drowned in a swimming pool on Peachtree Street and that an officer had already been sent to the scene. The neighborhood was one of Blair's favorites around town, full of older homes on quiet streets that were lined with pines, maples, redbuds and crepe myrtles. He strongly preferred it to the new subdivisions on bulldozed lots without a tree in sight.

Blair showered and dressed and looked in on his wife, who was shopping online and looked poised to spend money. He grabbed a Gatorade and headed to the police station, an old, collapsing structure with cinderblock walls, outdated paneling, and dingy fluorescent lighting. He saw no need for a huge office and had converted the previous chief's digs to a badly-needed conference room, then chucked the ancient electric typewriters in favor of a networked computer system. His captain was loyal, and the majority of the officers he now had were good, honest men and women. But Blair still felt the fear and distrust from locals after Gary Quinn, a second-generation Oakdale police officer, went berserk last winter and embarked on a killing spree before being shot to death with his own gun. The stress had no doubt contributed to Blair's heart attack.

Blair had radioed Pete Clark, the young officer who took the statements, and Clark was now in a folding chair across from Blair's standard-issue desk. Blair glanced at the mounted deer head on the wall behind Clark. Then he read Clark's report before giving the officer his customary expectant look. He liked getting up to speed on the facts before asking for further thoughts from whoever went to the scene.

"The deceased was positively identified as Sherry Rutledge," Clark said as he shifted in the squeaky chair. "By her daughter Nancy. I took a statement from her."

"Guess Sherry won't be running for mayor. Heard that through the grapevine."

Clark shrugged. He hadn't grown up here and knew little about local politics and the Oakdale social scene. But because Blair's wife ran a shoe store on the square and fed a daily dose of gossip to her husband, he was always in the loop.

"Way I understood it, Chief," Clark said, "Ms. Rutledge and her daughter had just come from a funeral down in Jackson."

Blair nodded. "Joan Morgan, Nancy's mother-in-law. Continue."

"They went to Jackson in one car, driven by Ms. Rutledge. Left this morning from the residence on Peachtree and returned at approximately five this afternoon. You may already know that Nancy and her husband live in Pleasant Acres, near the college."

Blair went to his poker face and nodded. He'd heard that Nancy and Mike Morgan, the morning weatherman on the Tupelo TV station, were having serious marital difficulties—it sounded like she was stepping out on her husband, and there'd been a scene at a dinner party when Mike tried to take Nancy home after she had several drinks and was mouthing off to everyone in sight. Blair didn't know how much the daughter imbibed, but Sherry was rumored to have had an intimate relationship with the bottle.

"After they got back from Jackson," Clark said, "Nancy got her car, went out to the house to check e-mail and phone messages, had supper, and then went back to her mother's, who was expecting her. Said she arrived at approximately 8:30."

"Where was Mike Morgan at this point? The husband."

"Damn, I forgot to put that in the report, Chief," Clark said. "His mother was from Jackson. He is, too, and Nancy kinda made it sound like he'd be there a while."

"Kinda?"

"She was vague, although real upset. I can certainly ask again, sir."

"What I'm saying is, I figure they'll let him off work for a few days, but I'm sure he'll be back on the TV soon. Anyway, Clark, we can get it later. Continue."

"Nancy has a key to her mother's house and let herself

in. Told me she didn't see her mother inside, even though her car—pink Cadillac—was visible in the garage. Went out back and found her in the pool. Called it in. That's pretty much it."

Blair looked at the report. "No blood, no noticeable trauma…?"

"No, sir. Now, a neighbor, Mrs. Priscilla Hall, was with Nancy when I arrived on the scene. She confirmed that Nancy called 911 from her home—Sherry Rutledge's, that is—after discovering the body in the pool. Mrs. Hall rode with Nancy and the deceased to the hospital."

"Could Sherry swim?"

"Yes, sir. Nancy said she swam just fine."

"Anything else that struck you, Clark?"

Clark shrugged. "No, sir. May be a simple drowning."

"We'll wait for the autopsy, then," Blair said. He thanked Clark and sent him back out on patrol. He reread the report once the door was closed. His wife, who had something good to say about almost everyone, used words like spiteful and vindictive to describe Sherry Rutledge. Although Blair didn't know Sherry well, he sensed that you were either with the woman or against her—Sherry had a reputation for holding grudges and playing for keeps and apparently expected the same of everyone else. Could she have pushed someone a bit too far…and gotten pushed to her death? Nancy, the grieving daughter and also a realtor, was an especially attractive young woman who seemed to run in the same circles as her mother. Blair turned off his computer and stood, figuring his wife was still shopping from home. His spouse would be a good resource if this was more than a simple drowning.

And something told him it just might be.

EIGHT

The next morning Webber left early to play golf at the country club. Monica made Eddie Ray a big country breakfast and matched him bite for bite. He watched her pack away the food and wondered again where she put it. As they were cleaning up, one of her casino friends dropped by, a tattooed, sassy gal who drank men under the table and cussed like a sailor. Monica poured tall glasses of sweet tea and led them to the sunlit patio, where they lit cigarettes and began prattling like the redneck hussies they were—he didn't doubt they'd open a six-pack before long. Eddie Ray wondered if Webber would introduce Monica to the country club scene. *That*, he thought with a grin, would be interesting. If so, maybe the man was legitimate after all. But if not, it would go a long way toward confirming for Eddie Ray that his new stepfather was only in it for the money.

Eddie Ray knew he needed to put Daphne at ease after being testy last night. It was her first time to the house since Monica returned from the cruise, and he was so taken aback at her news he didn't think to mention Webber. He would today, though. Daphne would be disappointed and perhaps angry that Webber was now, in all likelihood, in control of the finances. But Eddie Ray would be damned if he went to the man for a handout. He and Daphne would move in together and find a way to survive, even if it meant living close to the bone. What they couldn't do was have a slew of kids they couldn't afford. He knew families like that growing up, folks who lived hand-to-mouth and kept right on having babies. It was a wonder they didn't all starve to death. He would let Daphne know that one would be the limit, at least for a good, long while. He'd even start wearing condoms.

He showered and dressed, then grabbed his keys, wallet,

and cell phone, and felt the muggy air slap him in the face as he stepped outside. He shielded his eyes from the sun and recalled that a cheap pair of shades was in the Grand Am. He heard kids down the street, which was one more reminder that Daphne would have his child next spring if his calculations were correct. That would mean getting a real job, of course. He'd start looking on Monday.

Then he forgot his pregnant girlfriend for the moment. He glanced toward the house, where Monica and her friend were running their mouths. While he was riding around feeling sorry for himself last night, Monica had gone around the corner and spotted an ambulance and fire truck in front of Sherry's house. He wondered if there was police tape out front, like he saw on *Law & Order*. He'd sure heard a big fight between Sherry and one of her girls, and he hadn't dreamed up that bottle being broken out by the pool. He didn't know where else it could have shattered unless it was hurled against the house like a downfield strike from Peyton Manning.

And an ambulance was called? Was someone dead?

He checked across the street, not wanting that nosy Mrs. Ardmore seeing him again, and trotted around the side of the house and into the backyard. Monica had planted a flower garden near the patio, but there was nothing else back here other than the cluster of pines at the rear of the property—she had no interest in a privacy fence because it would involve removing several of the trees. Eddie Ray wasn't in sight of the patio yet and cocked his ear. His mother and her friend were laughing amid loud whispers, all caught up in their gossip and oblivious to his approach. He was certain he would see a neighbor or two, maybe some happy kids playing on the swing set in the yard next door. But everyone was either at the lake or watching their kids and grandkids play soccer. Maybe it was just plain too hot to be out, since there wasn't a soul anywhere.

He took several steps toward the Rutledge backyard and paused, aware that he stopped in this very spot last evening. He could see the pool and wondered if his eyes had played tricks on him: He didn't see any glass then, and he sure didn't now. A gentle breeze caught his attention, followed by cicadas that began buzzing high in the pines. He frowned and wished he could mute them somehow. Then he heard ring tones from a cell phone. The noise stopped instantly, as if someone had been waiting for the call. Eddie Ray didn't hear a voice and figured his mind was messing with him. The tones could have drifted from anywhere, not necessarily the Rutledge's place.

Then he heard another sound and looked up in time to see Nancy emerge from the tree house. A jolt of adrenaline shot through him, the way it always did when he saw her. She came down the steps which were nailed to the tree and hopped to the ground in bare feet. Good grief, she was fine. He feared she would see him and wonder aloud what he was doing, but she adjusted her sunglasses and strode toward the house. He watched her tug open the sliding glass door and leave it unattended. He knew she would return and moved a few feet away so she wouldn't spot him. He heard the door close seconds later and soon heard squeaks from the wood as she climbed the steps and went back inside the tree house. Someone else might be inside the *main* house, but he was willing to bet that she was by herself up in the oak. He moved a step in that direction before stopping.

What would he say to her?

Nancy was liable to tell him to get the hell off their property and his nose out of their business. If something tragic had happened, though, and even if Nancy was polite, what could he do, other than offer his sympathy? He imagined her turning suspicious and knew the best option was the truth: He'd heard an argument followed by broken glass, and was told late last night by his mother that an ambulance had been called to the house. He would assure his rich, snobby classmate that if she needed anything, he and his mother were right around the corner—all Nancy had to do was knock on the door. The cute little thing couldn't get upset at that, could she? At least not to his face.

He was steps from their yard when he heard Nancy conclude her cell call. He paused again, feeling like a bulls-eye in the middle of a target, and half expected Sherry or someone to come running with a shotgun pointed at him. He heard the flick of a gas lighter followed by Nancy inhaling from a cigarette, assuming that was her. She exhaled, and he could almost picture the smoke rings and smiled at the notion that she smoked where no one would see her—high-class ladies like Sherry and Nancy Rutledge didn't puff out in the open because such activity was beneath them. He listened carefully, wanting to make sure he didn't hear anyone else. Then he heard movement and knew she was about to come back down. He moved to within ten feet of the tree house.

"Hey, Nancy?" he called out. "It's me, Eddie Ray Chester."

Nancy stuck her head out and looked around until she spotted him. He knew right away that she wasn't wearing a bra under her tank top, which was the first place his eyes went. She adjusted her sunglasses, and he saw her blue eyes for an instant. They were bloodshot and looked bad. Maybe something awful really happened out here last night. Folks didn't call paramedics for no reason.

"Whatcha need?"

"Not spying on you or nothing, but I saw you go up in there a second ago and thought I'd walk on over." He imagined Sherry watching from the kitchen window with that signature nasty look on her face. Her daughter, Sherry would be thinking, was talking to a *little* person right there in her yard. "Can you talk a sec?"

"What is it?"

"Uh, you mind coming down?"

Nancy stuck her head back inside the tree house before emerging with her cigarette between her lips, which made the little beauty queen look a lot like a common redneck. Her tiny cell phone was between her fingers, one of those newfangled gizmos that probably didn't weigh an ounce. She reached the ground and took another drag before blowing smoke skyward. She crushed the butt against the tree and let it drop to the ground. Then she smoothed out her top and faced him. He indeed felt suspicion as she gazed up from behind the shades.

"Make it quick," she said. "I'm real busy."

Eddie Ray tried not to stare too openly at her firm, full breasts. He'd assumed a boob job long ago but couldn't care less. Her skin was soft, her legs were tanned and toned, her lips were full and her hair was thick and beautiful. Man, there were stories about her in high school. It wasn't just horny teenagers scoring with Nancy in the backseats of cars: word got around that the band director and the physics teacher—both married with kids— had steamy affairs with her. Interestingly, both left the school soon after he and Nancy graduated, and the band director, from what Eddie Ray heard, went through an ugly divorce and left town.

He knew there would always be a double standard. Girls from the trailer park who jumped from bed to bed were sluts— labeled that way by girls like Nancy—but it was apparently a badge of honor in the stuck-up crowd to do the same thing. Yet none of it ever hurt Nancy's reputation. She was queen of the prom and president of their class, and these days she drove a Beamer, modeled pretty gowns in TV ads, lived in a huge house in that ritzy Pleasant Acres neighborhood, and was married to that good-looking, smooth-talking weatherman. It made perfect sense that the dude was always in a good mood each morning as he gave his forecast. Eddie Ray figured he would be, too, if he were banging Nancy Rutledge each night before going to sleep.

He cared about Daphne and thought she was pretty hot, but Nancy was ten times as smart and had a better complexion, a smaller nose, a much flatter stomach—

"Eddie Ray, anybody home?"

"Uh…"

"Like I said, I'm in a hurry. What do you need?"

"Just wanted to make sure y'all was all right," Eddie Ray said as he cleared his throat and hoped he didn't look as stimulated as he felt. "Stepped out on the patio last night, heard some sort of, uh, commotion coming from here—"

"What commotion?"

He felt her on the attack, fiercely guarding their privacy. The unannounced visit was probably a mistake. But he was here to check on them, he reminded himself. As well as lust after her.

"Well, it was your mother arguing with—"

"What time was this?"

"—either you or your sister. Heard one of y'all call her by name."

"What *time*?"

Nancy's voice was a growl, like she didn't intend to ask again. She was an intense little thing and probably used to getting exactly what she wanted. That smile of hers, which couldn't look any more romantic in yearbook photos, was probably as fake as her perfectly-shaped boobs. He could imagine her turning into a pit bull when anyone dared get in her way. And that, based on what he'd heard about Sherry over the years, probably ran in the family.

"Trying to think." He rubbed his hands together to dry the perspiration on his palms. "I know it was after eight. Maybe 8:15 or 8:30, 'cause there was still a little daylight left."

Nancy nodded. Her eyes were still hidden behind the sunglasses. "Okay, 8:15. Now tell me exactly what you heard."

"Well, no offense or nothing, but your mama sounded a

little looped. Drunk, I'm trying to say. She was arguing with one of y'all girls, 'cause I heard whichever of you it was call her *Mom*. Then I heard this bottle break and right after that someone went in the pool. Thought that was weird because—"

Nancy raised a hand for quiet. Eddie Ray clammed up and watched her take a long look at the house, like she was thinking about inviting him inside. She turned back to him as an odd little shiver went through her. She hugged herself and inadvertently shoved her breasts forward. Then she rubbed her temples and shook her pretty head, as if trying to clear the cobwebs. He got another look at the bloodshot eyes and saw heavy circles below them before she straightened her shades. He didn't want to miss anything she said and again wished he had a way to silence the doggone cicadas.

"Can you meet me somewhere?"

He heard this loud and clear and tried not to look amazed. "Uh…I guess. Where?"

"You know where the county lake is, right?"

"Sure."

"Keep going south another mile," Nancy said after a glance at her phone. "Watch for an unmarked right turn onto a rutted old road. Take it and go maybe a quarter mile. Bunch of camp houses around a stocked pond out there."

"Yeah, I know where that is. Went fishing there once."

"Be there in an hour. Second cabin on the left. And don't tell anyone, hear?"

Eddie Ray nodded dumbly. Nancy spun without another word and started for the house. He gazed at her backside and wondered if she was hungover and horny. Did she and her TV star husband have a big fight last night, and would she want to get even by sleeping with a trailer-trash neighbor from high school? He didn't need to muddle his suddenly-complicated life even more, but the chance to jump Nancy's gorgeous bones even *once* in his life was probably worth almost any punishment he could imagine. He wouldn't care if she never spoke to him again.

But winning millions at the casino was more likely, Eddie Ray figured. Even though Nancy didn't give him so much as a smidge of information about last night, she sure seemed interested that he'd heard what he had. And she wanted to discuss it with him at a cabin out from town? Why not here in the yard, and why in an hour? What would she be doing between now and then? If something bad had happened, wouldn't she want the neighbors—even if she looked down on them—in the know, so they could help the Rutledge's in their time of need? Or, at the other end of the spectrum, protect their own selves from harm if a criminal was on the loose?

Would she show up dressed like that?

Damn straight he was going.

NINE

Nancy swallowed the valium tablet with a sip of diet cola and took a deep breath. It was her second pill of the morning and would make her super woozy, but she had a million things to do and would have a panic attack if her mind continued to race—if that happened, she surely wouldn't be able to pull off the genius of an idea she had while talking to that imbecilic Eddie Ray Chester. She was at her mother's computer after cleaning out Sherry's vast array of prescription narcotics, since Mommy Dearest would no longer need them. The same was true of everything in the liquor cabinet. She thought about Brad, who was still asleep when she staggered out of the hotel as the sun rose this morning. She would call him on her way to the cabin and get him up to speed.

First, though, there was some earth to scorch.

She drummed her fingers and considered how to word

the e-mail to Melanie Bryan. Melanie was a modern-day June Cleaver, a Junior League mom who taught Sunday school and never missed her daughter's school plays or soccer games. And because Melanie ran that oh-so-charming little bookstore and coffee bar on the square, all the important women of Oakdale stopped in and buttered her up and included her in the gossip. Nancy, like her mother, was jealous of the attention Melanie received but never made an issue of it. Lately, though, Melanie had been snippy to the point of disrespect. Nancy didn't know where the sass was coming from, but she sure wasn't going to take it. Not from Melanie Bryan.

Not when Keller had...

A tear-jerker of a note would be a good start, Nancy decided. It would turn the family upside down. But the Bryans needed a good dose of reality after years of being the perfect little nuclear family everyone liked and admired. She would make herself available to meet with Melanie, perhaps suggest a drink somewhere if Oakdale's favorite working mom wanted more information. The possibilities of what she could do to this unsuspecting quartet were endless, depending on how effectively she played Melanie.

Nancy closed her eyes and saw her mother at the bottom of the pool.

She shook her head firmly enough to make it hurt and tried to drive away the swirling fog of noise. The sooner she could get the funeral behind her, the better. She would handle everything herself, since she wanted nothing to do with Caitlyn and couldn't imagine the bitch wanting to be involved. But Caitlyn would be in for the shock of her life if this meeting with Eddie Ray Chester went the way she thought it would. He was in remedial classes as far back as she could remember, but they had study hall together in eighth grade. God, the way that boy *stared* at her back then. It made her skin crawl even worse than the drooling looks she got from her own father at home.

Life sure provided some strange twists and turns, she thought with a grim smile. Nancy would never forget the horror in her mother's voice when she announced that Monica Chester had paid *cash* for that house on Golden Drive several years ago and was moving in. She and Mike were still in Jackson at the time, and she was convinced it was a joke until she came home one weekend and saw Eddie Ray under his Grand Am in the middle of their driveway. It made her want to throw up. Mrs. Ardmore, the widow that lived across the street from the new neighbors, vowed never to speak to them and hadn't, if one believed anything she said. Mrs. Ardmore had called this morning to offer condolences—Priscilla Hall obviously couldn't keep her mouth shut, since word about Sherry had already gone around the neighborhood—and noted while doing so that Eddie Ray had gotten his slut girlfriend pregnant. Mrs. Ardmore knew this, she said, because she heard the announcement with her own ears.

That small fact wouldn't keep Eddie Ray from being any less hot and bothered out at the cabin, though. His eyes kept darting down her shirt as he talked in that slow way of his about what he thought he heard last night. And they nearly popped out of his head when she asked him to the cabin, like he'd been told Santa was coming in July this year instead of December and would be joined by the Easter bunny. She was willing to give him a gift to remember, too, although his help would be needed. And not just one time: This was a detailed plan, and a lot of things would have to go just right.

But Nancy sensed Eddie Ray would do anything she asked.

TEN

Eddie Ray found the rutted road and headed left when he reached the stocked fishing pond. Each cabin occupied about an acre of land and was surrounded on all sides by dense pines, crepe myrtles, sagebrush, and pockets of tall grass. There were several cars in front of the first cabin, and Eddie Ray spotted a pair of men toting large coolers as he rolled past. He reached the second cabin and saw a navy-colored BMW. Nancy was leaning against it, smoking a cigarette and batting at a mosquito as she talked on her cell phone. He pulled in and cut the engine of the Grand Am. He climbed out and heard a whole choir of birds and cicadas. Nancy was now in a blouse and jeans—so much for the see-through top and threadbare gym shorts. She ended her call and dropped the cigarette and stubbed it with a faded penny loafer. He noticed the large purse over her shoulder for the first time when she dug into it. A moment later she pulled out a key ring with a lone key and started for the door.

"We'll talk inside," she said. "Come on."

"Works for me."

He knew the property out here was coveted and expensive, but the cabin looked like it was about to cave in. The interior featured three mounted deer heads and was rank with stale cigar smoke. The electricity was thankfully on, though, and he watched Nancy adjust the thermostat in the corner of the room. He looked around and took in the kitchen behind him. They were in the living area, and a bedroom was down a short hall and probably included the bathroom. The whole thing couldn't be 800 square feet and had no furniture except for an old couch against the far wall. She nodded for him to sit. He did, and she took the opposite end and lit another cigarette.

"Stinks in here," she said. "Might be hard to sell."

"Y'all own this?"

"No, this was Bud Crisler's infamous little party shack. After he died, Gloria pretty much gave the whole thing to that ass Jim Pittman. I've heard she and Pittman were casino-hopping and sleeping together before Bud was cold in the ground. Gloria, in case you haven't seen her lately, has gained all her weight back and then some. Oh, and their gay son lives with her now—poor Bud's probably rolling over in his grave." Nancy paused to exhale smoke. "Anyway, Pittman sold the plasma TV, Bud's boat, his hunting rifles, and everything else in here, and had just listed the place with my mother. Realtor, if you didn't know. So am I."

Eddie Ray kept his frown to himself. Nancy had shared so much gossip in ten seconds that his head hurt. She sounded like the type who hugged your neck while stabbing your back and was probably like that with her friends. But word was that Crisler, the legendary Oakdale High football coach, was caught up in some serious crap before dying of that stroke after the playoff loss last year. It made Eddie Ray wonder what had gone on out here in the woods. He couldn't believe the macho coach had a gay son, though.

"Anyway." Nancy took off the sunglasses. Her eyes didn't look as bloodshot, but the dark circles were still there and she sounded wiped out. "Cigarette, something to drink? All kinds of things in the magic purse."

"Naw, I ain't thirsty," Eddie Ray said. He looked at the purse, then back at her. "Swear I'm not trying to mind your business. Just concerned, is all."

"We're cool, classmate. So you heard a commotion, as you called it. Last night."

She didn't seem as fierce without the shades. Eddie Ray felt his heart rate increase at the prospect of pressure, however. This almost seemed like a job interview, and if nothing else, he thought, it would be excellent practice for next week, when he would begin interviewing for a job that he hoped would support him and Daphne and the baby.

"Well, like I say, I heard some yelling coming from there."

"About 8:15, right?"

"I wasn't real sure of the time, now," Eddie Ray said. He stretched and heard his back pop. "Just starting to get dark, I'd say. Heard your mother out there, and either you or your sister. Don't know why her name escapes me—the basketball player—"

"Caitlyn."

"Yeah. One of y'all said the word, 'Mom.'"

"And you said my mother was drunk?"

"No offense, now," Eddie Ray said. "But it sure sounded like it."

"Okay. So what happened after that?"

"I heard a bottle break, real loud. Kinda spooked me, you know? Waited a few seconds, not sure what to do." He wasn't about to admit that he didn't show his face because he figured they would scream at his trashy butt to go home. "Heard someone go in the water, like they was gonna swim. Thing is, I didn't hear no splashing or nothing else, no more voices. Struck me as odd."

Nancy reached into the purse and removed a silver flask. He watched as she unscrewed the cap and took a long swallow. Then she capped it and put it at her side. She stared straight ahead.

"My mother's dead," she said. "Drowned last night."

Eddie Ray gasped. His first instinct was one of comfort and reassurance. He started to reach for her, but an internal voice told him that Nancy Rutledge *did not* want Eddie Ray Chester touching her, no matter how dire her situation.

"My God, Nancy. I'm sure sorry."

She gave him a slight nod. Death hit people in different ways, he knew. Some folks on *Law & Order* went to pieces, while others stayed cold as ice. Maybe drinking was Nancy's way of holding it together, although alcohol could unleash a fire hydrant of emotion in a woman, too. He'd heard plenty of blubbering drunken females up at the sports bar.

"I brought you here so we could talk in peace and quiet," she said. "Still trying to make sense of what happened last night. Mother knew I was coming, see. Sometimes we sit and talk on the porch swing, sometimes out at the pool. But she wasn't there, wasn't anywhere in the house. Car was there and the lights were on, so I knew she was home. Went out to the pool and there she was."

Eddie Ray pictured Nancy walking out there and finding her mother dead in the water. He tried again to hear the voice that argued with Sherry last night. The one that told her to go to hell, as he recalled, and do her own dirty work. Listening to Nancy talk, it sounded like it could be her. But Caitlyn, since she was Nancy's sister, would also sound like that. He wished he had a tape of their voices and could compare them.

"So if you found her," he said, "you're thinking Caitlyn's the one who argued with her?"

Nancy turned to him. Her baby blues were suddenly intense again. She took a long, deep drag from her cigarette before sending smoke toward the cabin ceiling. While Daphne always struck poses in silly, never-ending attempts to look like a movie star, Nancy Rutledge was the real thing. She reminded him of Shannon Doherty, that short, hot little woman who played bitchy roles on TV all the time and was convincing as hell.

"How well do you know Caitlyn?"

"Know *of* her," Eddie Ray said. "Always seemed nice. Sure can play ball. One day we were at City Park, and there she was, shooting by herself, draining one three-pointer after 'nother, nothing but net. Loudmouthed old boy bowed up and challenged her to a game, and man, your sister just wiped the floor with his sorry—"

"She has a dark side. And she and our mother never got along."

"I didn't know nothing about that. Now, I know your dad died a while back."

"Caitlyn's always had problems. Crap with her just never ends," Nancy said. Eddie Ray noticed that she didn't respond to the comment about her father. He watched her reopen the flask and got a whiff of strong-smelling alcohol. She took another swallow and replaced the cap, then put it by her side. "Just can't believe she'd kill our mother."

Eddie Ray felt his eyes bug out. "You think *she* pushed her in the pool?"

"You're probably right about Mother being loaded. Every once in a while she'd let off a little steam. We all do that once in a while, don't we?"

"Gosh, yes."

"Mother and I were out of town yesterday on business. When we got back, Mother could tell Caitlyn had been in the house. That's not cool, because she's not supposed to be there unsupervised. My husband's also out of town, so I went home to do some things, then came back out to see Mother and got there at 8:30." Nancy paused to zero in on him. "If you heard my mother arguing with one of her daughters at the pool at 8:15, it was *Caitlyn*. So I need you to go to the police."

Eddie Ray swallowed involuntarily at the thought of giving a statement about something he didn't see. She grabbed his wrist as if she could read his mind. Her cool fingers sent a jolt of current through him.

"Listen to me: Someone in the neighborhood saw a very tall, broad-shouldered, blond girl trot away on foot not long before I called 911. Said the blond girl was wearing a black golf shirt and tan shorts, and had frizzy hair halfway down her back. That sure sounds like Caitlyn, doesn't it?"

"But why would she kill her own mother?"

"Because she's sick," Nancy said, as she exhaled a mouthful of smoke. "Tried to kill herself when she was thirteen, still sees a shrink. What everybody sees, Eddie Ray, is this superstar athlete, but the Caitlyn I grew up with doesn't know right from wrong. What I heard, she and a bunch of teammates drive fancy cars they got from university boosters and take all kinds of gifts from them."

Eddie Ray smirked. "They all do that, I figure."

"It's illegal. Part of being a role model is acting like one. But she thinks she can do whatever she wants and get away with it. And the proverbial whistle, as they say, was about to blow. You with me?"

"Caitlyn was about to get in trouble?"

"Maybe not jail time, but I could see her losing that basketball scholarship." Nancy took a final drag from her cigarette and crushed it on the stained carpet below. She obviously didn't think this would hurt her chances of selling the cabin, and it probably wouldn't, seeing how men would be using it. "What I think, Caitlyn got in some big trouble and asked Mother for help, because Mother knew people in high places. Mother was a person of integrity, though, and she probably told Caitlyn she'd made her own bed and would have to lie in it. Truth is, it would be about Caitlyn's speed to sneak in and try to find something on Mother she could use as blackmail. I'm sure that's why she was in the house while we were gone. And Mother probably confronted her."

Nancy didn't say anything else. Eddie Ray watched her light another cigarette and wondered how much she smoked. Then she had another sip from the flask. He was aware that if she got blitzed, his chances of getting laid on this dirty couch in this stuffy little cabin would increase significantly. But the pressing concern was the request to go to the cops. While Nancy's story was sure possible, and although he'd heard the poolside argument, he simply hadn't seen anyone and couldn't identify the younger voice arguing with Sherry.

"Look," he said. "Not that I don't believe you, and I hate your mother died..."

Nancy let his thought hang in the stale air. She took a drag from her cigarette and sent more smoke toward the ceiling, where it was forming a hazy blue cloud—this was like being at the sports bar. Then she scooted closer. Eddie Ray noticed perfume, as well as the smoke and booze emanating from her. Her eyes were glassy up close, but she still seemed in control.

"I really need your help, Eddie Ray. I can't say who, but someone else said they saw Caitlyn trotting off just before I called 911. Someone who's likely to come forward if you do."

"Wait, she was on foot? I don't understand if she ain't allowed in the house."

"I thought about that. Probably parked at the Bryans, three houses up the street."

"Oh, sure, I know them. Real nice folks."

"Well, that's another story for another time," Nancy said as an odd smile formed on her face. "But Caitlyn and Keller are thick as thieves. He might be in on this, too."

"Now wait, Nancy, I sure didn't hear no one else's voice."

"I'm just saying he probably told her to park there. And I know this makes you uncomfortable, but it's your civic duty—your damn *responsibility*—to go to the police if you know something about a crime that was committed. And Caitlyn shoved my mother into the pool where she drowned, and now both my parents are gone!"

Nancy was beginning to sound emotional. Although he'd

started to embrace her minutes ago, he didn't want her bursting into tears. He just couldn't say no to a woman who was crying, no matter what she wanted. Which would doom him with Daphne, he knew. She would probably cry for jewelry, clothes, and—heaven forbid—more kids.

"I know, girl, and it just breaks my heart. But I didn't see Caitlyn push her in."

"Just tell them you saw her *leave*," Nancy said slowly. "The other person who saw Caitlyn fears retaliation, okay? But that person will come forward if you do. And juries convict in circumstantial cases all the time."

"On TV they do. I watch—"

"And in real life, believe me. Now, you definitely heard the argument and broken bottle at 8:15, and you know I found my mother at 8:30. Just tell them you stuck your head around the corner of your house and saw Caitlyn leave, okay?"

Eddie Ray cracked his knuckles. "Okay, let's say I talk to the cops. Then what happens?"

"Caitlyn'll hopefully be tried for murder. For God's sake, she killed our mother!"

"Meaning I'd be called as a witness. I don't know about that, Nancy."

She eased back to her corner of the couch and stared straight ahead. He couldn't tell if she was mad or hurt or both. She wanted him to testify in court to something he hadn't seen, though, and that was perjury—he sure knew that from *Law & Order.* On the other hand, it really sounded like Caitlyn did it. Stories about Caitlyn had floated around for years, so the mention of a suicide attempt didn't surprise him. But if she was unstable today, as Nancy claimed, she could very well have lost it last night and could do so again in the future. What a tough call.

"Heard about your mom and Arnold Webber," Nancy

said, breaking the silence and turning to him with a little grin. "I'm sure the last thing you expected was her coming back from the cruise with a husband."

Eddie Ray didn't bother to ask how she got the information, since gossip zipped around as fast as text messages. Ten different neighborhood women could have told Sherry, who most certainly would have passed it on to her gorgeous daughter.

"You know him?" he asked.

"Parents knew him, long time ago," she said. "I know his reputation. Trust him?"

"Not sure yet. He was sorta sprung on me."

"Be very careful around him. Tell your mother the same thing."

"That's who I'm worried about. Ain't no secret she got a lot of money when that contractor settled. Wonder if Webber'll try and get his paws on it."

"Very possible." Nancy broke into a smile. "And if my sources are correct, you and Daphne Kendall are expecting your first child."

She had to have gotten this from Mrs. Ardmore, who was in her yard when Daphne blared her news at the top of her lungs last evening. Eddie Ray felt hot blood flood his cheeks in a mix of embarrassment and anger.

"Well, I understand you may not think much of Daphne, but—"

Nancy scooted right up next to him. Now her eyes were really glassy, although she didn't sound drunk when she spoke. "Look, girls I run with are pretty impressed with themselves. I don't mind telling you that. But down deep, we're *all* from Oakdale. You and I grew up together and will always have that in common. Goes for Daphne and anyone else from the little place we call home. Sense of pride, know what I mean?"

"I suppose."

"Take my word. Now, having kids is a life-changing experience. You ready?"

"Well, this wasn't exactly planned."

Nancy's smile now looked supportive. Eddie Ray was amazed they were still talking. She almost seemed like an old friend, and maybe she was being truthful—beneath the snobbery she and her just-as-beautiful girlfriends displayed, perhaps there was a bond because they were all local folks. It would be interesting to hear Monica's take on that, since she'd lived all forty-eight of her years in Oakdale.

"Be honest, girl, what I wish I could do is get drunk and cry to my mama."

Nancy was in the midst of a drag on her cigarette and laughed. She sent little spurts of smoke everywhere when she coughed.

"But Daphne's having the baby, and I'm slap determined to be a man for the first time in my life," he continued. "Get us under the same roof and work my butt off to support her and the little one."

"Can I ask a nosy question?"

"Don't tell me: What'll I do for money, since Webber'll steal us blind, right?"

"You're smarter than the average bear. Tell me."

Eddie Ray shrugged and smiled. "Hell if I know. Driving a delivery truck is all I ever done, other than handing out towels up there at the hospital. I see you up there all the time, doing your spin class. Looks like you work real hard to keep in shape."

Nancy didn't reply to this and chose instead to take another sip from the flask. It had to be almost empty. She finished her cigarette and crushed it next to the other butts. "Well, let's think about this," she said. "Y'all need money, don't you?"

"Nancy, I will *not* ask that man for a handout. Maybe Mother, but not him."

"You won't have to. Just imagine ten thousand bucks in the bank and look at the magic purse."

Eddie Ray glanced at the purse. His mouth fell as he caught on. Nancy took his hands, which were in his lap. The simplest touch of hers sent voltage through him. He would start panting like a rabid dog if she actually came on to him, and she just might, with a bribe suddenly part of the deal. She probably didn't plan to walk out of here until certain that he would tell the police exactly what she wanted. And it sure sounded like Caitlyn did it. Besides, he knew from *Law & Order* that witnesses got scared and had to be talked into cooperating. That went for him as well as this mystery person who saw Caitlyn scamper from the Rutledge property.

"Envelope in there, baby, your name on it. Know what's inside?"

"Uh, do I want to know?"

"Ten grand." She crawled onto his lap. "And more later. Lot more."

Eddie Ray saw that she was going to kiss him and felt faint. His breath was fresh and he'd put on cologne, because getting laid was on his mind along with curiosity about what went down last night. They should have had this discussion right there in her yard, but it was too late now—she was making him an offer he couldn't refuse. He hadn't forgotten the reference to those people in high places Sherry knew: Nancy had to know the same folks and could certainly make things happen. She could gut her sister's basketball career and possibly get her sent to prison, maybe even come after *him* if he didn't go along with the program. And his ability to reason was disappearing in a hormonal fog.

"You need that money in the worst way," she whispered. She took his face in her cold little hands and looked almost motherly. "Does Daphne even have a job?"

"She says she's filled out a bunch of applications, but nobody's ever called about—"

"It's gonna take a lot to raise a family. And she'll want more than one papoose," Nancy said, giving him a tender little kiss on the cheek. "I know the last thing y'all want is to live on welfare, Eddie Ray. But bless Daphne's heart, all she's thinking about right now is *having* babies, not raising them. That's just the way girls are. And y'all were counting on your mama's financial support, weren't you?"

"Yeah," he said breathlessly. "Sure were."

"Well, that's gone with Webber running the show." She adjusted herself in his lap and pressed against the almost painful bulge in his shorts. She planted another little kiss right next to his mouth and ran her tongue up his jaw line. "But I can help. Because that's what we do around here: help the people we grew up with, especially at crunch time, which this is. So can I count on you?"

He squeezed his eyes shut and tried to block out an almost overwhelming urge to throw Nancy down and have her. He went back over the poolside argument in his mind one final time. Based on what he'd heard last night from his mother's patio, he could easily imagine Caitlyn hurrying from the house after shoving Sherry—who was drunk—into the pool. And it made sense that Caitlyn's car could be parked at the Bryans. He'd seen Caitlyn and Keller together many times over the years. It also made sense that the neighbor who feared retaliation was more likely to come forward if he did. Then something else crossed his sex-crazed mind, like a voice shouting at him from a long distance away.

Reasonable doubt.

He opened his eyes and grinned at Nancy. She smiled back, then yanked her shirt over her pretty head. She wasn't wearing a bra, and as she shoved him down on the couch and smothered his face with those huge boobs, he concluded that a jury of his peers would have a tough time agreeing on a guilty verdict if no one actually *saw* Caitlyn push Sherry Rutledge to her death. And Eddie Ray could live with that. He would talk to the cops and even go through the torture of testifying on the witness stand. Because the bottom line, which Nancy had nailed, was the bottom line.

He needed the money in the worst way.

ELEVEN

"Cool," Caitlyn said. She placed the word QUACK on the Scrabble board and covered a triple-word space. She recorded the tally on a scratch pad and waggled her tongue at Keller. "Down 150, dude. Throw in the towel now, or fight to the bitter end and really get squashed?"

The board game was Keller's idea. It gave Caitlyn's mind something to chew on beside the bizarre, unexplained death of her mother and the considerable baggage that confounded their relationship. They'd both slept poorly, and Caitlyn had dozed off and on all day and talked little when awake. At least she wanted his closeness. They made love in the middle of the night and again before lunch, and Keller held her and wished he could crush the pain and anguish inside her with his bare hands. In his heart of hearts, he didn't think she had anything to do with Sherry's death. But his mind wouldn't be completely at rest until an official cause of death was given. An accidental drowning would suit him just fine.

Caitlyn was his priority, although he remained upset that the sitter's boyfriend was at the house when his mother arrived home from her night out. Based on the ambiguity of Melanie's comments, the girl was new and hadn't been vetted well, if at all. That absolutely couldn't happen again. Holly could get in all kinds of trouble if left unsupervised, and there wouldn't be a do-over if she hurt herself or saw something she shouldn't. He wondered last night after taking Caitlyn to the hospital if Melanie was having an affair. It was a jarring sensation, but one that his mind deemed feasible after a time of kicking it around. He wondered if Caitlyn thought the same thing but wasn't comfortable saying so.

He gave her a cocksure look, trying to convey that he wouldn't go down without a fight, and hunkered over his tiles. They both looked up when a car pulled into the driveway of the duplex. The tattered curtains were open and allowed sunlight to filter through the crepe myrtle near the porch. Caitlyn stood and peered out, her curly locks bobbing a bit in the breeze from the ceiling fan.

"Well, if it isn't the princess," she said. "This'll be fun."

Keller got to his feet as Nancy climbed out of her BMW. She'd never seemed pleased, if that was the word, that he and Caitlyn were serious and might well walk down the aisle. Why, he couldn't imagine. It didn't seem to be a status issue, since Jack Rutledge and James Bryan were occasional golfing partners before Jack's death, and Sherry and Melanie—though not close—had many of the same friends. And it sure wasn't like Nancy cared who Caitlyn dated, or whether she even had friends. Keller, though, after years of smiles and winks and hugs from Nancy at church and other settings, picked up some ice from his former sitter once she was back in town and living with husband Mike Morgan in Pleasant Acres. The better he got to know Caitlyn, though, the unhappier he understood Nancy to be. He simply tried to be friendly around her and was prepared to do so now, although he wondered if her pink business suit represented trouble. He couldn't believe she'd be showing property after everything that happened last night.

Maybe she just met with her lawyer.

He watched her amble toward the duplex, keys in one hand and cell phone in the other. Mike Morgan would have gotten the CD this morning and may have already shown it to his lawyer, who could have gotten in touch right away with Rutledge family attorney Vince Cockrell. Nancy wasn't smiling and looked almost sinister in her sunglasses. She clomped in white flats up the cement steps to the porch, pulled open the screen door, and walked in without an invitation.

"Well, what a nice surprise," Caitlyn said. Sarcasm absolutely dripped from her voice.

Nancy ignored her and looked all around. She seemed to be appraising the interior, and Keller could almost smell the disdain. Maybe all realtors checked out each new place in the same way that musicians Keller knew eyeballed each other's guitars and drum kits. He wondered if Nancy's pure snobbery was on display when she showed property, though, and it would seem damn difficult to close sales that way. He was ready to force a smile and say hello, but Nancy didn't acknowledge him and turned to Caitlyn.

"I take it you don't have my cell number," Caitlyn said.

"I do."

"Well, a call would have been nice. I don't just drop in on people unannounced. But last night, I'm talking about. Would have appreciated hearing from you."

"I believe Priscilla called you." Nancy turned to face Caitlyn and stood at full height, which was five-two. Keller swiftly felt the tension in the room.

"She didn't, but the message found its way to me, so don't give it a second thought," Caitlyn replied. "Keller's standing right here, by the way. Say hi, if you haven't lost all your manners."

"Hi, Keller," Nancy said, staring straight at Caitlyn. "Look, I don't have long, and I'm in no mood for your crap today—"

"Well, that makes two of us, doesn't it, honey? So tell me what happened last night, since you couldn't bring yourself to call."

Keller felt his heartbeat increase at the prospect of violence and wished he could see Nancy's eyes. She sounded like she was ready to rumble, and Caitlyn, who was five-ten and tipped the scales at a muscle-bound 190, possessed a short fuse when it came to her family and could snap Nancy like a twig if she wanted. In fairness, Nancy had just lost her mother, too, and was a lot closer to Sherry than Caitlyn.

"I found her in the pool," Nancy said, enunciating each word like she was lecturing a small child.

"And that's it?"

"There isn't much to tell."

"Well, I know you guys went to Mrs. Morgan's funeral yesterday—"

"What does that have to do with anything?"

"What time did you find Mom?"

"Look, I told all this to the police," Nancy said.

"How 'bout you tell *me*, since you couldn't find time to do so last night."

Now Nancy really looked exasperated. "We got back around five. I went out to the house, made some calls, and had supper. Got back to Mother's about 8:30. Her car was there, but she wasn't in the house. Went out to the pool and found her. End of story."

Keller didn't detect a whit of discomfort in Nancy's voice. She'd gone to Tupelo, of course, and apparently had no compunction about lying her little butt off right to their faces. She was impossible to read, so he still had no clue if she'd spotted them last night from the doorway of the motel room and wasn't planning to let on—and get even—until ready.

"Had she been drinking?" Caitlyn asked.

Nancy looked away and seemed to stifle a laugh. Then she turned back to Caitlyn. "I knew you were gonna ask—would have put money on it. First, I have no idea. Second, if she was, be just like you to make sure everyone knew. Make sure her reputation gets good and trashed."

"That's from your playbook, not mine. Now what can I do for you, dearest?"

Nancy moved a step closer. Keller knew his long-ago heartthrob absolutely detested being tweaked by Caitlyn. He watched the scene with a certain amount of fascination as well as fear.

"There's a ton of stuff we have to do," Nancy growled. "And since you refuse to reach out to Mother's friends who've supported you all these years—"

Caitlyn snorted at the absurdity of the statement and Keller almost laughed as well. It was the dearly departed, after all, who led the fight to make sure everyone in her clique thought of Caitlyn as a second-class citizen. Nancy knew this, of course. She ridiculed and character-assassinated Caitlyn in front of the same people and had the nerve to look her sister in the eye and pretend otherwise.

"—but since you completely blow them off, *sis*, I thought I'd save you the embarrassment of having to work with them and handle everything on my own. I've been at the freakin' funeral home trying to make it as easy on you as possible and all I get is attitude."

Caitlyn clasped her hands and spoke in a mocking southern drawl. "Oh, Nancy! What a lovely gesture. I just hope you get your props, baby doll, because we both know that's *exactly* what this is about. Maybe the paper will run a glowing feature on what a kind, giving young lady you truly are."

Nancy whipped off her shades. Keller couldn't see her eyes clearly, but they looked like two little blocks of granite from his vantage point. "Go to hell. For all I care, you and Keller can skip the funeral and play Scrabble."

"You know, that's not a bad idea."

"Just take your crazy pills if you do come so you won't cause a scene."

Keller blinked. Although Caitlyn had acquired a thick skin over time, the way to wound her was to throw the state hospital in her face, to chide her about spending time in a rubber room and imply that her elevator didn't make it to the top floor. Nancy knew that like she knew the sun would come up tomorrow, and anything Keller still felt for her evaporated in that instant, overtaken by single-minded hatred he'd never felt for anyone before. But Caitlyn didn't look upset in the least as she leaned down toward Nancy. It reminded Keller of his mother and Holly, on those many occasions Melanie was trying to make a point to the little girl.

"Take all the cheap shots you want, *sis*," she said. "You're 'bout to find out you're nothing around here without Mother holding your little hand. Now, will there be anything else before you're on your merry way?"

Nancy's breathing had intensified. She reminded Keller of an angry Doberman as she aimed an index finger at Caitlyn's face. "You just watch your back."

"You're so cute when you get upset."

"You keep on, hot stuff. You could get hit from all sides and then some."

"That's enough, Nancy," Keller said. He could no longer help himself and moved to get between the women. "Go pick a fight somewhere else."

Nancy gave him a chilling little smile and leaned toward his face. For an instant he thought she was actually going to kiss him, and heat filled his cheeks and caused him to feel faint. "You should mind your own business, you darling little boy," she whispered in a voice ripe with insinuation. "I sure wouldn't want anything to happen to you, either."

Keller felt a firm hand on his shoulder. This was Caitlyn's way of telling him to stay out of it. He kept his mouth shut but felt humiliated. Nancy punctuated the little dig by shifting her weight to face Caitlyn again. Now he couldn't see Nancy's face, although he had a good look at his lover. Caitlyn looked angry enough to drop-kick her sister across the street. Her voice was clipped when she spoke.

"Thanks for handling the arrangements. Now get the hell out of my house and do *not* come back. For any reason."

Nancy stepped back and adjusted her jacket, then slipped the shades back on. "Fine, if that's the way you want to play it. Don't say I didn't warn you."

"I feel sufficiently warned. Now get lost."

Nancy stalked out, letting the screen door bang as she stomped off the porch and down into the driveway. Keller watched her strut to the Beamer. She cranked up and backed out hurriedly and just missed the mailbox. She put the car in gear and roared away, certainly trying to send a message of some kind, he figured. He turned to Caitlyn after watching the cloud of dust settle.

"I almost broke her little neck," he murmured. He heard the tremor in his own voice. "She has nerve to throw your meds in your face, with the stuff you say she takes."

Caitlyn gathered him into her arms and squeezed. She outweighed him by twenty pounds and was every bit as strong. Although he played all sports growing up and lettered in baseball in high school, he'd come to terms long ago with the fact that his girlfriend was unquestionably the better athlete. She'd also matured into a strong person, and he reminded himself that although she showed incredible poise in the five minutes Nancy was here, Caitlyn was conflicted and in more pain than she wanted to admit. He needed to put Nancy's ugliness out of his mind and take care of her.

"Anyway, sweetie," he said, "I'm sorry about all that—"

"I know you were in love with her once," Caitlyn said quietly.

Keller felt more blood in his face. He kept his head on her shoulder. "That's overstating it."

"Well, you had feelings for her. We can agree on that."

"I was in junior high, Caitlyn. It was a silly crush."

"Just know *that's* the real Nancy. She isn't the little angel your parents and everyone else sees, the big sister who babysat you all those years ago. She's a miserable, narcissistic human being, just like Mother. Fact, I'd venture to say she's unstable. And I don't just throw that word around."

"How'd you keep from punching her lights out?"

"She was trying to provoke me, and I wasn't going to give her the satisfaction."

"Then you're a better person than me," Keller said. "But what about the threats? I really wonder if they saw us."

"She's all talk." Caitlyn kissed his cheek. "Go check on your mom. I can tell you're worried about her. And tell her that her son is taking good care of me."

TWELVE

"Get you anything, sir?" Officer Pete Clark said as he and Eddie Ray entered a windowless room in the Oakdale police station. "Coffee, water, soft drink?"

"Love some water."

"I'll get it," Clark said. "Have a seat. Be right back."

Eddie Ray settled in a folding chair as his eyes adjusted to the gloomy fluorescent lighting and equally depressing bare walls. He sure didn't need any more caffeine after guzzling a

Mountain Dew while gathering the nerve to make the call that he knew would change his life. Nancy had absolutely worn him *out* on that couch in Bud Crisler's old cabin, and he accepted the envelope of cash in a lovelorn stupor and promised to stick to the script when he talked to the police. He took down her cell number and promised to call afterward with a report.

He now felt so scared he wondered if he'd have a heart attack sitting right here.

He looked at the scuffed conference table, which was the only piece of furniture in the room besides the pair of rusty chairs. It probably got downright claustrophobic in here for someone with something to hide and a pair of cops firing questions from point-blank range. This would just be Clark, though. Eddie Ray reminded himself of the story he rehearsed while driving downtown. He didn't need to get creative and talk himself out on a limb. Folks who blew it with the cops probably did just that.

"Okay, down to business," Clark said, bustling back in and closing the door. He handed Eddie Ray a chilled bottle of Dasani and took the seat across the table. He set a spiral notebook and ball-point pen in front of him, ready to take notes and look for holes in the story he was about to hear. Eddie Ray felt cool air coming from a vent in the ceiling and was glad for that. The damn place would probably feel like an oven without it. "You heard some things on your patio last night that might relate to the death of Ms. Rutledge, huh?"

"I hate you was paged," Eddie Ray said for no reason he could think of. "For you to have to come in on your off-time, that is. They said they would have to page you."

Clark looked surprised. He was Eddie Ray's age or younger, a clean-cut, stocky man who might be five-ten and looked strong enough to bench-press a John Deere. He wore his hair in a buzz cut. "Hey, part of the job," he said, holding his palms outward. "And it sure takes folks out in the community helping us, so I appreciate you coming in. Now start at the beginning, and take your time."

"Well," Eddie Ray said after a sip of water. "Embarrassed to admit I still live at home."

Clark's grin looked friendly, not mocking.

"It's like this: My mom got remarried, and my stepfather just joined us. Little uncomfortable at times, which is why I went out back for some fresh air."

"What time are we talking about?"

"Before the sun set, about 8:15," Eddie Ray said. He measured his voice for nervousness and heard none. He reminded himself again to stay on point: He didn't need to explain that he and his mother were looked down upon by the neighbors, or that he graduated with major-leaguer Brad Valentine. "All quiet, then this argument broke out."

"At the Rutledge residence."

"Yes, sir."

"How'd you know it was them?"

"Because Ms. Rutledge referred to herself at one point. Said, 'Nobody messes with Sherry Rutledge.'"

Eddie Ray looked at Clark, expecting a reaction. Clark simply scribbled on his pad and nodded for Eddie Ray to continue.

"I knew it was her, along with another female. At one point the girl said, 'Go to hell, Mom.' So it was one of the daughters— she got two of them. And right then a bottle exploded. I jumped about a foot in the air." Eddie Ray paused. "Be honest, Officer, Ms. Rutledge sounded a little drunk."

"And you think it was one of the daughters. You just don't know which one."

This was a jolt. He wasn't sure if Clark's response was a statement or question and wondered for a panicked second if the cop saw right through him.

"Not right then," Eddie Ray said carefully. "Then I heard a splash, as if someone went in the pool. Now, there are several houses with pools in the neighborhood, but Ms. Rutledge has the only one right nearby. So I figured someone went for a swim."

"Then what happened?"

Eddie Ray paused again. He was about to tell his first lie to a card-carrying, gun-toting officer of the law, and he wondered if the guilt percolating inside him was plastered all over his stupid face. He wished to God he hadn't blundered over to see Nancy this morning. And he might not have made the trip to the cabin if the little honey was in an ugly housecoat instead of gym shorts that left little to the imagination and a top with her boobs practically hanging out. But it was too late to fret over that now.

"It was strange," he said. "They'd just had this nasty shouting match, and someone broke that bottle all to pieces, and then someone went in the water, and suddenly I didn't hear a thing. Expected to hear someone splashing around, maybe a voice or something."

"But you didn't hear anything, from the water. So what'd you do?"

"Waited a few seconds and started that way," Eddie Ray said. "Didn't see anyone at the pool. Looked across the back yard, and also at the house. Figured I'd at least see someone because this argument had just happened."

Clark held up a hand. "Hold on. How long from the time you heard the splash until you could actually see the Rutledge pool?"

Eddie Ray was prepared for this one, having thought of it while parking the Grand Am. "No more than half a minute. Stood on our patio maybe ten, fifteen seconds, waiting to hear something, then started over there. Didn't take long to get where I could see."

"Okay. Go on."

"Like I say, I was expecting someone in the water, or near the pool, or maybe going toward the house. What I saw was Caitlyn, the younger daughter. She was kinda trotting out of the yard."

Clark wrote some more. Then he looked up. "Going where?"

"Out toward the street. Sidewalks up and down Peachtree, you know?" Eddie Ray felt his fear spike back up at the onset of uncharted territory. "Saw her get to the sidewalk and start up the hill. Walking north, I guess."

"Walking or running?"

"Running, kinda, till she got to the sidewalk. Then a fast walk. Just a few steps and she was out of sight. Big girl, long stride."

"Then what happened?"

"I went back home." For the first time, Eddie Ray felt embarrassed about his lack of action last night, even though he knew he couldn't have prevented the death. "I should have at least looked in the pool, I guess, but Ms. Rutledge sounded drunk, Officer, and I didn't think it was my place to interfere in a family squabble..."

"But you went to look, didn't you?"

He felt himself turn red. "Uh, yes, sir. But like I say, I turned around and went home, thinking that Caitlyn and Ms. Rutledge had some sort of fight, and maybe Caitlyn thought she'd go for a walk and cool off. I went out riding and forgot about it. Got back, and Mother said there'd been an ambulance at Ms. Rutledge's house. She heard it and went outside to see where it ended up."

Clark wrote for several seconds before looking at him. Eddie Ray was dying for a look at the officer's chicken scratch but didn't dare peek. "So your mother knew Ms. Rutledge was dead at that point, or not?"

"No, sir. Just knew an ambulance went to their house."

"You tell her what you heard on the patio?"

Eddie Ray felt himself blush again. "No, sir. Mother's kinda gossipy, you know? Hell, everybody in that damn neighborhood is."

Clark smirked and said nothing.

"But it was pretty late by then. Come this morning, though, I was real curious about if someone was seriously hurt. Went out back, looked over at Ms. Rutledge's house and happened to see Nancy, the older daughter, out in the yard. Went and talked to her, and she told me her mother was dead." Eddie Ray hoped they were about done. His façade didn't have much left. "Knew I'd better call y'all, and here I am."

"Did you tell her everything you just told me, about what you heard?"

"Yes, sir, I did."

"And what was she like?"

Eddie Ray couldn't begin to read Clark and wondered if his discomfort at answering questions for which he wasn't prepared would show. Whatever he said, the trip to the cabin was off-limits. At best, Clark might doubt his story about what he heard from the patio. At worst, though, the cop across from him might wonder if he was somehow involved in Sherry's death.

"Seemed shocked, I guess," Eddie Ray said. "Didn't talk all that much."

"She seem glad you came over? To talk about what you heard and saw?"

"Yes, sir, she did."

"She ask you to call us?" Clark said.

"Yes, sir. She said it would be helpful. But I would have even if she hadn't. I'm a little sorry I didn't go over there last night, be honest."

"Anything else?"

"No, sir, I don't guess."

Clark pushed on the table for support as he got to his feet. "Then I thank you for coming in. Write your phone number and address down for me, and we'll contact you if we need you."

Eddie Ray felt relieved as he scribbled on a clean sheet in Officer Clark's pad. He apparently wouldn't get the third degree, and now he needed to get out of Dodge as gracefully as possible. He shook hands with Clark, whose grip was tight to the point of pain. He grabbed his water and started down the hall with his eyes on the stained linoleum floor. He reached the front door and resisted the urge to look behind and see if anyone was watching him, then stepped out into the brutal sunlight and humidity. He was sweaty, even though the interior of the building was at least twenty degrees cooler than the outdoors, and his head was spinning after the few minutes with Clark. Hopefully nothing would ever come of the statement he'd given the officer.

Right.

He cranked the Grand Am and turned on the air and aimed a vent at his face. The guilt at what he'd just done to Caitlyn hit him like a discharged airbag, and he sucked in a deep breath and held it in an attempt to ease the rapid tightening in his chest. An internal voice reminded him that Caitlyn—unlike her older sister and late mother—had always been nice. Monica had suffered a nasty fall in the garage a couple of years ago while unloading groceries, and Caitlyn, who was still in high school and jogging along Golden Drive that day, saw her and came sprinting up to help. Eddie Ray arrived from the sports bar to find Caitlyn and his mother chatting it up over glasses of sweet tea, which Caitlyn had poured after putting an ice pack on Monica's swollen ankle. She'd also propped his mother on the couch and refrigerated all the perishables. Monica told Eddie Ray it was one of the kindest displays she'd ever seen and always had a soft spot for Caitlyn thereafter.

And he'd just sold the poor girl down the river.

Everybody said Caitlyn was the real deal on the basketball court, a future superstar at the pro level. But that could go right down the crapper, now that Eddie Ray Chester had lied to the police about something Caitlyn may have had nothing to do with. He'd lied on the advice of older sister Nancy, of course, who pretended to be his friend before bribing him with an envelope of cash and perhaps the best sex he'd ever had. Yes, he desperately needed the financial help, and yes, Caitlyn *may* have shoved Sherry into the pool. But was he so pathetic that he would do anything for the approval of Nancy Rutledge, the naughty little vixen who might just be using him in a high-stakes game of sibling rivalry? And was he so gullible that he assumed everything Nancy said at the cabin was the gospel truth?

Eddie Ray felt a powerful headache coming on. Because Nancy was so bent on ruining her sister, he realized for the first time, would she be willing to invent a few convenient details to make her story work?

Or even make the whole thing up?

THIRTEEN

Chief Blair sat behind his desk and ran his hands through his crew cut. Officer Clark was in the folding chair across from him. Brawny lead detective Rob Higgins stood to the side. Higgins preferred to stand, and the cologne-drenched son of a gun was never still: He was always shifting his weight and cracking his knuckles and humming to himself. The hyperactivity got on Blair's nerves, but Higgins was a dedicated and thorough investigator if a bit stubborn about following his first impression. And his instinct, as he'd just stated to Blair and Clark, was that basketball star Caitlyn Rutledge was guilty as hell of murdering her mother.

"Remember, y'all, I grew up here," Higgins drawled. He

kept playing with the opening of his shirt, as if he was warm and trying to ventilate his chest. "Everyone knows Jack Rutledge drove smack into that wall. Man was one strange bird."

Blair caught Clark's eye and nodded. The consensus around town was that Caitlyn's daddy definitely killed himself, no matter what was reported in the newspaper. Blair, though he'd been in town five years, still deferred to Higgins on matters of the town's often infamous history since Higgins seemed to know just about everyone.

"Now, having said that, I'm proud as anyone Caitlyn's doing so well. Great for her, great for Oakdale," Higgins continued. "She was in the state hospital growing up, though. That's the dirty little secret, Chief. Everybody sweeps it under the rug these days, but we all know what happened."

Blair had talked to his wife minutes ago and described the statement Eddie Ray Chester gave Clark. Blair was forced to listen while his wife lamented the blunder Eddie Ray's ditzy mother Monica had just made: The hick-turned-rich-gal married a con man named Arnold Webber, and his wife's sources predicted the marriage wouldn't last six months and fully expected Webber to clean Monica out and send her and her son back to the poor side of town.

As far as Eddie Ray was concerned, all she knew was what Blair himself had heard: Eddie Ray was no rocket scientist, but he, like his mother, hadn't dumped all his redneck buddies after moving up in the world. That was in contrast, Blair understood, to Sherry Rutledge, who also came from the sticks but married into money and elbowed her way into the elites. In the end she'd looked down upon her trashy brethren with all the contempt an authentic Southern belle could muster, despite being a pretender to the throne.

"Do you know this Eddie Ray Chester?" Blair asked Higgins.

"Yeah, I've talked to him at the sports bar. Nice enough fella."

Blair turned to Clark. "And he struck you on the level, huh?"

"Yes, sir."

"Seem to have a reason to lie?"

"None that I know of, Chief," Clark said. "But I can go put some heat on him."

"Let me talk to Caitlyn," Higgins cut in. "Find out where the hell she was last night. And I know, Chief, without you having to tell me, that all we got right now is circumstantial evidence that ties exactly no one to a crime."

"Couldn't have said it better myself, Higgins."

"But that family has a history—girl sure does. Could Sherry have gotten liquored up and fought with her daughter? Sure. And could Catilyn have lost it? Better believe it."

Blair could picture such an altercation, especially if Mama Rutledge was drunk. Eddie Ray had described Sherry as slurring her words and said a bottle shattered near the pool. Had Sherry come after her daughter, and if so, had Caitlyn pushed her while defending herself? It was possible. But if that had happened, Blair reasoned, wouldn't the youngster have tried to save her mother if she saw that Sherry was in trouble? Instead of doing that, though, she'd apparently left the scene.

Trotted away, according to Eddie Ray Chester.

"Okay," Blair said. "Bring her in, Higgins."

FOURTEEN

The knock on the duplex door roused Caitlyn from a nap. She sat up and rubbed her eyes and wondered if Nancy had returned to argue some more, maybe even confront her about playing George Eastman Kodak last night. She'd downplayed

Nancy's tough talk in front of Keller because she didn't want him worrying about it, but Nancy, like their late mother, was truly in her element when making plans to avenge an enemy. Keller could be exactly right about Nancy seeing them last night, then circling the wagons before picking that quintessentially perfect moment to strike back.

What a mess, she thought, as she started across the room. She should have stayed out of her sister's marriage, regardless of what Nancy did to Mike Morgan and his poor mother. Intent on teaching Nancy a lesson, however, she'd taken and sent pictures that could explode into a *national sports story* because of Brad Valentine. Worse, she'd never forgive herself if Angie got hurt over her role in unearthing where Brad hid while in the area. As to her own mother being dead, Caitlyn supposed she was sorry it happened. But she couldn't say she would miss her. She knew that grief, in some capacity, would work its way to the surface. Then she would cry. And that, she knew, would make Keller feel better. The tears, actually, might come when she found the words to express the gratitude she felt toward her soulmate for being such a wonderful and compassionate friend.

She opened the door and mentally prepared to face Nancy. But a big man in a cheap suit was on the other side of the screen. She felt the intense humidity and saw the lengthening shadows as she took in a navy-colored Crown Victoria behind the Jeep. He held a badge where she could see it.

"Miss Rutledge?" he said in a voice rough from cigarettes. She smelled them now, as well as a generous splash of cheap aftershave. "Detective Robert Higgins, Oakdale police. My condolences about your mother."

She'd seen this man around town over the years and knew he was an Oakdale native, although she had no idea he worked for the police department. He was probably ten years ahead of Nancy and not much younger than James Bryan. Like everyone from this little place they called home, Higgins had to be well-versed on the Rutledge family misadventures. But what got Caitlyn's attention was his posture. He looked ready for an argument. And, maybe, to arrest her.

"Thank you, sir," she said as her heart sped up. "How can I help you?"

"Need to ask you some questions down at the station. Right now, please."

FIFTEEN

"Mom?"

"In here," Melanie Bryan called out.

Keller walked past the den of his parents' house and saw Holly in front of an animated movie. The den served as the playroom and still had the outdated paneling and orange shag carpet that came with the house. Nearly every other room had been remodeled, and the living room sported matching leather sofas and handsome cherry tables as well as the shelves James Bryan labored over all summer a few years ago—Melanie spent days arranging books, photos and knickknacks before deciding everything looked just right. Keller stepped into the room and found his mother on one of the sofas. The muted plasma television was tuned to the Discovery Channel as classical music played softly on her Bose system. Everything looked completely normal as Melanie rose and came forward for a hug. She was five-seven and attractive, Keller felt, for a woman of forty-three. She was a devoted mother, ran a successful book business, was active in the community, and appeared to be as happily-married as any woman in Oakdale. But last night's call, although to relay the shocking news about Sherry Rutledge, had him looking at her in a new light.

With her husband on a business trip, what was she doing

on a date?

Her stuttered explanation of her whereabouts—*dinner with a friend*—now had the seed planted firmly in Keller's mind. And what was with the failure to vet the sitter? It sounded like someone Melanie really wanted to see dropped in with no notice, which led to last-second arrangements. He knew he shouldn't judge his mother without proof. But he hadn't forgotten her gloomy stretch after Holly was born. He even asked his father if she had a terminal illness she couldn't bring herself to discuss. James Bryan finally confided that she no longer enjoyed teaching eighth-grade English and needed a change, and that year they bought a failing business on the square and opened the bookstore. Looking back, it bothered Keller that his mother never said a word to him—she moped around for months without explanation before gradually regaining the bounce in her step. It was possible that because he was only thirteen then, she didn't think he was mature enough to handle a career crisis.

If that's what it was.

Or did she reluctantly give up an affair that year? And if so, had it started back up?

Keller loved his dad, but it had taken some thoughtful comments from Caitlyn for him to truly appreciate the way James Bryan provided for his family. His children, while having every-thing they wanted within reason, were expected to volunteer at church and around town to help the needy. Moreover, he'd taught Keller not to brag or even hint that they were better off than anyone else. Caitlyn pointed out that while Sherry, especially after Jack's death, made sure everyone knew how much she made on real estate commissions and stock trades and where she and her friends vacationed, James was every bit as successful and never rubbed anyone's face in it. Melanie's parents, though as kind as anyone you could hope to meet, eked out a living to feed and clothe their three daughters—it was

James who opened his wife's bookstore with inheritance money. And he spent months decorating every last square inch so she would feel totally at home in her new place of business.

Keller tried to push all of this from his mind and kissed his mother's cheek. She smelled great. "Where's Caitlyn?" she said.

"Resting. Couple things I want to talk about confidentially. Holly okay in there?"

Frustration spread across his mother's facial features like time-lapse photography of storm clouds blowing through on a sunny day. "Little heathen's going to bed early for throwing a fit in the damn grocery. Always seeing what she can get away with," Melanie said. "Anyway. What's up?"

Keller shifted his weight so he would see his sister if she emerged from the den, since Holly, like all children her age, didn't miss a thing and wasn't bashful about asking ticklish questions. He told his mother about the bogus will Mike Morgan found in his file cabinet and noticed that Melanie seemed to listen impassively, rather than display the shock he expected after such an outrageous tale.

"If Mike knew about this," she said when he was finished, "why didn't he confront Nancy?"

"I asked the same thing. He told Caitlyn that because his mother was so close to death, he wanted to wait till after the funeral and speak to his brother. Wanted them to handle it together."

"But why talk to Caitlyn and not Nancy? Nancy is his *wife*. Sounds to me like Mike and Caitlyn were plotting against her."

Keller frowned and wondered if he hadn't been clear about Nancy's role in the will. "I don't know. Guess Mike needed someone to talk to. But there's no question it was tampered with—"

"And just how do you know that?"

Now Melanie had a little grin on her face. Keller's roommate Patrick was fond of taking a position opposite of whatever Keller felt strongly about, but it was almost always to mess with his old chum in good fun. Melanie, though, sure sounded like she was siding with Nancy. And Keller wasn't happy that his mother seemed to be hinting at something conspiratorial between Caitlyn and Mike *against* Nancy, the poor, defenseless princess.

"I haven't seen it, if that's what you're asking," he said. "But you and I talked about how sick Mike's mother was, Mom. They had round-the-clock sitters by the time this revision was supposedly signed, and she was completely bedridden by then. And Caitlyn said Mike and his brother got along fine. There's no way Mrs. Morgan ever would have cut one of her sons from—"

"What the hell makes you such an expert on this family?"

Melanie rarely used foul language or lost her temper. The noisy retort startled him, and he gave himself an extra second and turned his palms up to her. He didn't need to get mad and have Holly come running into the fray.

"Look, it's not worth arguing about," he said.

There was that smirk again. His mother's approach to this conversation seemed all wrong, and in that instant she took a half step back and raised an eyebrow as if reading his thoughts. Now she looked defiant.

"You're old enough to do your own thing," she said. "But I didn't raise you to attack your friends. Nancy Rutledge is a dear, sweet girl I love nearly as much as my own children. She was your babysitter, Keller. And in case you've forgotten, I seem to recall a little puppy-dog crush on *her*."

This sent hot blood to Keller's face. He was embarrassed at being reminded of it and angry that the information was being used now: it seemed a cross between a taunt and a guilt trip. His next words were out before he could get them back.

"Look, you know all about Nancy and Brad. She's hardly pure as the driven snow."

The words hung in the air as a hard look formed in Melanie's eye. A moment later a purple vein was in plain sight on her forehead: Melanie Bryan was *pissed.* Keller, who'd planned to cover what went on in Tupelo last night, wasn't about to get into that now. He dearly wished his dad was home because both his parents needed to know about the molestation Nancy had endured, not to mention the valium and drinking binges. And yes, they needed to know about the marital infidelity and the bogus will, too: it all added up to an unstable woman that didn't need to be left alone with a young, impressionable girl like Holly. Melanie *had* to know that before calling Nancy for help in the next babysitting jam. But if she was this hostile toward anything negative about Nancy, she'd go ballistic if he got into the heavy-duty stuff.

"Let me tell you something, chum—"

Keller was bracing for a blast of artillery from his mother when the phone rang and startled them both. Holly called out that she would get it, but Melanie yelled loudly at her not to get near the phone.

"Put your sister to bed while I take that," she snapped. "Tuck her in and tell her I'll be right up."

Keller walked to the threshold of the den and tried to calm down. Holly was watching *Cars* for about the hundredth time and constantly sang "Life is a Highway" in an adorable, off-key voice. She looked a lot like Melanie, with the same blue eyes, dark hair, and smile. She was dressed for bed, and he saw that the movie was ending: Holly had the remote in her hands and looked poised to watch the special features. Keller crept up behind her and snatched it away.

"Mom—hey, give it back! Mom, Keller's being mean!"

"Time for bed, kiddo."

"Uh-uh! You don't tell *me* to go to bed," Holly said with eight-year-old indignation oozing from every pore and a priceless pout on her face. Keller stopped the DVD, picked up his sister and put her over his shoulder. He started out of the den and headed for the stairs.

"I'm talking to you, mister," she said. "You can't put me to bed anymore. New rule."

"You didn't behave at the grocery, huh?"

"Well, I wanted candy," Holly began in an abashed voice. "And Jenny's mom buys her candy all the time but Mommy wouldn't buy me any. It's not fair. And Mommy hurt my feelings when she yelled so loud. Everybody at the store stared at us."

Like she yelled just now? "A grown-up young lady like you isn't supposed to throw a fit."

"I didn't throw a fit. Not a big one. And Mommy really yelled loud. It made me cry."

He started up the stairs after making sure he had a firm grip on his sister and that his weight was balanced. Both of them, over the years, had tumbled down the wide, carpeted steps a time or two, and Keller had no interest in a repeat performance with Holly in his arms. He imagined himself in traction after giving up his body to save her.

"Make a deal with you," he said. "Miss Caitlyn and I will take you to the park tomorrow—"

"And McDonald's?"

"Yes, if you're good at church in the morning. *And* if you stay in bed tonight until you fall asleep, even though the sun hasn't gone down. Can't get out of bed, got it?"

"I hate going to bed early! Nobody else has to go to bed this early!"

"There are consequences when you don't behave, young lady."

"Quit calling me that!"

"Let's just plan on having a better day tomorrow, okay?"

"I wish Daddy could tuck me in," Holly said. "I really miss Daddy."

"He'll be home in a few days."

"Mommy said we'll never see him again."

Keller's eyes popped. He'd often told Caitlyn that he would have a big advantage over friends who were never around little kids before getting married and having their own: He'd changed many diapers and was good at not only watching his mouth around Holly, but being careful not to overreact to the things she said. This was a big flag, though. Why on earth would Melanie say *that*, especially to her daughter? He would ask later but ignore it for now.

"She meant we wouldn't see him this weekend, sweetie. He's in Chicago, Illinois, and he'll be back when he's through doing his business up there."

He reached the top of the stairs and put his sister down, then took her hand and led her down the hall. His old bedroom was the first door on the right. It was open, and he glanced in out of habit and stopped when he saw the telescope on the desk. Holly saw what he was looking at and pulled away. She trotted into the room, went straight to the desk, climbed into his chair, and got on her knees. She leaned forward until she could look through the viewfinder.

"Come here, Keller. This is so cool."

"Why is that out, Holly?"

She turned to him with a charming little-girl smile. There was nothing devious about it: She was as proud of herself as could be. "I told Miss Jeannie you had a telescope," she said. "And I told her I would set it up so we could look outside."

"Who's Miss Jeannie?"

"The babysitter, dummy," Holly said with a comical roll

of her eyes, as if Keller had asked an idiotic question. "Both she and Mr. Doug looked, after I did."

Keller glanced at the phone extension a few feet away. The red light at the bottom was blinking, so Melanie was still on the phone. Doug, apparently, was the boyfriend who was here when Melanie arrived last night. It angered Keller that those two allowed Holly to unpack his SpaceProbe-130 from its box on his bookshelf and set it up, since none of them should have been in the room. That would be one more thing he would discuss with—

"And I saw Miss Caitlyn push Miss Sherry in the pool."

SIXTEEN

Keller felt a bolt of current zip through him. He didn't want to panic in front of his sister, though, and feigned interest in the telescope. It had been left exactly where he used to peek at Nancy and friends in their bikinis at the pool: There was a tiny pencil mark on the faded desktop where he set the leftmost corner of the SpaceProbe-130. Once it was anchored there, all he had to do was adjust the focus.

"I mean Miss Nancy," Holly said.

Keller glanced at the base of the phone again. Then he gathered himself and looked his little sister in the eye. If he wasn't careful, Holly would pick up on his consternation—his unbridled *terror*—and ask what was wrong. Then, depending on his reaction, she might blurt the information to their mother. Little kids just opened their mouths and said things without thinking them through, and Keller didn't want Melanie hearing of this until he knew exactly what Holly had seen.

Or what she thought she'd seen.

He tried to push the notion that Caitlyn might actually have done it from his mind.

"What did you say?" he asked, trying to keep his voice light.

"Miss Nancy pushed Miss Sherry in the pool."

"Miss Nancy or Miss Caitlyn?"

"Miss Nancy."

Keller felt himself relax a bit. "When?"

"Last night."

"Did the babysitter tell you this?"

"No, I saw it," Holly said. "With my own two eyes."

"When was this?"

"I told you, Keller, last night. I mean, duh!"

"I understand," he said calmly. "But was the sitter with you when you saw this?"

"No. Miss Jeannie and Mr. Doug were watching the movie. See, they wanted me to watch a DVD, so I told them *Cars*, and she put it in. And I got bored, 'cause I've seen it a million times," Holly said with another eye roll. "I had to go to the bathroom, then I was gonna go in my room and find a toy or something, and I thought of the telescope. So I came and set it up all by myself."

Keller nodded and forced himself to slow down. This was an eight-year-old child he was interrogating, after all—*who might possibly have to testify in court.* He looked again at the phone and wondered who Melanie was talking to. She was probably grateful that her son was putting the little munchkin to bed, but she would get off soon and come bustling up here to say goodnight. He didn't have much time and had to find a way to wrap up and change the subject. Otherwise it would remain on Holly's fertile little mind and she would inevitably start babbling to Melanie.

If she hadn't done so already.

Did she tell Mom that CAITLYN did it? Is that why Mom's acting so weird?

"So you and Jeannie and Doug came up here and got out the telescope…?"

"I showed them how it worked. They were really impressed!"

"But you guys looked at it, all three of you. And you came back up here later?"

"I got tired of the movie. I mean, I've seen it twelve million times."

"And you came back up by yourself. Is that right?"

"Yes, Keller. I mean, duh!"

"And you got up in that chair and looked through the telescope and saw what?"

Holly smiled that proud-of-herself smile again. "I told them I swam down there sometimes with Miss Nancy."

This made Keller's knees almost go wobbly. He decided he would stay half the night if necessary in order to tell his mother everything he knew about Nancy Rutledge, even though his dad was hundreds of miles away. It didn't matter how angry Melanie got. Holly was never to be at the Rutledge pool again for any reason, regardless of who was with her.

"And that I get to swim in the deep end because I'm a good swimmer," Holly added.

"But you set up the telescope to where you could see the pool, right?"

"Yes. So I could show them where I swim."

"Now tell me again what you saw?"

"Well, I'll tell you," Holly said, enjoying her moment on stage. The reports from Holly's teacher, though ranging in behavioral descriptions depending on the day, pretty much added up to the same thing: The little girl loved attention, which made sense because she was basically an only child with her brother in college and on his own. "Miss Sherry and Miss Nancy were out there."

"And?"

"Miss Nancy pushed Miss Sherry in. And I laughed,

because sometimes, Keller, at the pool at the hospital, when there are two lifeguards—one way up in the chair and the other with us in the water—they say it's okay if we push each other in, because the lifeguard is always there to—"

"I need to know exactly what you saw."

"I told you, Keller!"

"Anything else? Did you see Miss Sherry get out, or Miss Nancy go in the water with her?"

"Well, Miss Nancy walked away. I thought maybe she was going to get her suit on to go swimming. Then Miss Jeannie called for me and I went running down the stairs. I almost tripped, but I got my hand on the railing just in time."

Keller looked down and saw the phone line wink out. Melanie would be up in seconds. "Okay, but do you remember what Miss Nancy was wearing?"

"A black dress."

This was crucial. Keller felt his heart leap. "You're sure about that?"

"Yes, you silly goose, I'm sure."

SEVENTEEN

Daphne Kendall wasn't sure how long she'd be carrying Eddie Ray Chester's kid. But she'd accomplished the first part of her goal, which was to trap him into a pregnancy. She made eyes at him at the trailer park growing up but wasn't sure the cute, older boy ever knew who she was. She forgot about him once her figure developed and men of all ages began hitting on her. But he'd walked up that night in the bar and started talking about the old days and kept buying her drinks. As she did with many men, Daphne got drunk and slept with Eddie Ray, and she had to admit he was dynamite in the sack. But it took being sober the next morning to appreciate what a damn fine house the boy lived in. She asked if they could date only each other, and soon she was whispering that she loved him. Because after all, everyone knew what happened to Eddie Ray after his daddy got killed in that accident.

He and Monica got rich and left the trailer park for good.

So Daphne, who lived in a falling-down trailer with her ailing mother and barely had a dime to her name, got it on with Eddie Ray whenever, wherever and however he wanted. Some folks said he was learning-disabled, while others said he just talked real slow. But he babbled that he loved her, too, and he'd bought her a couple of outfits and pretty earrings and insisted on paying every time they went anywhere. Monica, who'd always been real nice, always fixed lots of food—that was one more reason for Daphne to make herself part of the household. She felt not a shred of guilt when she missed her period and the pregnancy kit tested positive after weeks of lies about the birth control she supposedly took very carefully. By gosh, if Eddie Ray and his mama won life's lottery and could leave the trailer park, Daphne decided, she and her mother would ride their coattails.

It would help a lot that the women were tight. Monica would hear how bad Patricia's cough was getting—you could hear it across a damn football field—and she'd see how Patricia had started carrying on conversations with herself and forgot who she was talking to in real-life half the time. Hopefully Monica would put her old friend in the best nursing home money could buy, but if she didn't, Daphne would tell Eddie Ray to give his mother a little nudge. Because they were now one big happy family, she would remind him, with a little one on the way. *That* would sway Monica for sure. You didn't have to be around the woman long to know how badly she wanted a grandchild, and, for that matter, how strongly she and her son felt about abortion. Daphne saw that firsthand when a teenage girl got knocked up during a made-for-TV movie they were watching: Monica and

Eddie Ray got so red-faced and loud Daphne felt like she was at a tent revival in the dead of summer.

She wasn't opposed to marrying Eddie Ray so long as he bought her a rich person's house and a hot car. And no nanny, no baby: The nanny could mess with diapers and formula and getting up at all hours, while Daphne would be sleeping late, watching TV, and surfing the Internet. She joined him on the love seat in a living room dominated by Western scenes and a huge plasma TV, and as she looked through the open curtains and saw the beautiful pines and oaks and the neatly-trimmed hedges and flower beds, she prepared to assure Eddie Ray that she'd pump out all the babies he wanted—but that he and Monica better plan on sharing the wealth. Living in this house, actually, would work fine if they built the nanny a guest cottage out back. Daphne would mention that, too. And the nanny would be busy: Daphne planned to get drunk and stoned whenever she felt like it, not to mention the eating for two she'd be doing whether pregnant or not. If Eddie Ray had a problem with any of that, well, tough.

"First, I 'pologize for last night," he began. "I know I hurt you. And I didn't mean to, baby. Lot on my mind."

Daphne met his eyes and shrugged. Then she turned away. The plan was to act cool for a few more seconds. She was more surprised than upset at his reaction last night and certainly wasn't hurt. She was definitely pregnant, and nothing other than an abortion would change that fact—she held all the cards, to her way of thinking. She didn't object when Eddie Ray scooted close and took her hands in his.

"Two weeks ago I'd have moved you right in," he said. "Problem is, Mother got married."

Daphne's last boyfriend was a mean drunk, but he was a wisecracking sort who was quick with a joke or funny line. Eddie Ray, who wouldn't hurt a flea, really didn't have a sense of humor. Sure, he smiled and laughed at things, and he seemed to follow those *Law & Order* episodes he loved so much. But his mind worked slow as molasses. That was why, she figured, he never cut up or acted the fool. So what he'd just said was no joke. Daphne asked him to repeat himself.

"You know that cruise she went on," he said. "She met up with a man named Arnold Webber, older fella she knew back before she met Daddy. Justice of the peace married them. He sold his house in Texas and put his stuff in storage and moved in when they got back from the Bahamas."

Daphne stared as resentment began to surge through her. Everything had worked out as planned, and now idiot-face Monica Chester had gotten *married* after running into an old flame on a freakin' cruise? Eddie Ray, of course, mistook the snarl on her face for profound amazement.

"I couldn't believe it, either. And I heard the slimy jerk's a con man—don't get me started on that. But he wants me out."

"What you mean? He done told you to your face? Hell, this is y'all's house!"

"They're newlyweds and want their privacy. Can't blame 'em for that, I guess." Eddie Ray squeezed her hands again. "And I was trying to find the right time to explain and hadn't done it, and here you was talking about the new house and car you want and I guess it got to me."

Daphne yanked her hands away. "You best look here, Eddie Ray—"

"Wait a minute, before you get all mad. I didn't say I's kicking you to the curb. I'd never do that, not with a child inside you, girl! We'll just have to do the best we can in a place of our own."

This made it sound like her access to Monica's money was still intact. Daphne's blood pressure fell, and she scooted next to him and caressed his thigh. "Remember when we was riding the other day, and there's that new neighborhood they're building out south? Right near the country club?"

Eddie Ray rolled his eyes and smiled. "In your dreams. Mine, too, believe me. But even with both of us working our butts off—you at least up till you have the baby—we'll most likely live in the projects. Maybe a trailer. Ain't like we're qualified to be president of a bank or something."

He wasn't joking about this, either. She let the words hang as she pulled away from him again. She took a deep breath and wished for a cigarette. A beer, too, although she'd be tempted to break the bottle over his head.

"Eddie Ray Chester, your mama got all that money from that contractor, remember?"

"Like I'm trying to tell you, Daphne, Mother done got married."

"What, this stepfather of yours is suddenly in charge of the money? Like hell!"

"It's Mother's, not mine!"

"You honestly think," she said in a quiet but firm voice, "that I'm going to live in the *projects* with you, let alone have a baby there?"

"Look, that's not my first choice—"

She stood and grabbed her purse from the coffee table. "Here's the deal: You grow a set. You be a man, and go to your mama and stepfather and tell 'em the truth: That you ain't worn no condoms in all the time we been together, and now I'm pregnant. I *know* your sweet mama will make sure me and the baby will be taken care of, as well as my own mama, who barely even knows her name no more."

Eddie Ray jumped to his feet. "Listen to me, Daphne, it just ain't that easy—"

"No, you listen to *me*: Sounds like you're trying to hoard all this money for yourself. I mean, really, Eddie Ray. Idea of us on welfare and all that, while your mother has all that money?

That pot you buy from that boy at the bar really has messed up your head."

"Please sit down," he said quietly.

She sat and was prepared to slap his hand away if he tried to put an arm around her. He was at least smart enough to pick up the ice and keep his distance.

"Of course I'm gonna tell them about the baby—"

"If you want me to have it, that is."

A mixture of fear and anger instantly appeared on his face, as she knew it would.

"You know I want to," she said. "But I won't if we're gon' live like Mama and I do now."

He took a deep breath. "All right. I'll talk to them about borrowing."

"She's your *mother*. She'll give it to you, for God's sake—she wants the best for her grandchild. And I'll tell you what: You don't ask them, I will."

"Won't be no need for that, okay?" Eddie Ray sighed heavily enough to rattle the cover of *Southern Living,* which sat atop the coffee table. "Something else we need to talk about. Now, you can't tell nobody about this. Not either of our mothers, not your girlfriends, not nobody. Hear?"

Intrigued, Daphne gave him a reassuring nod. She listened as he described a visit he had with an Oakdale cop following a chance meeting with Nancy Rutledge in her backyard. The familiar hostility toward *snotty rich people* flared in Daphne's mind at the name. Yet that bunch had a history, with the daddy dying in that wreck everyone insisted was suicide, and Caitlyn, who was admittedly an awesome basketball player and dating that cute Keller Bryan these days, being in the loony bin a few years ago after she tried to kill herself. Daphne's rule of thumb about rumors was that if everybody was talking, it was most likely true, so she believed everything she heard about the

Rutledge clan and hated them because they had money.

Eddie Ray really got her attention when he said Nancy *paid* him to lie to the cops. He showed her an envelope of ten grand and said more was on the way if Caitlyn was convicted of murdering their mother, who'd drowned in the family pool last night. Daphne went to her poker face and simply listened from there on out: the poor, stupid thing was freaked at perhaps having to testify in court to something he didn't see and looked like he was about to cry. When he finished talking she put her arms around him, kissed his neck, rubbed his pectoral muscles, and assured him he'd done the right thing: Reasonable doubt in the minds of the jury, as he'd just suggested, would certainly be enough to get Caitlyn off—and, yes, it would also keep payments coming from Nancy Rutledge. He whispered that he took the money to take care of her and the baby, and she smiled a smile he couldn't see as she led him to the guest room and undressed.

Now she *owned* Eddie Ray Chester. His clueless mother, too, for that matter.

EIGHTEEN

Keller and his mother were in the den after putting Holly to bed. She never said who called and resumed berating him for attacking Nancy. As she rattled off credentials that sounded a lot like talking points (Girl Scout, church pianist, high school valedictorian, regular volunteer at soup kitchen), he almost walked out in frustration. Caitlyn, just before Jack's fatal crash and Nancy's abrupt departure for Jackson six years ago, discovered a journal under a loose plank in the Rutledge tree house. She photocopied over forty pages that described in horrific detail the sexual molestation Nancy endured as well as her history of alcohol, pills, and rampant promiscuity. The information, which Caitlyn hadn't shown to him until a few months ago, broke his heart and made him physically ill as he read. But he would insist that his parents read every last word if Melanie continued to act as if Nancy was Oakdale's version of Mother Teresa. They just couldn't leave Holly alone with her again for any reason.

Was Nancy the friend Mom had dinner with?

That scenario was easier to stomach than his mother being with a man other than her husband. And it seemed possible: If Nancy called, say, late-afternoon with something urgent to discuss, Melanie could have lined up the sitter as Nancy raced to Tupelo in her BMW. Nancy had returned to Oakdale after her escapade with Brad and went to see Sherry, and whatever had taken place at the pool, Keller understood that Nancy rode to the hospital in the ambulance with Priscilla Hall. He supposed Nancy could have called his mother at some point in there—especially with such a dramatic change in plans—and perhaps Melanie went racing to the hospital to offer whatever support she could.

In his mind's eye, Keller saw them in the darkened hospital parking lot.

He'd seen Nancy smoking a joint with his own eyes and would bet everything he owned that she drank last night. Caitlyn said Nancy kept a flask in that huge purse she carried with her, and he could imagine his mother holding Nancy as she sobbed and having a few sips herself to calm her nerves. Thing was, though, James and Melanie Bryan just *didn't drink.* So it wouldn't take much alcohol for her to get fuzzy-headed before she drove home and called her son with the shocking news. But would Melanie have omitted so much crucial information on the phone last night?

Maybe Nancy had given his mother a set of instructions on how to deal with her son.

He smiled the best he could and interrupted the litany of Nancy Rutledge accomplishments.

"Look, we're all trying to figure out what happened last night." He paused for an instant and hoped his segue was subtle.

"By the way, tell me who watched Holly last night, so I'll know not to use her if you and Dad go to the coast or something and I have her a week."

"That's none of your damn business," Melanie said.

"Excuse me?"

She jumped to her feet and started from the room. "I heard something about McDonald's tomorrow. What time should I expect you to get your sister?"

Keller charged after his mother. "You said this girl had her boyfriend over!"

"You can let me know tomorrow, then. Good night."

She marched into the kitchen and left him standing by the grand piano. The front door was ten feet away. He looked that way and thought about leaving. His mother clearly wanted him out and was probably a lot more shaken by Sherry's death than she wanted to admit, especially with her husband away. She was a kind, nurturing woman with a high level of intelligence, but he and Caitlyn agreed that Melanie Bryan leaned on her husband for emotional support much more heavily than James relied on her. He started toward the kitchen, intent on giving his mom a reassuring hug before he hit the road. He would keep quiet about Nancy until his dad was home.

He arrived in time to see his mother yank open the fridge with a determined look on her face. She grabbed a quart of orange juice and fished a plastic stadium cup from the cupboard. Then she opened the pantry and removed a bottle of vodka. Keller couldn't believe what he was seeing. He'd never seen alcohol in the house, not even champagne on New Year's Eve. Melanie, though, made herself a mammoth screwdriver, the kind of drink an enterprising upperclassman would serve to a wide-eyed freshman belle at a frat party. She stirred the concoction with her index finger, took a healthy swig, then turned to him and set her jaw.

"Didn't I just ask you to leave?"

"Look, all I wanted to say—"

"So help me *God*!" Melanie shouted with gritted teeth, sending droplets of her drink onto the linoleum floor as her hand shook. "It's none of your damned business who watched your sister last night!"

Keller stared as his mother's voice reverberated through the kitchen. Hopefully Holly was singing to herself or talking to her stuffed animals and hadn't heard the explosion. Melanie looked angry enough to slap him, as if his query constituted a deeply offensive invasion of her privacy. That didn't make sense under normal circumstances, though, he thought, and the question absolutely begged to be asked after what Holly told him. With both parents out last night, why on earth would his mother *not* want him to know who sat for Holly? He'd followed his mother in here to give her a quick embrace, but the booze changed everything.

Maybe she did have a date last night. She wouldn't be this desperate to hide anything else.

And who'd just called her? Nancy? Or was it the would-be boyfriend, wanting a little more action? Maybe the sitter knew about them and was sworn to secrecy. For that matter, maybe *Nancy* knew about them! He tried to force the paranoia from his mind and focus on learning whatever he could about last night. But Melanie shocked him again when she plucked cigarettes and a little butane lighter from atop the fridge. He stayed rooted to his spot as she strode away. He heard her rip the sliding glass door open and moved to the kitchen window in time to see her appear on the patio.

He watched her light a cigarette and inhale before blowing smoke toward the soft blue sky.

This was like watching his mother play a part in a movie, their house and yard part of a big soundstage with Steven Spielberg in a director's chair with a bullhorn. Melanie set the cigarettes and lighter on the gas grill, then gulped down some more of her drink. She was going through it the way Caitlyn guzzled Gatorade after basketball practice, and the thought of Holly sneaking downstairs and encountering their mother in this state broke Keller's trance. He hurried to the sliding glass, stepped onto the patio and eased the door closed. Holly's window overlooked the patio. Hopefully she wouldn't look outside.

"Go away," Melanie said. "I'm not going to tell you again."

Her voice reminded him of a snake poised to strike. Keller desperately wished his father was here and would call him at the first available opportunity. But what would he say? He'd never seen his mother like this—not even close—and now felt frightened. Was Holly safe? If Melanie planned to get smashed, at least she was already at home and could stagger into bed. But did she actually tell Holly that they would never see—

"Mom," he said slowly, "did you really tell Holly we'll never see Dad again?"

She turned to him. Keller wasn't sure what he expected on his mother's face, but he was caught off guard when that smirk reappeared. She took another sip of her screwdriver. Then she inhaled and blew more smoke.

"Bastard walked out after twenty years of marriage, just like that."

This made Keller's knees weak.

Could it be true?

James Bryan, like Keller's grandfather until his death a decade ago, consistently went the extra mile with suppliers as well as customers. That was a big reason why the little haberdashery had done so well for so long. An Independence Day journey to Chicago to save an important clothing line didn't surprise Keller, and James probably jumped in his truck and roared up I-55 because getting a last-minute flight on a holiday weekend was impossible. That said, though, Keller, hadn't lived in this house in a year. Maybe things weren't very joyous between his parents anymore. Did James have someone on the side, someone he saw while making his business trips?

If anyone knew *that* little factoid around here, Sherry and Nancy Rutledge would.

Keller just couldn't imagine his dad walking out on the entire family, though, especially Holly. But his mother wasn't just worked up—she was like a different person. He saw her with Nancy again, but instead of Melanie holding the younger woman as she sobbed, they were crying on each other's shoulders and using language salty enough to melt the pavement. They *had* to have talked recently if Melanie was suddenly so protective of her, and Keller wouldn't put it past Nancy to impart entirely fictional stories of James Bryan's infidelities and send Melanie with booze, cigarettes and maybe even pills to "take the edge off." Nancy didn't do supportive things out of the goodness of her heart, of course: she played angles when she saw something to be gained. But what, in this case?

"Look, Dad left a note," Keller heard himself say in a voice he hardly recognized as his own. "That's what you told me Thursday when I came by the store, when you had Holly up there and were doing inventory. He's in Chicago on business. He's made tons of trips like that over the years—"

"You got that right."

Melanie took a dramatic drag to punctuate a reply that clearly insinuated infidelity. Keller couldn't help but notice she looked like she knew what she was doing with those cigs. Maybe she'd smoked long ago and quit before picking it back up. She turned her gaze on him.

"Kids think they know a little something about everything," she said. "But you don't have a clue how the world works. So get off your high horse and stop pretending you do."

Kids? Anger crackled inside him at her smug look and the seen-it-all posture she'd adopted as she sipped again. This was the woman, an internal voice pointed out, that left her eight-year-old daughter in the hands of an unfit sitter last night. But he sure wouldn't get anywhere arguing about that. Something was dreadfully wrong, and he needed to close this down before she screamed at him again and got the attention of the neighbors. He would call his father the minute he was off the property.

But was Holly safe in their mother's care tonight?

"...hardest part of being a parent is watching your children make bad choices."

This brought Keller to the present. "What choices? Who are you talking about?"

"You and Caitlyn, damn it! She fooled every last one of us."

"What the hell are you talking about, Mom?"

Melanie dropped her cigarette to the patio and busied herself with lighting another. Hopefully the butt would burn itself out. He could see her lingering out here, her head wherever it was, and inadvertently setting the yard on fire. She had a sad smile on her face when she met his eyes again.

"Sherry."

It took him a second, but he realized Melanie was all but accusing Caitlyn of murdering her mother. He looked up into the trees and focused on a point in the distance. Was this why Melanie Bryan was drinking and smoking in front of him and generally acting out of her head?

"Do you realize what you're saying?" he whispered.

"Go home," Melanie growled as her gaze became fierce again. "I want you out of my sight."

"I'll read to Holly till she falls asleep. I don't want her seeing you like this."

Melanie turned her back on him and puffed away. He opened the sliding glass door, slipped inside and closed it, and headed for the stairs as acid burned his stomach. The blast of cool air felt good, but now his head throbbed from cigarette smoke as well as stress. Keeping Holly in her bedroom was a good move in an awful situation, he felt, but it would backfire if their mother got sloshed in the next few minutes and came charging into the room and frightened the little girl. If that happened he would forcibly remove Holly for the night, and things might get really ugly. But hopefully their mother would do whatever she had to do outside and go straight to bed in a few minutes.

His cell rang when he reached the top of the stairs.

He reached into his cargo shorts for the phone and prayed that this was his dad. If so, he'd go right back downstairs and put him on with his mother and stand a few feet away and see what in the world they said to each other. He frowned when he saw *Angela Bartman* on the screen, however. He punched a button and held the phone to his ear.

"This is Keller. What's up, Angie?"

"Hey, bud. Caitlyn asked me to call you. You still at your mom's?"

Keller felt his blood pressure soar at the prospect of trouble. He was two steps from his old bedroom and close enough for Holly to hear him. He had no doubt she was still awake.

"Yes. What is it?"

Angie paused. "Police want to talk to her. My lawyer's on her way from Tupelo. I told Caitlyn to keep her mouth shut until she gets there and not answer any questions."

NINETEEN

"Hello, Chief Blair," Tina Littlefield said after introducing herself to Caitlyn. "Can I have a minute with my client, please, sir?"

Littlefield was Angie Bartman's attorney and a brunette

of perhaps fifty with gray at her temples. Wearing a navy suit, she'd marched into the stuffy, windowless interrogation room carrying a briefcase that reminded Caitlyn of what Jack Rutledge took to the office each day. There was no doubt she was in control, and Caitlyn's first impression was that an honest, competent lawyer had her back. The phrase *my client* was chilling, however. It drove home the certainty that all of this, from the shocking death of her mother to the crazy notion that the police might consider *her* a suspect, was real. She knew she'd done the right thing by lawyering up, as they said on TV: There was a reason Higgins asked her down here, and she couldn't imagine what it was. All sorts of scenarios had played out in her head as she drove downtown after frantically calling Angie for help, including the possibility that Nancy knew Higgins and put him up to this.

For that matter, had Nancy killed their mother? She was now wondering.

Littlefield saw Blair, Higgins, and a uniformed female officer out of the room and closed the door behind them. Then she returned to the table and sat across from Caitlyn. She wore a wedding ring and looked like she might have grown children, maybe even a grandchild. She had a businesslike air about her, but Caitlyn saw warmth in her eyes.

"Okay. Please tell me you didn't answer any questions, young lady."

"Didn't speak at all," Caitlyn said, "other than to tell them you were coming."

"Excellent. Ready to leave?"

Caitlyn looked at her in surprise. "Now?"

"We'll talk in the next day or so." Littlefield stood and picked up the briefcase, then jerked a thumb at the door. "I'll put them off, tell 'em we'll set up a meeting in a day or so. Which we'll never have, far as I'm concerned. Meantime, I'll work on finding out why you were brought in."

Caitlyn got slowly to her feet. Littlefield had driven from Tupelo, and the forty-five minute wait after Angie's reassuring follow-up call (which Caitlyn took as she parked the Jeep several steps from the front doors of the police station) seemed to have taken hours. Her temples throbbed, her chest was tight, and her palms, armpits, and brow were damp. She was dying of thirst, too.

"I can't thank you enough for responding so fast, especially on Saturday night."

Littlefield smiled. "Glad to do it. Angie's a friend, and she adores you."

"Higgins—the detective—was *pissed* when I said my lawyer was coming," Caitlyn whispered. "Oh, and that woman kept looking at me, and I finally realized it was the mother of a girl I played ball with in high school. She used to work at the sheriff's department. She didn't say anything, but Higgins all but accused me of killing my mother. Tough keeping my mouth closed."

"I'm glad you did. And let's get one thing straight, Caitlyn: You don't talk to *anybody* about this. Not without checking with me first."

"Yes, ma'am."

"And I'm sorry about your mom. I really am."

"Thanks."

"You're local, so you know about the Gary Quinn shootings last winter," Littlefield said as she also lowered her voice to a whisper. "Strictly between us, the D.A. made Henry Blair look like an idiot. Blair stepped up and admitted poor judgment in pushing for that low bond and letting Quinn back on the street, and the D.A., who could have insisted that Quinn be tried on charges involving that thirteen-year-old, didn't. If he had, Quinn wouldn't have been back on the street to commit those murders. I know Neal Cramer, and, believe me, he doesn't like talking about that."

"I bet he doesn't."

"Anyway, dear, he needs a high-profile conviction in the worst way to save face with voters in this area, and Blair needs the same thing to keep his job. I've met Blair and he seems like a decent sort, but I'll be watching them *very* carefully. Just put your mind at rest about this, okay? I know you've got a lot on your plate. Now let's go."

Caitlyn nodded. Like Keller, Angie was a wonderful sounding board. And Caitlyn could describe to her friend the paranoia she'd felt around Keller all day: She wondered if he was thinking, deep down, that maybe his girlfriend had finally snapped. He hadn't said anything, but it was just a feeling Caitlyn had. And if he was already suspicious, it might increase once he learned that the cops were interested in her. But Keller just couldn't pull away.

Her sanity would crack faster than the faulty foundation beneath the duplex.

TWENTY

Scott Perry sat in his cubicle in the newsroom at the NBC affiliate in Tupelo, his cell phone pressed to his ear to block out the occasional bursts from the scanner. It was a quiet Sunday morning. As always, he'd arrived at work several hours early to get a jump on the newscasts at five and ten. In addition to being the news anchor and senior reporter on weekends, he also produced the shows. He checked the news wires and made calls before the small crew of reporters and photographers straggled in at two. By then he was ready to huddle with the team about beating the streets in search of local news.

Scott was from Dallas and a graduate of Syracuse University. He interned at a hometown station before landing his first full-time job in Tupelo. His goal was to report and produce for CNN, FOX, or one of the broadcast networks—he'd learned from good people and knew to absorb as much as he could during this two-year stretch in Mississippi, instead of griping and goofing off the way some of his co-workers did. Part of his routine each weekend was to phone his contacts at police departments and sheriff's offices all over the area. He'd impressed his news director by driving his personal car on days off to make those contacts: He gave out business cards and urged the small town law enforcement folks to call him with news tips. Once in a while they did, but Scott had struck gold several times by coaxing information from those who weren't quite brave or assertive enough to get in touch on their own.

His contact at the Smart County sheriff's office was a part-time dispatcher named April. He'd met her on one occasion, and she struck him as in the loop and eager to please: it didn't hurt that he was a fixture on the air and famous to a degree in the eyes of the local folks. April answered on the first ring.

"What you want, Scott Perry?" she asked. Usually she sounded happy-go-lucky, but he couldn't read her tone today.

"Didn't know if you'd be home. Just looking for a scoop on a Sunday."

"Try Baskin-Robbins."

Scott smiled. "Very funny. Anything cooking over there in Oakdale?"

"Other than the chicken I'm frying up for me and my niece? Which you still ain't driven out here in the country and tried, Mr. TV Star, like you said you would. Make you a plate of down-home food that'll knock you to your knees."

"One of these days, I promise," Scott said. "Anything I should know about?"

There was a long pause. Scott felt a bite on the line and grabbed a pen and his reporter's notebook and poised himself to write.

"You didn't hear this from me," April said softly. Scott guessed April's niece was in the room, and that this tidbit wasn't for her ears, either. "Know that rich woman who drowned in town?"

He realized April was referring to what happened in Oakdale. They'd led with the Sherry Rutledge death Friday night at ten, although details at that point were sketchy. The Oakdale police chief was vague yesterday about anything new, so Scott's follow-up report was a rehash of what they already had. If April had an update, though—

"Sherry Rutledge," he said.

"Right. Now, her daughter—the basketball player at the college—was brought in for questioning yesterday evening. Name's Caitlyn, which I'm sure you know."

Scott looked around. He was by himself in the newsroom, and the master control operator was the only other employee in the building before noon on Sunday. Caitlyn Rutledge was a big deal in these parts, an SEC basketball star and a really nice person to boot: Scott met her when she was on hands and knees several months ago while building a Habitat for Humanity home with fellow church members in Tupelo. He had no idea she was the daughter of the Oakdale woman who drowned—apparently the idiots in sports didn't know, either—but he wasn't about to admit that to April.

"What, y'all bring her in?"

"Naw. Police department did," April whispered.

"They charge her with anything?"

"Don't sound like it."

Scott lowered his voice. "They think she killed her mother, though?"

"I don't know. Honest. But they definitely brought her in for questioning. Lawyer came down there, and Caitlyn left with her—Caitlyn wouldn't talk. Now, Scott?"

"Yeah," he said, writing furiously.

"You didn't hear *none* of that from me."

TWENTY ONE

"Here she is," Keller said as Melanie's minivan came into view. "This should be interesting."

"I'll watch Holly." Caitlyn kissed his cheek before getting to her feet. "Take all the time you need. We'll swing, do the merry-go-round, whatever."

He and Caitlyn were at a cement picnic table shaded by a massive oak at City Park, which was almost empty on a Sunday morning with everyone at church. Puffy white clouds were already beginning to dot the horizon on a sunny day that would be breathtakingly steamy by afternoon. He watched his mother park a few feet from Caitlyn's Jeep and felt his stomach churn at the prospect of more trouble. Some of the tension evaporated when the middle door opened and Holly jumped out and sprinted off toward the monkey bars.

"Looks like she's okay, at least," he said.

"I'm sure she's fine, babe."

"Hope so. Mom was pure ice on the phone."

"Hangovers do that to people."

"Hey, she was talking crazy last night way before she started drinking." Melanie had cut the engine but remained in the van, Keller saw. He thought she might be on her cell phone but wasn't sure. "Keep her good and occupied, okay? If I set Mom off again, I don't want it to be in front of Holly, and if she goes off on you I'm liable to knock her into next week."

"Just stay calm," Caitlyn said. "You'll know what to say. You always do."

He'd heard Melanie reenter the house last night after he began reading to Holly and braced himself for another fight. But

Joe Lee

she returned to the patio a minute later and never came up the stairs. Holly wasn't in a deep sleep until it was dark outside, and Keller turned off her light, opened the door, and crept down the hall to the master bedroom. It was empty, and Melanie wasn't in the living room, either. He'd peered through the kitchen window and saw her slumped over in a lawn chair, the overturned plastic tumbler at her feet and her phone and cigarettes and lighter in her lap. She'd passed out, and she reeked of cigarettes and booze when he got out there and didn't respond when he called her name from two feet away.

He'd gathered her into his arms and carried her up to bed before leaving the house near tears.

He tried his father's cell phone twice on the way back to Caitlyn's and got the voice mail both times. He was angry and emotional when he reached the duplex and paced as he described his mother's bizarre behavior. Caitlyn assured him that Holly would be fine overnight and that his father, hardly a techno-geek, had forgotten his cell or left it on silent and would apologize from head to toe when he got all the messages from his son. Caitlyn didn't know what to make of Melanie's words and actions any more than he did, though. They talked for hours, and Keller stared at the ceiling long after Caitlyn drifted off—he'd already downed a large Coke this morning to get his motor running. He was watching Caitlyn sneak up on Holly when a door slammed shut. He turned toward the minivan.

Oh, God.

His mother was in a pink halter that revealed her shoulders and midriff. Faded blue-jean shorts that left little to the imagination clung to her hips and gave way to bare feet. He didn't know she had clothes like that, let alone would dare wear them in public—girls *his* age wore that kind of thing to the pool and crawfish boils and perhaps around guys they wanted to seduce. She wore sunglasses and was moving slowly, her brown purse

106

just barely over her left shoulder and looking like it might fall to the ground. He wondered if some of the alcohol from last night was still in her system.

Or if she drank this morning in front of Holly.

"Morning," he said when she was six feet away.

Melanie said nothing. She dropped the purse on the table and went right for her cigarettes. She shook one from its pack and lit up before sitting across from him as the sun went behind a cloud. She inhaled before tilting her head skyward to expel the smoke from her lungs. He thought back to his mother's funk several years ago. Maybe she was a depressed person who'd masqueraded for years as a cheery wife and mother. Had she reached some sort of boiling point this weekend? She was going to explain herself, though, no matter how uncomfortable it got out here. Caitlyn would know to lead Holly to a different part of the park if necessary.

"Rule number one is this," she said hoarsely. "I don't have to give you a reason for anything. So get that through your head."

Keller peeked to his right. Caitlyn was pushing Holly in a swing fifty yards away. He turned back to his mother and watched her smoke. At least Melanie had a memory of his visit last night. Caitlyn expected her to be blank as a stone, but she was still angry, apparently, that he wanted to know who babysat Friday night. There was no telling what else she might be upset about.

"I hope you're not doing that in front of Holly," he said.

There was that infuriating smirk again. She said nothing.

"I love you, Mom. Anything you want to talk about?"

She blew smoke into his face. It made his eyes water, but he resisted the impulse to react.

"I'm just saying I'm here. I know you got your hands full with Dad—"

She whipped the shades off. Underneath were bloodshot eyes that looked like absolute hell. He wondered if she'd puked her head off in the middle of the night or this morning. She probably felt like crap if she'd had two tumblers of vodka and orange juice. The drink he saw her make would have equaled at least three in a bar, and he assumed she went back for a refill while he read to Holly.

"Don't you defend that creep. Don't you dare," she hissed as she leaned over the table and nearly gagged him with acrid smoke breath. He was treated to an unwanted display of cleavage and couldn't help but notice that his mother wasn't wearing a bra. The sight made him as uncomfortable as anything she could say to him, he figured. "It's time to grow up and see things for what they are, little boy. You're not half the man you think you are."

Caitlyn said last night that some people seemed to handle death a lot better than others. James Bryan, who'd already lost both his parents and was a pallbearer at three other funerals in recent years, was typically quiet but always dignified, strong and comforting in the face of death. When Phil Roland, Keller's high school math teacher and now the husband of Melanie's bookstore employee Gina, lost his first wife to cancer, it was James who immediately stepped forward and embraced Phil when the old man broke down at the cemetery. The hug must have lasted half a minute, and Keller had never been prouder of his pop.

He and Caitlyn agreed that Melanie was much more fragile in that regard, yet Keller just couldn't see his mother having a nervous breakdown over *Sherry's* death. There had to be something else playing out in her head: something causing her to mouth off about her husband, not to mention the smoking, drinking, and the trailer-trash get-up. Was Melanie Bryan even cognizant of the fact that she was acting like this in front of her kids, especially an eight-year-old daughter that could be permanently scarred by what she saw and heard?

"Okay, then, talk to me," Keller said, trying to feign a calmness he didn't feel. "You were always a good teacher. Both in the classroom and at home."

For a moment it appeared she would open up. He imagined holding her while she sobbed and would get Caitlyn's attention and signal for her to keep Holly busy—Holly didn't handle it well when she saw people crying. He would spend the whole day with his arm around his mother if necessary. But Melanie merely sniffed, as if he'd said something stupid. She put her shades back on and smoked with her eyes fixed on a point in the distance. She seemed to be enjoying letting him hang, and Keller, who was already on edge, felt anger build inside him. But he'd vowed to keep cool. This meant keeping his emotions in check and acting, if he had to, as if he was as unenlightened about the world as his sister.

"Then Mom, if you think I need to grow up," he said, "I'm all ears. Please talk to me."

Melanie threw back her head and howled. Caitlyn's psychiatrist popped into his head for the first time as he watched little puffs of smoke dissipate in the air. Keller had never met the man but understood him to be bearded and older and warm. Maybe *he* would be able to reach Melanie Bryan, since Keller sure couldn't. And his father would have to take her. Hopefully James would call this morning and announce that he was headed home from Chicago after apologizing for not returning his son's messages promptly. And Keller made an executive decision in that moment: He would watch his sister until their father got home. He stood and wondered if he would need therapy of his own after seeing most of his mother's naked body.

"We'll go ahead and take Holly to McDonald's and maybe a movie," he said. He wasn't about to tell his mother that Holly would spend the night with him—maybe several nights—

out of fear for his sister's safety. He was also uneasy about his mother being by herself in this state of mind, but he was certain he was doing the right thing by taking charge of Holly. He'd have to go to the house later today for clothes and her toothbrush and a stuffed animal or two, and that might be horribly awkward. But he'd fall off that bridge later. "You gonna hang out here a while, or…?"

"Sit your butt back down. You think you're old enough for the truth?"

Keller lowered himself onto the cement bench as a shiver went through him. Whatever Melanie's thought processes were at the moment, maybe she'd always exercised a maternal instinct not to involve him in things that weren't his concern. Sure, she wouldn't want her son knowing about an extramarital affair. But all parents, he'd heard James and Melanie say many times, wanted their kids to just be *kids* as long as possible—they didn't want their precious babies being forced to grow up too fast. His mother's almost sinister tone, though, told him that he was about to get the information he wanted.

And that it wouldn't be pretty.

"Don't interrupt me," she said. "Or I won't talk."

As long as you don't start in on Caitlyn, he almost said. He bit his tongue and nodded. Then he waited while she lit another cigarette. Melanie, who had her emotional moments like everyone else, had sounded at the end of the call Friday night like she was about to cry. Maybe part of it was alcohol, assuming she was tipsy, but she said she loved both Rutledge girls. Keller didn't doubt her: She adored Caitlyn and hadn't been subtle about her hope that Keller would marry her, and while Melanie had been conspicuously quiet about Nancy in recent years, it was hard to imagine his mother *not* feeling something for the girl who sat for their son so many times as he grew. If Melanie was hurting, though, it was concealed behind a mask of rage.

"The sitter is Jeannie Hanson," she said as she exhaled smoke. "All right?"

Keller nodded. The name meant nothing to him, but he could work on that later.

"James can go to hell."

"He's in Chicago, right?"

"I don't know where he is, nor do I care." Melanie gazed high into the trees and shook her head. "Talk about being the last to know. But at least I do now. Cheating bastard."

Keller swallowed hard and kept his mouth shut. Caitlyn, for her part, utterly refused to believe James Bryan was having an affair and had left his family. Her insistence made Keller feel better, but his confidence wavered in the face of his mother's hostility. He was dying to ask what she knew and where it came from, but she'd warned him not to interrupt. She leaned back and stretched as a little smile spread across her face. He heard her back pop and couldn't help but notice her breasts pressing against the thin fabric of the halter. His roommate Patrick returned from a trip to his grandparents when he was twelve and said he accidentally walked in on his mother as she was wrapping a towel around herself after a shower. Patrick said he spun on a dime and backed out before his mother ever knew what happened, but he assured Keller he'd seen everything there was to see. It apparently didn't mess with Patrick's head in the least, but Keller felt like he was violating his mother and needed to serve hard time behind bars, maybe spend a few days on a chain gang in the blistering sun.

"And if he is, I am," Melanie said. "Fair is fair. And since Derek was right there in the store, I said, 'Come on with it. Do this country girl like you used to.'"

The words clanged off Keller's brain like rounds of automatic gunfire.

Let her talk. You can decide what you want to believe later.

"See, Derek's from Hollandale. First boyfriend," she said. She sounded almost dreamy now, like she was sharing this information with a girlfriend—*Nancy?*—during Happy Hour over a bottomless glass of beer. "He's a lawyer. Also wrote a damn good legal thriller, which is no surprise because he's a damn good lawyer."

"Book signing?"

Melanie chuckled at this and lapsed into a coughing spasm that became so fierce he thought she might be sick. Her shades even fell off, and Keller—after shooting a glance at the merry-go-round and spotting his sister playing with another little girl—hopped up, reached down for the sunglasses, and handed them to his mother. She put them back on without a word and lit yet another cigarette when she realized she'd dropped the previous one in the grass while coughing. Keller, not wanting the park to burn down, stomped on it before taking his seat. His stomach was howling from the stress, but he tried his best to focus on his mother's tale and act as neutrally as possible.

"What?" she said. Now she did look blank.

"Book signing. Friday."

Melanie smiled again. "Poor thing didn't sell a single book. Nobody came at all."

Keller frowned at this. His mother talked up her author events to every single person who set foot in the store, and she advertised in the newspaper and distributed flyers like bank tellers handed out suckers to little kids. She always had regulars and at least a few others at signings, and while some events didn't make money, it was hard to believe there wasn't a soul in the store Friday afternoon.

"His book is really good," she said. "He felt like a fool, and I said, 'Look, let's go have a drink, get a bite to eat.' Then I thought, 'Hell, there's no need for all that when we can just go to the back, you gorgeous thing, and *do* this country girl.'"

Keller saw the bookstore in his mind. The display window facing the street was as attractive as any on the square, with hardbacks and paperbacks on small wooden stands juxtaposed against a stained-glass backdrop his father made for her. Inside, university memorabilia was everywhere, and built-in bookcases, similar to the ones in the living room at home, lined the walls. The café was in back and had room for a dozen people. It had proved a great move because almost everyone who stopped for a snack walked out with at least a magazine or newspaper and helped keep the store afloat. Behind the café was her office: it was a cramped room with a computer desk, folding chair, lamp, and couch.

Which folded out into a bed.

There were just as many holes in this scenario as there were with his mother and Nancy huddling in the hospital parking lot Friday night. *But it was possible.* She'd told him in the past that she had no choice but to turn down authors who'd published their own books and didn't have anyone promoting their work, because *that's* when you had nobody turn out for someone nobody had ever heard of. If this Derek guy really was an old boyfriend, though, he might have leaned on her to do a signing— especially if he had designs of scoring with his old girlfriend. And if his mother was being truthful about what she supposedly heard about her husband, maybe she did line up a sitter at the very last second. Jeannie Hanson, a voice said. He'd have to commit that to memory. But how did Nancy figure into all this, if Melanie was being so protective of her? Could Nancy somehow know this author and gotten Melanie hooked up with the sitter?

He forced himself to analyze later and focus on his mother. The last thing he wanted was chapter and verse about her time with this man—real or imagined—and he dared take control of the discussion. This was almost like being a police investigator and trying to get as much out of a witness as possible. The tone of his voice could easily shut whatever window he'd opened in her.

"Well, what happened when you got home?" he said. "Fire truck, ambulance and such?"

"Oh, Derek followed me, like I knew he would," she said. She sounded almost wistful now. Keller pictured her telling this man during a final embrace that she needed to put her daughter to bed, but letting it be known with a wink that she wouldn't mind some company later in the evening. "Got there right after I did. Can't remember the name of the boy with Jeannie—"

Doug, Keller thought to himself. Holly had mentioned the name.

"—but he was about to do to her what Derek just got through doing to me—"

She's totally off her rocker. No mother says this in front of her son. If she even knows it's me.

"—and the little punk sassed me when I said to get the hell out of my house. That's when she ran in and told me about the fire truck and ambulance."

"Holly, you mean."

Melanie took another drag and let it out with a milder coughing fit. "Talk about getting in the way—I mean, go play with your damn dolls. But like I always say, timing's everything. Derek picked that exact moment to knock, bottle of wine in hand. 'Dad, what the hell are you doing here?'"

For a moment Keller was confused. Holly had been carefully shielded from such language, and she would have been thrilled to see her father, not shocked. But James wasn't there, Keller reminded himself. Then it dawned on him that Melanie was talking about the reaction of the *sitter*: Derek, the dashing high-school boyfriend from Hollandale and damn-good-lawyer-turned-author, was the *father* of the irresponsible idiot who'd agreed at the last minute to watch Holly?!? This was such a remarkable coincidence—apparently—that Keller forgot his anger and upset and stared.

"Oh, Jeannie went nuts," Melanie said. "Raced out of the house, got in her car, and tore off up the street, the boy right behind in his truck. Derek went off after her. Figured he'd come back after getting everything settled, but he didn't. I'll hear from him, though. Always do. Grew up with his first two wives. This new one I don't know, but I'm sure she's as vindictive and hateful as the rest."

This made it sound like his mother had had an ongoing affair that might date back to her grim period when she left teaching. Keller hated himself for becoming judge and jury and taking his father's side, but down deep he felt Caitlyn was right: There was no way James Bryan was cheating. None. And Keller honestly felt that his mother, in need of something or someone she didn't think she had, just might. Was it possible that she was on some sort of medication he didn't know about—

Given to her by Nancy???

—and was simply out of her head right now and would be fine in a couple of days? He desperately wanted to give her the benefit of the doubt and believe that everything was fine with the Bryan marriage. He heard the happy shouts of Holly and the other little girl, shot a look over there, and saw that Caitlyn and a young mom were side by side pushing the girls in the swings. Keller felt a bead of sweat drip down his right temple and realized how sticky he already was. He hadn't eaten anything this morning because of nerves, and he needed some food to soothe his stomach. He also needed a shower. And maybe, once Holly was situated, to cry on Caitlyn's shoulder—

"And you'll love this," Melanie said. "Nancy said James has a thing for her."

TWENTY TWO

Keller had started to get up and announce, once and for all, that he and Caitlyn were taking Holly to McDonald's and that he would call later in the day. He'd gotten everything he felt he could handle emotionally, but his knees went weak at this tidbit, which hung in the air like the smoke from his mother's cancer sticks. He slumped forward. Melanie seemed not to notice.

Not Nancy and Dad. Please, God.

"She said when Jack died, James was real sweet and supportive. But the day she left for Jackson, she had her car packed and went out to the cemetery one last time. James must have seen her in traffic and followed her out there. Said some suggestive things. *Did* some suggestive things. And just won't leave her the hell alone."

Keller closed his eyes and tried to picture the scene.

Don't sweat this right now. Just LISTEN.

"He got her cell number somehow," Melanie said. "Called her all the time, even after she got married. Got real bad when they moved here. She went in his store one day and told him to stop. She said she was coming to me if he didn't, and he still wouldn't leave her alone. So she told me."

Now Melanie was looking at him like she expected a response. Keller had no idea what to do.

"I know you'll defend him to the hilt," she said with a mean smile. "Like always."

She coughed again, then ground her cigarette right there on the table and suddenly looked livid. Keller sat completely still and wished he could vanish into thin air. But he knew he had to stick this out and get what information he could from her. Then he would leave with Caitlyn and Holly as gracefully as possible.

"If he thinks he needs a little honey because I'm too old

and not pretty enough and not skinny enough anymore, well, all men are like that," Melanie said. "But the *babysitter*? I mean, he might as well have gone to Hollandale and started screwing my sisters right out in the open. If he isn't already. I'd put nothing past him. And you can bet he's with someone right this second. Nancy says she's heard it all."

It sounded like Nancy and his mother had indeed been in contact. He could see Nancy serving as an emotional scratching post as well as a pharmacy and liquor store, which might account for his mother's frame of mind. But could Nancy have slept with his father? It made his heart hurt to think about it, but yes, it was possible. Nancy left town so quickly after Jack Rutledge's death that maybe she wanted to escape a lot of things—including an interlude with Mr. Bryan down the street. Keller thought back to the day when he saw, through the SpaceProbe-130, Nancy holding a razor blade to her wrist while sobbing in the tree house. Her father's car crash was just days later, and since then Keller had learned about the molestation. But was she crying about *James Bryan* that day? He didn't need to start passing judgment and making decisions until he'd talked to his father, though.

Wherever the hell he was.

"She said plenty about Caitlyn, too," Melanie said.

Keller jumped to his feet as if stung by an insect. He mopped sweat from his brow and took a deep breath. He was at his own breaking point and might slap his mother's sunglasses right off her head if she mentioned anything about Caitlyn pushing Sherry into the pool. It was very possible that his mother had talked to Nancy *this morning* before coming out here.

"I'll call you later. We'll take Holly to McDonald's, then a movie—"

"You go right ahead and live in denial," Melanie said. She stretched again, then pushed on the table for support with wobbly arms and managed to get to her feet. She put her cigarettes and lighter in her purse, then put the purse over her shoulder and reeled past him. She stumbled as she reached the sidewalk but righted herself. "Don't say I didn't warn you."

This, thought Keller, was approximately what Nancy said to Caitlyn yesterday. He was now willing to bet that alcohol and/or medication was responsible for his mother's mindset, and that she might be a danger to herself. He looked again toward the play area. Holly and the other little girl, thankfully, were now in the sandbox. Keller watched his mother amble along in her hideously short shorts and wondered if she would wreck the van—it was probably a miracle she'd gotten here safely. Holly looked up when she opened the driver's side door. She started to run that way, but Caitlyn, also watching, looked at Keller. He shook his head firmly, and Caitlyn reached down and scooped Holly into her arms and positioned her so they could both wave at Melanie. Melanie cranked up, backed out, and headed for the entrance of the park.

Without waving at her daughter, Keller saw.

He let out a heavy sigh and flicked more sweat from his forehead. Then he started for the play area. Caitlyn was putting Holly down, and Keller could see her talking to Caitlyn—where's Mommy going and why didn't she wave? Caitlyn wouldn't know how to answer and was probably trying to say something reassuring. Holly would nod, but then she would ask Keller the same thing in just a moment.

And he wouldn't know what to say.

TWENTY THREE

"First, honey, I know you're not attracted to your mother," Caitlyn said quietly. She and Keller were in the kitchen of the townhouse he shared with his roommate Patrick, another neighbor she'd known since early childhood. Patrick, God bless him, was playing racquetball with friends and would be gone a couple of hours. Caitlyn had positioned herself at the edge of the hallway to keep an eye on Holly, who was watching a rented copy of *Shrek* in the living room after eating chicken nuggets and fries at McDonald's. "Second, I'd be surprised if that author's even a real person. And third, I honestly think your dad forgot or lost his cell phone."

"Then why not call from his hotel room or wherever he is?"

"He may have tried your mom. Eventually he'll try you if he doesn't get home first."

Keller hung his head. She knew he was worn out from worry over his dad's whereabouts as well as Melanie's suddenly incomprehensible behavior. The cigarettes and alcohol was one thing if Melanie felt especially stressed following the death of a neighbor. Caitlyn had kept a close eye on Melanie while playing with Holly this morning, though: The word *hooker* came to mind as Melanie staggered toward her son, and Caitlyn got so caught up in watching Melanie smoke that she was almost knocked flat while pushing Holly in the swing. Everything Keller reported from their discussion was anticlimactic to Caitlyn's way of thinking—there was something definitely wrong with Melanie Bryan, as Keller said, for her to go out in public dressed that way.

If nothing else, Caitlyn thought, while berating herself for being selfish, the love of her life didn't seem to think *she'd* killed her mother. And the sudden crisis with Keller's parents had taken her mind off Detective Higgins and Chief Blair and Tina Littlefield to a degree. Caitlyn hadn't said so aloud to Keller, but she was beginning to think something happened between mother and the *preferred* daughter at the pool—and Nancy lost it. If Keller was correct about Nancy and Brad spotting them in Tupelo, were she and their mother fighting about how to proceed? And after dismissing the thought last night, Caitlyn now wondered if Keller was right about his mother and Nancy having been in contact. He seemed to think Nancy gave his mother the cigarettes, vodka and possibly some pills to pop. While that sounded far-fetched, they were in definite agreement that Nancy would throw Melanie under the bus as fast as she would anyone else.

"I'll talk to Gina tomorrow and see if they really had an author," Keller said. "And I'll ask Mr. Barksdale if Dad left a number where he was staying. But who the hell is Jeannie Hanson?"

"You got me. Ask Gina about that, too. Maybe your mom set up the sitter while still at the store." Caitlyn paused. "You'd have said if there was mental illness on either side of your family…?"

Keller looked irritated. "Yes, Caitlyn. And you know Mom's folks and her sisters all seem fine, other than Grandpa's arthritis and Grandma's diabetes. Grandma would have *died* if she'd seen Mom. Melted right into the ground."

"Let's research bipolar disorder tonight after Holly goes to bed."

"Oh, man. That's what this is?"

Caitlyn drew him into a hug. "I don't know, babe. But this is *not* the Melanie Bryan we know and love. I spent more time at your house than mine in high school, and unless you and James saw something I never did—"

"I swear we didn't."

"I believe you. And I'm no doctor, but as someone who's reliant on medication, I've done a lot of research over the years. Lot of stuff stays dormant for a long, long time before symptoms appear."

"Meaning she's had something a long time?"

"Possibly. Maybe a touch when she was teaching, but she pulled herself back together. I know it's driving you nuts because you want this to make sense. But we won't know till she's checked out by a professional." Caitlyn paused again. This next part would never be easy to talk about, even to Keller. "Think back to the end of eleventh grade and the field trip to the blues museum in Memphis. I've told you I tried to come off my meds and what a disaster it was. You know I need them the way diabetics need insulin. And your mom may need something, too."

"You see her in restraints at the state hospital, people forcing lithium into her so she won't hurt herself or anyone around her?"

Talk about cutting to the quick. Caitlyn flashed back to the psych ward and saw herself—at thirteen—planting her hand in a male orderly's chest and shoving him backward so hard that he fell. Four men wound up holding her in place so the nurse could give her the injection. She pushed the image from her mind and focused on Keller.

"I hope not," she said. "That's worst-case scenario."

Keller didn't reply. Caitlyn could almost hear the thoughts whirring in his mind.

"You're thinking that even though most of what your mom said was off-the-chart crazy, there were a few kernels of truth in there, right?" she said. "Like maybe—*just maybe*—your dad and Nancy?"

Keller looked her straight in the eye and nodded.

"If he really left here for good—I mean just flat *walked out* on you guys—I'll never suit up for another basketball game in my life. And baby, I just can't see your dad having an affair. By that I mean sneaking around and leading the proverbial double-life."

"But a one-shot thing?"

Caitlyn sighed. "If Nancy made the first move and threatened to blackmail him, yeah, maybe. But like you say, don't prejudge your dad until you talk to him. Of course he's the one who'll take your mom to see someone, not you, so don't worry about that. And again, I'm real proud of you for stepping up with Holly."

"That's a no-brainer."

"It is for people who care. Not everyone does."

"I'm real worried about Mom," Keller whispered. "I'm not sure she's physically strong enough to use Dad's hunting rifle. But he has that little revolver his dad gave him, and I'm sure she knows where it is. If she gets enough vodka in her…"

This hadn't occurred to Caitlyn. She felt a shudder ripple through her. "I know Holly needs a few things if she's spending the night. Let's go over there later, see what kind of shape she's in."

"Not sure I'll know what to say."

"We'll deal with that when we get there," Caitlyn said. "When'd you try your dad last?"

"Just before we went to the park."

Her cell rang and startled them both. She grabbed it from the waistband of her shorts and came back to the present with a jolt when she saw *Tina Littlefield* on the screen. She pushed a button and held the phone to her ear.

"Hey, Tina. What's up?"

"Angie just called," Littlefield said. "Someone leaked your police visit to Scott Perry, the TV reporter. They're doing a story."

Caitlyn gasped. She held up a hand to keep Keller quiet when he stepped forward. "Oh, God. I swear to you I didn't say anything—"

"Perry got the info and went to the school. They sent him to some kid with the athletic department who gave him a statement. In so many words, Caitlyn, they're deeply saddened by the death of your mother, have no comment on the investigation into her death, and you, as a model student and star athlete, have their full support."

Roger Conrad had to be the spokesman and was probably sweating bullets talking to Scott Perry. Caitlyn thought of the

Nancy/Brad photos and wondered if Conrad would rat out Angie if he got scared. She would never forgive herself if Angie lost her job, and a firing over something like this could finish her in coaching.

"This is going on TV?"

"At five and ten tonight," Littlefield said. "And since I live minutes from the station and know the aforementioned talking-head, I'm on my way there now and will insist he put me on camera. I will absolutely *blast* the Oakdale police department for letting this out, Caitlyn—I'm not pulling any punches. Then I'll assure their vast audience that you haven't been charged with a damn thing and that they damn well better speak up if they have something."

Caitlyn swallowed hard. She felt her heart beating fast and took a deep breath, trying to beat back the rising panic inside her. "We need to talk, Tina."

"We will," Littlefield said. "I know it's of little reassurance, but try not to worry about this. I just wanted to confirm that you didn't talk to anyone—"

"I didn't."

"—and to prepare you in case you watch the news tonight. Goes without saying that if anyone calls—*anyone*, Caitlyn—don't speak about this. We square on that?"

"Yes, ma'am." She glanced at Keller. "But we still need to talk. This is a lot more elaborate than my mom being found in the pool."

TWENTY FOUR

Scott Perry and his news director, Zack Bowen, were in a soundproofed edit bay in the newsroom. Perry had just interviewed Tina Littlefield and had a treasure trove of sound bites at his disposal—she'd all but called the Oakdale police department corrupt and was demanding a public apology for the leak about Caitlyn Rutledge. Bowen, one of those fast-track guys who wanted to produce newscasts at the national level one day, had watched the interview from the control room. He agreed that they had an obvious lead story because of what was implied: The hometown-girl-made-good with the huge basketball future might not be such an angel after all. Perry could see from the look in Bowen's eye that his boss was several moves ahead: another plaque from the Mississippi Broadcasters Association for outstanding news reporting would look just dandy in the station foyer.

"So we've got Littlefield reaming the cops a new one, and the bite from the kid in sports at the university," Bowen said through a mouthful of chips. "Chief Hayseed will absolutely go *off* when you put him on camera and won't say where you got your info."

"Won't like having the Quinn fiasco thrown in his face, either."

"Hit him with that, Scott."

"I will, believe me."

"Once Joe Six-Pack in Oakdale realizes his trusty PD let this leak, he'll want to know why. I do, too." Bowen lowered his voice. "I'll deny this if you ever tell anybody I said it, but I'm not convinced that man had a heart attack."

"Blair? He looks like he's lost about two kids, Zack."

Bowen looked skeptical. "Crash diets are everywhere, and I wouldn't put it past him to have worked out something with his doctor in order to gain a little sympathy, win back support he lost around town. Anyway, sports department has plenty of footage of Caitlyn playing ball…"

"I have her working on a Habitat home, on my save tape."

"Excellent," Bowen said as he clapped Scott's shoulder. "You guys move. I want this turned around for five."

Perry tilted his head and projected his voice. "Billy-Bob, let's go!"

"Y'all get over here, man."

Perry followed Bowen across the newsroom to his own cubicle, which was near the scanner in a high-traffic area of the room. He'd been on the Internet earlier and was still logged on, and he found the bearded photographer at his desk and staring at the Drudge Report.

"*Un*-Happy Valentine's Day," Billy-Bob read aloud. Perry zeroed in on a site link that was in red font instead of the normal black. "Atlanta Braves outfielder Brad Valentine whiffs in Tupelo, Mississippi motel room. Discretion advised."

"Clever," Bowen said as he crowded in for a look. "Open it."

The photographer clicked on the link. The first image came up, and the three men gasped in perfect unison.

"Yeah, that's Valentine, all right," Bowen said. "Joint in hand."

"I believe that's Mike Morgan's wife Nancy," Perry said.

"You're right," Bowen murmured. "Look at that rack—the half I can see. Gorgeous little thing. She's all over ads for something we produce…?"

"A boutique in Oakdale," Billy-Bob said. "And didn't Mike's mom just die?"

"Funeral was Friday in Jackson. He'll be out all this week." Bowen reached for the mouse and scrolled down to read the story. Perry saw that Drudge had linked to the NBC affiliate in Jackson. "I know their news director," Bowen said. "I'll call and see what I can find out. Looks like they posted the story in the last hour—Valentine's from *Oakdale*? I thought he was from Tupelo. This gets more interesting by the second."

Perry imagined getting reactions from Oakdale residents about the high-profile fling and splashing them, tabloid-style, into their newscasts. Everyone around here would watch, the way folks across the country viewed CNN, FOX, and MSNBC for hours on end whenever Paris Hilton and Britney Spears did anything. It was hard to focus on the Oakdale police chief after this bombshell, and Bowen, as if reading his thoughts, backed away from the screen and addressed him and the photographer.

"Go get the bite from Blair and come straight back," he said. "Once the five is in the can, go back to Oakdale and get reaction to Valentine. Local wunderkind blows it, pun intended."

TWENTY FIVE

At six-six and 330 pounds, curly-haired, gray-bearded Stan Earle looked like the TV character Grizzly Adams. The high-school dropout ran a windshield repair company in Ripley, and the hand-crafted furniture he made in his shop had provided a valuable second income over the years. The shop was behind the house and littered with sawdust. It smelled of linseed oil and sweat and didn't have heat or air-conditioning. Perspiration dripped from Earle's nose as he looked up from the end table he was sanding when the news came on. His ears perked up when the clean-cut young anchor mentioned local baseball legend Brad Valentine. Then the anchor tossed to a reporter in Atlanta. Earle lumbered to the ancient black-and-white TV in the corner of the room and cranked the volume.

"...a photo which was taken in front of the Hampton Inn in Tupelo, Mississippi two nights ago according to the time stamp, while Valentine was reportedly on personal leave to attend to his ailing father who lives in nearby Oakdale. This was an absence that was sanctioned by the ball club..."

Earle gaped at an intentionally-blurred breast which was hanging from the dress of a dark-haired girl he actually thought he'd seen before. Valentine had one hand on her, and the other, as the picture zoomed in, on a little item Earle recognized from back in the day. The digital image was pixilated, but it sure looked like his old friend Mary Jane. Unbelievable.

Earle wiped his face with the back of his hand as the report continued. His oldest boy loved the Braves and worshipped Valentine, even after the twerp refused to sign an autograph for him in Atlanta last year when half a dozen other players were signing balls and programs for a sea of star-struck kids. Valentine was far from the media darling that exploded onto the stage three years ago, though: Rumors of steroid usage, an off-season bar fight, an ugly contract dispute, and a horrible batting slump had soiled him with Braves fans, who booed him like crazy these days. Now he was in trouble again.

Earle's smile faded when the anchor went to the next story and crime-scene tape in front of Sherry Rutledge's house appeared on the screen. He turned up the TV again and stood a foot away. He felt his heart sink when the news anchor mentioned her death—Sherry was *dead?* He gathered that it happened Friday night and realized he hadn't watched the news all weekend. Scenes from his past were beginning to blur in his head when footage of Caitlyn playing basketball for the college ran next. Earle jerked back to the present. Lord, was she dead, too? What the hell had happened?

"Stan?"

"Quiet, baby!"

He turned the TV up even louder.

"…the attorney who's representing Miss Rutledge. Here's what she had to say."

"*Let me be perfectly clear: Caitlyn Rutledge has not been charged with anything. And it would seem to me, Scott, that the Oakdale police department has a lot of explaining to do, since it's clear they leaked her name in connection to her mother's death.*"

"*Why do you think they would do that?*"

"*Maybe that's something you news people can find out.*

Meantime, I strongly suggest that the police chief get a handle on his department. I think it's safe to say that the good people of Oakdale are still reeling from the shock of losing two beloved members of the community to a deranged officer who Chief Blair insisted be back on the street before his trial last December. They don't need one of their favorite daughters besmirched for political reasons, if that's what this was."

"Are you considering legal action?"

"I have no comment on that, and nothing further to say."

Earle stared as the Oakdale police chief, apparently interviewed in his garage based on his t-shirt, gym shorts, the towel around his neck, and the treadmill in the background, heatedly denied that his department leaked the information. That little lawyer, though, was right about the suspicion folks had for the way that cop was handled before the shooting spree. Earle and his friends all wondered if their own sheriff—heck, lawmen everywhere—might circle the wagons just as closely if one of their own had issues. But that wasn't his problem at the moment. He suddenly had one thing on his mind.

"Stan?"

Drops of sweat flew when Earle swung his head to look at his wife, whom he didn't realize was still standing there. She was his age, a modestly attractive woman of forty-eight who worked for H&R Block and was by no means slender, but cast a much smaller shadow than her king-size husband of eighteen years. He reached over and turned off the TV.

"Sorry, baby. Just trying to hear that."

"Gonna ask what you want for dinner. Make you some meatloaf, heat up some black-eyed peas and make some cornbread, or—"

"Need to run to Oakdale." He brushed past her. "Lemme get a shower and be on my way."

"Now? Why?"

"Take too long to get into. I don't think I'll be long, though. Go 'head and start that meatloaf."

TWENTY SIX

The air conditioning at the police department had just gone on the fritz, which made Chief Blair even angrier. His wife had pleaded with him not to get upset because of his heart condition, and Blair was trying to keep himself under control. But he was ready to turn his desk over as he stared at Pete Clark, Rob Higgins, and Dorothy Flagg. He'd called them in for an emergency meeting, and he'd just shut his door and gone behind his desk after ordering the dispatcher not to disturb him unless there was a crisis involving assistance from every law enforcement team in the state. His three employees were on their feet, as was he. It was six p.m.

"I don't know if any of y'all just watched the news," Blair growled, "but we got a problem. Someone let on that Caitlyn Rutledge was down here. And damned if that item didn't find its way to the TV station in Tupelo, where it went out over the air. So I'm asking whoever's responsible to speak up. You do that, and your punishment won't be near what it'll be if I find out some other way it was you."

None of the group spoke. Clark seemed surprised, while what looked like amusement registered on Flagg's face. Higgins didn't react at all.

"Then, I'll amend that: Whoever did it has five seconds to speak up. Or *all y'all* are fired!"

Clark stepped forward. He'd turned red and was suddenly breathing heavily. He was a muscle-bound kid who looked like he could whip any man's butt he came across, and he had a hot temper when riled up and looked plenty upset. Blair did his best to steady himself. He knew he needed to maintain at least a measure of control.

"Wasn't me, Chief," Clark said. His voice trembled with adrenaline flow. "And unless you have a shred of proof it was, I wouldn't talk that way. Because if you do fire me for something I didn't do, and it's proven I didn't do it, I'll sue your ass clear across the great state of Mississippi."

Blair heard Flagg suppress a snicker and felt hot blood rush to his cheeks. "Now, you just listen a second, Clark—"

"I ain't listening to nothing." Clark turned and started for the door. "You give the third degree to these two you *inherited* when you got here. And after you learn from them how this got out, come let me know. I'll be at my damn desk."

Clark slammed the door so hard on his way out that Blair thought it might break from its hinges. He felt the electricity in the room and took a moment to get his bearings. Being upbraided by a subordinate—especially with other personnel standing right there—would ordinarily merit instant dismissal, but Blair had a hunch Clark was exactly right about how the information got out. And the young officer hit a nerve: Higgins and Flagg were buddies with the previous chief and had thrown their hero in Blair's face more times than he cared to count. Blair wouldn't put it past either of these two to stir up trouble, and he made his decision in the instant he opened his mouth.

"Both y'all go home," he said. "Suspended with pay, pending a review by the department."

A little smile crossed Flagg's face. "You think you can fire me?"

This didn't surprise Blair after the attitude he'd gotten from the quiet, sulky woman over the years. "There's no thinking about it, Flagg. I can fire you and anyone else around here, as y'all work at my will and pleasure." He slammed his desk with his fist. "And I will *not* tolerate this crap!"

"Well, then, I cannot tell a lie." Flagg jerked a thumb at

Higgins. "Your boy did it."

Higgins looked stunned before hatred colored his pock-marked face. He turned to Flagg, his retort coming out in a slow, stony hiss that reminded Blair of a coiled snake. "*You lying—*"

Blair was out from behind his desk and between them before the big detective could assault the woman. Higgins spun and stalked to Blair's door, threw it open and marched off down the hall. Flagg stood there and held Blair's gaze with a defiant look on her face.

"Go home," he said.

"I really will sue you. Let loose all the sexual harassment that takes place in this pit."

"Go home, Flagg. *Now.*"

Flagg sneered at him and walked out. Blair followed, making sure both were out of the building before walking back through the double doors. He ignored the dispatcher when he saw her staring at him and stomped through the station until he reached Pete Clark's desk. He told Clark to follow, waited until Clark was in his office, and closed the door behind him. He approached until they were nose to nose.

"Son, don't ever threaten me with a lawsuit or anything else," he said. "One more outburst like that, for any reason, and you can hit the road. We clear on that?"

Clark sighed. "Yes, sir. Whatever disciplinary action you think is appropriate..."

Blair waved this away and walked to the water cooler in the corner of the room. He filled a paper cup to the brim and drank it down, then did it a second time. He walked back to Clark and kept his voice down.

"You didn't hear this from me, but they're both gone."

Clark nodded. He didn't look surprised.

"There'll be a review. But off the record, we won't work with them again." Blair set his jaw. "And if either one of them wants to sue me, this department, the town of Oakdale, or Procter and Gamble, I say bring it on, by God."

A half smile crossed Clark's face. Blair went back to the cooler and was refilling his cup when his phone buzzed.

"What is it? I thought I told you—"

"Chief, a man just walked in and said he needs to talk to someone about Caitlyn Rutledge," the dispatcher said quietly. "Said he was on Peachtree Street Friday night."

Blair looked at Clark in surprise. "We're coming," he said. He walked across the room, yanked open the door, and strode down the hall toward the front of the building with Clark right behind. He gawked at possibly the biggest man he'd ever seen, a towering hulk with long, curly, graying hair and a bushy beard. The man was in a denim work shirt and blue jeans with ratty tennis shoes on his huge feet. He smelled of after-shave. Blair stuck out his hand.

"Chief Henry Blair," he said. "This is Officer Pete Clark."

"Stan Earle, Chief," the big man said in a deep voice. His hand engulfed Blair's. "I'm Caitlyn's biological father."

TWENTY SEVEN

Nancy sipped her glass of Grey Goose and sat in the second-floor bay window that overlooked Pleasant Acres. She'd taken another valium and knew the whiskey would make her even woozier, but it was the only way she could think straight. Blurry and slow was preferable to her neurons firing all over the place and prompting another dreaded panic attack. If it happened now, she might grab her mother's gun from the huge purse and blow her head off.

She'd unplugged the land line and turned off her cell phone after the barrage of calls from shocked but mostly sympathetic girlfriends who'd seen the Internet pictures and viewed infidelity as a badge of honor. One who never took a shine to Mike suggested he'd been spying on her like a typical jealous husband, complete with a private eye that commanded a huge fee. If Mike was in on it, though, he had more chutzpah than she ever gave him credit for—took stones to boohoo the way he did in front of her at his mother's funeral while knowing she was hours away from a trap back home.

Her hunch was that some powerful people had it in for Brad. He was super-handsome and built like a brick house, but the boy must have had Sherry's DNA. He was used to getting his way because of his athletic prowess and the Valentine old-money influence, and there was nowhere for him to go but down because he'd knifed so many people on his way to the top. Having run seriously afoul of the ballclub this time, he was hauling back to Atlanta after making abundantly clear to her who came first in his life. There was no longer any point in pretending he loved her.

At the moment, though, there were more important crises to worry about.

One girlfriend who knew the Brumleys confided that the old matriarch was furious about the pictures and especially livid that her model was wearing a Brumley dress for the world to see. It sounded like Nancy would be canned from her modeling job as soon as her mother was cold in the ground. Worse, Mrs. Brumley had pitched her for a similar contract with an upscale clothier in the fashionable Germantown area of Memphis. That career enhancer was certainly gone.

But the real jolt was a call from one of the other realtors, a witch who'd savaged the Rutledge women to others while being nice to their faces. After offering transparent condolences, she hinted that Nancy's days as a realtor were numbered. Nancy wasn't surprised that Mrs. Brumley was angry. She hadn't thought about the real estate job in that context, though, and because Oakdale was so small the company might decide Nancy was radioactive—that she might drive away business the way people fled from skunks. It would definitely happen if the other women were sabotaging her with Sherry gone. Forget absorbing her mother's active listings, Nancy thought. She might not have a job at all.

What the hell would she do, now that Mike was gone?

Death, actually, wasn't such a bad idea. Her father had opted for such an escape when he felt the walls closing in. He was a despicable bastard and deserved eternal residency in the hottest recesses of hell. But Nancy felt in some ways that her mother was even more evil. Sherry came from humble beginnings and insisted, as Nancy grew up, that status came above all else. And because Nancy viewed herself down deep as having failed her father—why else would he have looked upon her as a sex object?—she'd felt an almost gravity-defying need to win her mother's approval. She dutifully kept the molestation to herself despite the anguish and self-loathing it brought her over the years. She allowed her mother to steamroll their marriage, because Sherry taught her that men were to be trifled with. Even men she had feelings for, like Brad and Mike.

And father and son Bryan.

The decision to break away, oddly enough, was made after screwing Brad's brains out and getting high with him at the motel—little did she know someone was snapping pictures nearby. Was it guilt after watching Mike cry as his mother was lowered into the earth? Not really, Nancy knew. It was a grown woman finally ready to stand up to an overbearing, selfish mother. Sherry could do her own dirty work, rather than assign such tasks to her daughter and demand half of everything collected, the way an agency would. Nancy told her mother so at the pool Friday night, explaining that she had no intention of pursuing half of Joan Morgan's estate through a bogus document that the dying woman signed while almost completely incoherent.

In fact, Nancy said, she'd shredded her own copy.

Her mother burst into drunken laughter.

Then, though slurring, Sherry got her point across: She'd gone behind Nancy, copied the paperwork, and made sure Vince Cockrell had it. *She* was going forward with the phony will, and Nancy, by God, would get on the stand and describe the countless hours she spent caring for her sick mother-in-law in a tear-jerker of a sympathy plea. And if she didn't, Sherry added, why, she might just roll on her own daughter. After all, it was Nancy who got the signature, not her.

A tsunami of hatred had finally exploded to the surface—

Nancy lit a cigarette and took a deep drag, trying to focus. She needed to go to the funeral home first thing tomorrow and make the final decisions. She would arrange a Tuesday night visitation and a Wednesday morning burial. This would buy her several days before everyone fired her, since no one would dare do so beforehand. Mike would be ready to go to war over the will. But the damned pictures had changed everything. Was it possible that whoever was out to get Brad had alerted Mike ahead of time? If that was the case, maybe Mike's lawyer was about to land on her with both feet. Well, Vince Cockrell would just have to take them apart. Mike was a good guy, and she'd done awful things to him. But she refused to fold her tent and go to prison if her mother never faced justice.

Nancy puffed again. At least Eddie Ray Chester had come through, since Caitlyn had been brought in for questioning. She would find out more about that tomorrow morning, too. Maybe the psycho would be arrested before the funeral. Seducing James Bryan was something she thought about every time she was in the Bryan home in the old days, and babysitting little Keller back then served a twofold purpose: It got her away from her father, and it gave her the chance, after putting the boy to bed, to stare at the photographs of James and imagine being with him. The ironic thing was that by the time she finally had James that day under the huge oak at the back of the cemetery, she'd moved on.

Because she was falling for Keller.

He was thirteen that summer. In addition to being incredibly cute, he was already displaying the quiet strength possessed by his dad. And Keller was in love with her. She knew from the high color in his handsome face whenever he was around her, the way he always seemed to be peering at her. She fled Oakdale to escape the specter of her father's death and her overbearing mother, but she thought constantly of Keller—even as a newlywed in Jackson—and vowed to return for him. She hated the big city and was thrilled when Mike took the weather position in Tupelo, and she and her mother fought him for different reasons about buying a house in Oakdale instead of the city where he worked. Keller had his driver's license by the time they moved here, which only fueled Nancy's fantasies of sneaking him in while Mike was at work. She would leave Mike for him, and he would marry her and move them far, far away from her hellish hometown and the horrors she'd endured growing up.

But disaster had already struck.

Not only had Keller and Caitlyn become friendly while she was in Jackson, *they were sleeping together.* Nancy could tell in the first five seconds she was around them. Her fat, ugly, uncouth, illegitimate half-sister had lost weight and was more upbeat, but it was Keller's discomfort that gave it away. His eye contact was poor, his hug super-stiff. He even held Caitlyn's hand in front of her, as if sending a clear message that he'd chosen Caitlyn over her. He wouldn't be so red-faced, Nancy reasoned, if he hadn't once felt something for *her.* She was willing to give the silly high-school romance time to run its course, though, and bided her time. It never did.

She'd never seen a couple that looked happier together

and hated them for it.

The easiest person to get back at these days was James, since he had the most to lose. Her note to Melanie would hopefully rock the foundation of that marriage pretty good, if not blow it sky-high. She'd thought of killing Keller and Caitlyn over the years, but she knew in her heart of hearts she couldn't hurt him. The beauty of this ploy involving Eddie Ray Chester was that if Caitlyn actually went to the Big House, Nancy would have a clear path to Keller: Not only was Sherry gone, but Mike Morgan was out of her life. Brad Valentine, too, for that matter. Yes, Keller had betrayed her, but she could forgive him. Caitlyn was the enemy.

She would tear them apart if it killed her.

TWENTY EIGHT

"A man named Stan Earle is my father," Caitlyn said. "Not Jack Rutledge."

She and Keller were sitting on his bed and holding hands. There was nothing on the sheetrock walls except a university pennant and a basketball poster with Caitlyn in the team photo. His TV was on a hand-me-down chest of drawers. The computer desk was next to it and displayed their Oakdale High senior prom photo. She was all smiles that night and looked as pretty as he'd ever seen her, although she looked tired and sad at the moment. Keller was vague with Patrick about his parents, but his room-mate picked up the tension and asked what he could do to help. He'd taken Holly to Pizza Hut so Keller and Caitlyn could talk after her visit with Tina Littlefield. Keller had no idea who Stan Earle was, but he'd long suspected that Jack, polite but quiet and difficult to read, wasn't her dad.

"But before I get into that—because there's a reason for doing so—Tina said you really need a lawyer. Said this could become an unholy custodial mess if your mom's incapacitated and something happens to your dad. Not to mention Nancy may have done it and Holly may have seen it."

"I know," he said. His mother was nowhere to be found when they drove to the house to get Holly's things, and Keller had packed clothes, books, stuffed animals, and toiletries for several days. Nor had James Bryan answered his son's most recent call. "May pop in on Clint Young tomorrow."

"Good. Now, Tina thinks I'm in the clear about the stuff at school, but Angie could be at risk if everything gets out. Tina asked her to find her own lawyer because representing both of us would be a conflict, if it came to that."

Caitlyn sighed. Keller kissed her cheek and stroked her hair, having learned long ago to be silent for as long as it took when his girl was opening up. There were days he was amazed she did so at all, given how eerily quiet she was in junior high.

"Did say that if Brad put the fear of God in Roger Conrad and Roger went to his bosses and they sacked Angie, Roger would get tossed, too," Caitlyn said. "Not like he wasn't complicit. And that'd be the end of his career in sports."

"Brad's in enough trouble without going Mafia on Roger," Keller said. "The Braves suspended him indefinitely."

Caitlyn didn't reply to that. Keller listened to her slow, deep breathing and wondered if she was going to nod right off—she sounded that weary. But she sighed again.

"I'd seen Stan once before, when I was thirteen," she said quietly. "Two months after Jack's funeral. Nancy was already in Jackson."

Although she resembled Sherry, Caitlyn didn't look a whit like Jack and possessed different mannerisms, a huskier voice, and a body type, most notably, that none of the Rutledges had. But it was *Sherry* who planted the seed in Keller's brain over the years: While Jack carried off his role as Caitlyn's pop effectively enough, his spouse—though definitely Caitlyn's biological mother—treated her daughter in public with aloofness and disdain generally shown to unwanted step-children. Keller knew about the week Caitlyn spent in the state hospital after Jack's death, although the love of his life had never discussed the particulars. He mentally prepared to hear them now.

"Garage door was down like always when I got off the school bus," she began. "This was before Mother had the remotes installed, and I assumed she was showing property. Pulled the door up and not only was the Cadillac there, big Harley was next to it. Went in the kitchen and heard Mother's laughing voice coming from the bedroom. She was drunk and I knew someone was with her. Should have run."

Keller imagined walking in on one of his parents at thirteen. What Caitlyn was describing took place right in the middle of his mother's own bleak period. It was possible that if he'd cut school one day in eighth grade and come home, he might have walked in on his mother and the damn-good-lawyer-turned-author. If such a person, as Caitlyn had pointed out, even existed.

"I heard this deep, drunk voice: 'Baby, I got *plenty* more where that came from,' and I just couldn't help myself," she said. "Went down the hall and looked in. They were both naked as jaybirds, Mother with rouge and mascara smeared all over her face, eyes bloodshot as hell, and this *huge* man, build like a damn redwood, with long, dirty, curly hair and scraggly beard. He saw me first, got this look on his face. I knew in my bones he was my dad, and that's when I ran. Don't remember how I got to Shelly Carpenter's house, but I remember blood in their bathroom and her brother kicking in the door."

Caitlyn paused. Keller rubbed her back and kept quiet.

"You should have seen Mother," she continued with a mirthless little chuckle. "Crying those crocodile tears and acting brave and resolute in front of the psych staff. Then she came in my room one morning and closed the door, had her game face on. 'You are *nevah* to talk about what you saw, young lady,'" Caitlyn said in her debutante drawl. "I knew how much her reputation meant to her, that *that's* what the little speech was really about. But believe it or not, in a way I felt she was putting her trust in me, crazy as that sounds."

"You were just thirteen. And we all want to please our parents."

"Yep. I've wondered if that was how Mother kept Nancy quiet. Her journal even alluded to hating Mother and dying to please her at the same time, remember? Anyway, Mother said she hooked up with Stan at a party back when she worked for the Chamber of Commerce—a weekend when Jack was out of town and Nancy was at a lock-in at the church." Caitlyn turned to face him. "As God is my witness, Jack never touched me or said anything inappropriate, ever. Just want you to know that."

"I believe you."

"Thank you, baby. Stan, by the way, paid a visit to the neighborhood only one more time. It was Friday night," she said as a wry smile crossed her face. "He was right there on our street two nights ago."

TWENTY NINE

Keller heard the door open downstairs and knew Patrick and Holly were back. Hopefully his roommate—and especially his little sister—could give them a few more minutes, since this was a potentially huge break in this train wreck. Caitlyn cocked her ear, having caught the sound, and gave him a knowing look. She, too, knew they needed to finish up.

"Talk about the mother of all surprises," she said. "Blair called in Tina for a chat after the TV interview. Seems that Stan— my dad, which sounds so weird to say out loud—was parked across from the house in his truck Friday night and saw me come and go when I came for my phone. Blair said he lives in Ripley now. He has a family and got saved and quit drinking long ago. And that he thought for years about trying to get in touch with me and picked Friday of all nights to try."

"Forgive me for being skeptical, sweetheart, but—"

"I'll worry about his motivations if I decide to meet him, and that's the last thing on my mind right now," Caitlyn said. "But he came down the street, found the house and was all set to knock on the door. Told Blair he got cold feet and went around the block. You know where the Garvers live…"

"Directly across from you guys and next to the Halls."

"Yes, and they have a carport, which I'd forgotten. He told Blair no cars were there and no lights were on, so he figured no one was home. Good a spot as any to idle along the curb while getting up his nerve. And I drove up."

Keller frowned. "There was a truck there and you never saw it?"

"I was totally focused on getting in and out of the house. Pulled to the curb and hopped out, probably looked right at him and didn't notice. Left the Jeep running and went inside, heard Mother out back, went in my room and got my cell, and went back out to the Jeep and split."

"But he's certain he saw you?"

"Said he recognized me from playing ball. Started to get out and speak but just couldn't. Here's the thing, though: He said I wasn't in the house more than a minute, and that I came and went through the front door and didn't get near the sidewalk— which someone claims I used to leave the scene on foot." Caitlyn paused and let the tension build. "Nancy pulled up not ten seconds after I drove off."

Keller whistled. He pictured Nancy arriving as Caitlyn was *about* to leave and imagined the girls speaking. If Nancy knew he and Caitlyn had just been in Tupelo, would she have said anything right there in front of Sherry's house? And would Sherry still be alive? If Earle was accurate about the ten seconds, a stoplight might have been the difference in Nancy and Caitlyn encountering each other.

"Did your dad see her go in?"

"Yes. Described the Beamer and the black dress. Said he'd seen her in the Brumley's ads." Keller nodded. This, once and for all, established the guilty party at the pool Friday night, and it most definitely wasn't Caitlyn.

"He said that totally killed his nerve about talking to Mother, so he turned around and went home. Said he saw the news this afternoon and didn't know Mother was dead until today, and that he had no idea the cops had already talked to me. Jumped in his truck and drove straight to Oakdale to see the police."

"So you're off the hook?"

"Hopefully. Blair told Tina they would *re-interview* someone," Caitlyn said with a nasty look on her face. "Wouldn't say who."

"Someone who supposedly saw you leave on foot. Who besides Priscilla?"

Now Caitlyn looked sad. "She's sweet, Keller. I hope it wasn't her."

"She's sweet to your face. She and your mother were big buds, and Nancy's the little princess in that crowd, remember? And Nancy went racing over to Priscilla's after calling 911 and they rode in the ambulance."

"You really think Priscilla Hall told the cops I killed my mother."

"Not necessarily. I think Nancy told her that, and Priscilla may have put you at the scene. Don't forget Joan Morgan's will."

Caitlyn gasped and covered her mouth. "You think Nancy

killed Mother over *that*, then bribed Priscilla into framing me?"

"Wouldn't rule it out." He stood and pulled Caitlyn to her feet. "Patrick will watch ESPN half the night for updates on Brad. Once Holly's good and asleep, let's run back over to the house. If Mom's there maybe we can sit with her a while, see what comes out of her mouth. If not, we'll turn the place upside down and find a number where Dad's staying, or maybe something that would explain Mom right now. Not like I'll be falling asleep any time soon."

THIRTY

Eddie Ray Chester was really scared now.

His mother had called and announced that while on their way home from a rip-roaring good time in Memphis, she and Webber stopped in Tunica for a few hands of casino blackjack. They'd won some money, gotten a little trashed, and opted to get a room for the night. That was fine with Eddie Ray, because not only did it keep his mother out of danger, he and Daphne could keep partying like it was 1999. Although she'd pledged last night to take care of herself while pregnant, Daphne didn't see how one last blowout would hurt the baby. So Eddie Ray called a buddy who sold him a nickel bag of pot, and they swung by the liquor store for a gallon of cheap wine and frolicked the night away. They'd lounged all day today, eating pizza and ice cream and watching music videos and gradually sobering up in anticipation of the happy couple's return. Once Monica called, though, Eddie Ray was just as eager as Daphne to cut loose a bit more. She was drawing a bubble bath when the doorbell rang.

It was Officer Clark.

He said he had a few more questions he needed to ask down at the station and sounded friendly enough. Daphne, thankfully, had the pot and wine in the bathroom, and Eddie Ray, who answered in his boxers, told Clark he'd be there as soon as he got dressed. With relief pouring through him at not getting caught with the cannabis, Eddie Ray told his naked girlfriend where he was going and that he expected to return in half an hour or less, based on the time he spent with Clark yesterday. He heard Daphne coughing as he left the house and smiled to himself. She held pot smoke in her lungs for so long at a time it was a wonder she could breathe at all.

Like yesterday, Clark offered water after leading him to the stuffy, windowless interview room. Clark's mood, though, seemed to have changed when he returned with the beverage. He didn't seem mad, but his eyes looked different. A second later a red-faced, grim-looking man walked in and closed the door. The man glanced at Clark, and something Eddie Ray couldn't make out seemed to pass between them. Then the red-faced man returned his steely gaze to Eddie Ray, not taking his eyes off him as he walked around to the end of the table. He remained on his feet. Clark did, too, and Eddie Ray saw that they were flanking him and felt intimidated. The older man spoke first.

"Mr. Chester, I'm Chief Blair."

Eddie Ray swallowed hard. All of a sudden there seemed to be very little air in the room. He was aware when he walked in that the building wasn't very cool, and he realized he didn't hear the air conditioner. Was the electricity off? No, the lights wouldn't be on.

"You gave a statement to Officer Clark yesterday," Blair said. "About seeing Caitlyn Rutledge leaving her mother's backyard on foot Friday evening."

"Yes, sir," Eddie Ray said. "Yes, sir, I did."

Blair backed away and ran his hands through his crew cut. Then he wiped his brow with the back of his hand and flung droplets of perspiration away. He approached again and stopped exactly where he was before. Eddie Ray smelled coffee on Blair's breath and felt his heart thudding away. He thought of Daphne, who was probably lying in the tub with her eyes closed and feeling very little pain, while he sweated like a pig in this cinderblock microwave. He'd told her he would be back in half an hour. That didn't look so good now.

"Well, that's interesting, sir," Blair said at length. "Because a man came in here little while ago and told us a story that completely contradicts yours."

Panic zipped through Eddie Ray's bowels and made him jerk. His throat suddenly felt like it was closing up. Was the heat on in here? He reached for his water and gulped down half the bottle. He saw the chief and Clark exchange another look. Then Blair zeroed in on him again and looked like he wanted a response. Eddie Ray had no idea what to say.

"Gotta be honest: That bothers me," Blair said. "A lot."

"Well, how you know he's telling the truth, and I'm not?"

"He was pretty convincing." Blair leaned even closer, and Eddie Ray saw Clark approach a bit from the corner of his eye. "And frankly, you aren't."

Eddie Ray blinked. He wondered if they were about to charge him with some sort of crime, since they seemed to know he'd lied. He'd watched tons of *Law & Order* with his mother over the years, and those pony-tailed lawyers with their plaid sport coats and horn-rimmed glasses always came running in to represent the thugs the wise-guy detectives brought in for questioning. Where'd those lawyers come from? Did they have offices in the police department? Did one work here? Officer Clark cleared his throat and brought Eddie Ray to the present.

"Look, you got a lot on your plate right now," he said. He sounded almost reassuring. "Have to move out, now that your mama got married, right? And I know you were shook up about what happened to the late Ms. Rutledge, seeing as how you didn't go right over there when you heard that splash. I know you wish you'd done that."

"Guess I do," Eddie Ray heard himself say.

"Did you really see Caitlyn leave the backyard on foot and start up that sidewalk?" Clark asked gently. "Because that man who talked to us said she drove up, parked along the curb in front of the house, went in there for a minute or less, came back out, and went straight to her vehicle and drove off. Never was on that sidewalk."

Eddie Ray's heart was pounding so hard he felt faint. He gulped down more water. Then he looked at Blair. "Uh…y'all got a lawyer who works here?"

Blair looked confused. Then he almost smiled. "No, we don't. This is a police station, not a law firm. Now, if you think you need a lawyer, you're perfectly within your rights to get yourself one."

"You think I should?"

"I can't make that decision for you."

The moment was at hand. Eddie Ray felt salty tears in his eyes, as well as a mess of perspiration on his forehead, chest, back, thighs, and in his hair. He had to confess if he wanted to escape this monstrously hot little room. He didn't know any lawyers or how to find one. His mother might, but she and Webber were either up to their necks in poker chips or passed out in their hotel room. She'd never hear her cell phone ring. And Daphne, if she hadn't drowned in the tub amid pot smoke and cheap wine, sure wouldn't know any lawyers. She barely knew how to write a check.

"All right," he whispered. "I didn't."

"Didn't what?"

"Didn't see Caitlyn out there. Didn't see nobody."

Blair slammed the table with his palm. For an instant Eddie Ray thought he'd wet his pants but realized it was more perspiration.

"Then what the *hell* were you doing yesterday?" Blair shouted. "You came down here on your own accord and said you needed to speak with someone about the death of Sherry Rutledge, and you told Officer Clark you heard voices Friday night and went over there and saw Caitlyn leaving the property on foot and go up that sidewalk!"

"Uh..."

"You understand what's at stake here, son? A woman is *dead*. And you told us you saw her daughter Caitlyn go trotting out of that yard and sure made it sound like you thought she killed her mama! Now you're telling us that didn't happen? Okay, what exactly did happen, then?"

Eddie Ray felt tears dripping down his cheeks and covered his face.

"Mr. Chester, would you like some more water?"

Eddie Ray looked up. Clark pulled out the chair across from him and sat down. He looked much more humane than Blair, who had backed several feet away. Eddie Ray couldn't read the look on the chief's face and turned to Clark.

"Uh, yes, sir, I would."

"I'll get it in just a second," Clark said. "But why don't you tell me and Chief Blair exactly what happened Friday night. Because like the chief said, one of your neighbors is dead. And we all want to find out what happened."

"I told you everything that happened Friday night. All true, except about me seeing Caitlyn."

"Then to recap, you heard an argument," Clark said. "You were sure it was Sherry Rutledge and one of her daughters, but you didn't know which one. Is that correct?"

"Yes, sir."

"And you heard a bottle break and someone go in the pool, and you got a little spooked—I think that was the word you used—and went over there after thinking about it a few seconds."

"That's right."

"But you didn't see anyone. Is *that* right?"

Eddie Ray sighed. "Yes, sir. That's the absolute truth, I swear."

Blair stepped back up after wiping more sweat from his face. "Then why'd you lie to us?"

"What trouble will I get in?"

That was the last thing he meant to ask. But it didn't matter: They had him cornered like a cockroach that couldn't find a crack in the floor to squeeze through, and they were about to step on him. They knew he'd lied. And since he didn't know any lawyers, how would he find one he could trust? He'd heard all kinds of lawyer jokes. Most lawyers were greedy and ruthless, sounded like. He looked at Blair, ready to confess his sins. But Blair really looked upset now.

"Depends on what you did! You shove Sherry Rutledge in that pool yourself?"

"*No!*"

"You know who did?"

"No, sir, I don't! I swear!"

"Then why you asking what trouble you'd get in?"

"Because I did something I shouldn't have."

There, Eddie Ray thought to himself. He'd said it. He'd gotten the ball rolling and would finally spill his guts. He drained the last of the water and placed the bottle on the table. He looked expectantly at Clark, but the young officer didn't move to bring him another one.

"Why don't you tell us exactly what you did," Blair said. "*Now.*"

Eddie Ray cracked his knuckles and wiped his damp palms on the table. "Nancy told me to."

"Nancy Rutledge Morgan, the older daughter? That who you're talking about?"

"Yes, sir. I graduated high school with her."

Blair moved closer but almost sounded conversational when he spoke again. "Now, you told Officer Clark you talked to Nancy in her backyard yesterday morning, a few hours before you called down here. That right?"

"Yes, sir."

"And Nancy asked you to do what? Be as specific as you can."

They'd never answered about what jail time, if any, he might face for lying. But something told Eddie Ray that the more information he gave them, the better off he'd be. Maybe he could give Nancy's money to the police department, and they could return it to her. But if he did that, he couldn't imagine how he'd ever hope to pay for—

"Mr. Chester? I'm really running out of patience."

"All right. She told me to say I saw Caitlyn leaving the yard on foot. Said if I did that, she'd pay me ten thousand dollars. Cash."

Eddie Ray saw the men share a glance. Blair looked stunned but was calm when he continued. "She say when you might receive that money?"

"Already got it," he whispered. "Gave it to me after I promised I'd call down here, talk to someone." He wiped his eyes with the back of his hand. "Said there'd be more if..."

"If what?" Clark asked gently.

"If Caitlyn went to trial."

"For the murder of her mother?"

"Yes, sir. That's what she was getting at."

"She say how much more?"

"Just said a *lot* more. And I know it was wrong," he added quickly. "Caitlyn's a sweet girl, always been so nice to my family, while those bitches Sherry and Nancy wouldn't give us the time of—look, can I give y'all that money or something, maybe get y'all to give it back to her?"

Blair didn't speak for a long moment. "I can't answer that, any more than I can advise you to get a lawyer. Now, at any point did Nancy specifically tell you that *she* killed her mother? Think hard."

"No, sir."

"So she told you Caitlyn did it?"

"More or less. Said she knew Caitlyn had been in the house, never said how." Eddie Ray looked at the empty water bottle. "She said she got there at 8:30 and found her mother. Told me to tell y'all I saw Caitlyn leaving the yard at 8:15."

"Where'd y'all work all this out?" Blair asked. "Her backyard, when you went over to talk to her Saturday morning?"

"No, sir," Eddie Ray said. "Out at that cabin used to be owned by Bud Crisler. She didn't want to answer no questions out in the yard, sounded like. Fact, she asked me not to tell anyone we'd talked, just to keep it zipped up till I got there. See, I didn't even know Sherry was dead until we was at the cabin."

Blair looked over at Clark and shook his head. Then he turned back to Eddie Ray. "So Caitlyn's name hadn't come up at that point, or had it?"

"No, sir, it hadn't."

"You mind telling me why you went out there in the first place? To the cabin, I'm talking about. Based on what you're saying, you and Nancy weren't big friends or nothing."

Eddie Ray felt like a natural-born idiot. But there were other idiots like him, he knew, who'd been in this very room and sweated buckets and broke down and told why they'd made such idiotic choices. And something told him he wasn't the first man to fall hook, line, and sinker for a beautiful, conniving woman who batted her eyes at him.

"Thought I might get laid," Eddie Ray murmured. He wasn't sure the men would have heard him if the air conditioning was humming and it wasn't so deathly quiet in here. "Always had a thing for her, even though I'm way below her on the status meter."

"I see. Did you?"

"Yes, sir."

"Then she gave you ten grand and instructed you on what to tell us."

Eddie Ray closed his eyes. "Yes, sir."

Blair didn't reply. Eddie Ray looked up and saw the men staring at each other. Nothing was said for a second. Then Clark started out of the room. He didn't say anything as he passed Eddie Ray, didn't even look at him. He left the door open, and Eddie Ray felt cooler air seep into the room.

"Okay, Mr. Chester," Blair said. "You can go now. But do not *ever* pull anything like this again, understand? If you have something to tell the police, or if the police ever need anything from you, it damn well better be the truth—the first time. We clear on that, young man?"

"Yes, sir."

Eddie Ray pushed on the table and got to his feet. He wanted to stick out his sweaty hand and convey sincerity to the police chief, but he was afraid Blair would scowl at him. He slinked out of the room and into the main hallway and kept his head down. It was a little cooler out here, but not much. Maybe the air conditioning was out all over the building. It would be his luck that it wouldn't work in the Grand Am. If that happened, he'd shower when he got home, as cold as he could stand it. He thought of Daphne and wondered how long he'd been questioned by Blair and Clark. Daphne would want to get frisky, but Eddie Ray just wanted to get drunk.

Nancy wasn't the type of person you crossed.

And he had, in a big way.

THIRTY ONE

Keller felt his heart thump away as he eased along Peachtree Street and wasn't surprised the house was dark when it came into view. He pulled into the driveway and reached up to hit the button on the garage-door opener. The door went up, and the garage was empty. He hadn't expected his father's truck to be inside. He'd hoped, though, that his mother was getting some much-needed rest after whatever she did all weekend. But it didn't look like she was here, either.

"Still want to go in?" Caitlyn said.

"Yes."

They entered the kitchen from the garage. Keller disabled the security alarm and flipped on the overhead fluorescents in the kitchen. The air conditioning was on and the cool air felt great. He looked around and took a deep breath and didn't smell anything odd, nor was anything out of place. He checked the top of the fridge and wasn't surprised the cigarettes and lighter weren't there. He grunted to himself when he couldn't find the vodka in the pantry. Had his mother moved it or taken it with her? He checked the plastic trash can under the sink, but the bottle wasn't in there. He walked into the living room, Caitlyn a step behind, and flipped on the patio light. He pulled open the sliding glass and immediately felt the vast difference in air quality—it still felt tropical outside. The folding chair hadn't been moved, and he and Caitlyn saw cigarette butts scattered in all directions. He had no idea if they were from last night, this morning, or since they'd seen Melanie at the park. It was very possible she hadn't been home. He'd called her cell an hour ago, and it went straight to voice mail as if she was on the phone. She hadn't returned the call, though.

"Think she went to Hollandale?" Caitlyn said as they

started back inside.

"Maybe." Keller slid the door closed, locked it, and shut off the patio light. He walked to an end table and turned on a lamp. "But if she went to see her folks, they'd have tried Dad immediately if she was out of her head like this morning."

"They may already have, sweetheart."

"If they couldn't get him they'd try me next. They have my cell. And she could have gone to Hollandale but not to her folks' house." He looked at the enlargement of his parents' wedding photo above the plasma TV and wondered again if this was simply a bizarre comedy of errors, or if the Bryan family was coming apart at the seams. If so, care for his sister would land squarely upon his nineteen-year-old head. "Guess I need to call them in the next day or so."

"One more thing your dad can do. I remain convinced he simply lost his phone."

Keller looked away and nodded. He knew Caitlyn was trying to be helpful and didn't want to sound gloomy, but it wasn't like James Bryan not to stay in close touch with his family while on the road. He called nightly when Keller still lived at home—

"Lemme check the caller ID, see if Dad called here," he mumbled as he looked around for the nearest phone. A cordless was on an end table next to the lamp. He was there in two strides, picked up the phone, and hit a button to review the most recent calls. There were several unidentified numbers (which meant telemarketers), a message from a friend of his dad looking for a golf game, and one from the local blood bank. But James himself hadn't called, nor had anyone on either side of the family. Keller put the phone back on its stand and shook his head.

"I'm sorry," Caitlyn said quietly.

"You may be right about the cell. But he'd call from a land line unless he's had an accident."

She walked over and put her arms around him. He rested his head on her shoulder and imagined his father injured and abandoned in the woods after a couple of punks robbed him and stole his truck. That idea was better than him being dead, and a death—especially a traffic-related fatality—would have led to the dreaded knock on the door by a somber-faced highway patrolman. It occurred to him that nobody would be here to answer with his mother away, but if something awful had happened and law enforcement couldn't find anyone, Keller was certain a trooper or patrolman would start knocking on nearby doors until they found someone that knew the Bryan family. And someone would tell them how to contact the grown son.

"Let's focus on your mom right now, babe," Caitlyn said. "Where do you want to look?"

He pulled away and started back to the kitchen. Caitlyn followed and watched as he inspected the fridge for a note and looked near the phone. She followed him to the den and lingered in the doorway as he did the same thing. He gave her what he knew was a hopeless look and started up the stairs. He walked into his old bedroom, Caitlyn right behind, and flipped on the overhead light. They stopped at the telescope and stared at it. He thought about Holly and knew Caitlyn was thinking about her, too.

"Whose fingerprints would be on this?" she said in a burst of quiet.

Keller hadn't thought about that and narrowed his eyes in concentration. "Holly for sure. Possibly the sitter, maybe the boyfriend. Maybe some old ones of me. I haven't touched it since I moved out. I'm wondering if the police are going to be involved with this real soon." He looked at Caitlyn and felt the need to fess up about something else. "I used to spy on your sister from here."

Caitlyn laughed. "That's a clever way of putting it."

He felt himself turn red. "You knew?"

"Not for a long time. I remember you showing this to me in about tenth grade, I guess. But it wasn't till we really got to know each other that I put together how you felt about Nancy back then. That's when I knew what it was *really* used for." Caitlyn poked a finger into his chest and grinned. "You'd have freaked if you'd seen me in a bikini at thirteen. I can just see you and Patrick trotting up here to look at Nancy and her friends, and there I am with a big poster: 'Hi, Keller, I know you're watching.' Seeing how I weighed two-sixty back then, I damn sure didn't get near a bathing suit."

"Well, you look great in one now."

Caitlyn gave him the shy smile that always melted his heart. He kissed her, then took her hand and led her down the hall to his parents' bedroom. He turned on the light and looked around, hoping to find a clue in plain sight about what was going on around here, perhaps something affixed to his mother's vanity mirror or the one on the dresser. There was nothing, however. He took a moment to gather his courage. Then he opened the top drawer of the night table on his father's side of the bed. Caitlyn knew what he was looking for, so he didn't have to explain his heavy sigh.

"This is not good," he said quietly. "Not at all."

"You think your mom has it, then?"

"No. I think Dad does. Which scares me even more."

THIRTY TWO

"I know where to go, Keller!" Holly said indignantly as she tried to pull free. "You don't have to hold my hand like I'm a little baby."

Keller shushed his sister as they walked through the parking lot of Smart County Hospital to the daycare. It operated year-round, with summer camps for kids through twelve years of age. With both Bryan adults running businesses, Holly had been a summertime fixture for years. Keller was comfortable leaving her here, but he hoped the manager on duty didn't start asking about his mother. It seemed inevitable, though: Melanie's routine was to catch a step class or treadmill in the wellness center after dropping off Holly each morning, followed by juice and a bagel before she headed downtown to open the bookstore for the day. He was now consumed with worry about both his parents and slept just as poorly as the previous night. He and Caitlyn remained in agreement that they couldn't let on a thing to Holly. Not until they had some answers.

"I said, mister, you better stop, 'cause Mommy always lets—hi, Miss Jeannie!"

"Hello, there, Miss Holly! How are you, darling?"

Keller looked up as his sister yanked her arm away and trotted toward a tall blonde in blue hospital scrubs who was approaching the double metal doors from the other direction. He assumed she was a nurse at first glance, but the woman's badge simply featured the wellness center logo, not the typical L.P.N. or R.N. designations displayed on the nursing badges.

"I'm fine, Miss Jeannie! Keller and I went to McDonald's for breakfast!"

"Morning," Keller said. He stuck out his hand after collaring his sister. "Keller Bryan. I'm Holly's brother. Jeannie…?"

The woman shook his hand with a firm grip. "Hanson."

THIRTY THREE

Jeannie Hanson reached the double doors and held them open. Keller felt Holly try to pull away again and let her go this time. He watched as she raced down the carpeted hall and disappeared into a room at the end. He turned to Hanson and got a good look while she waved at another little girl. *This* was the female who'd supposedly watched Holly on Friday night and had a guy over? She wore a wedding ring and looked at least thirty, maybe closer to forty. She probably had kids of her own if she managed the daycare and certainly wasn't a sex-crazed teen that would have fooled around with her boyfriend under the pretense of sitting. She turned and gave him a smile he couldn't read.

"Good to meet you," she said. "You're on the emergency pickup list."

"Yes, ma'am. I'm a student."

"Where's Melanie this morning? Didn't see her in step class."

At least he'd been prepared for this. He went to his poker face and resolved to give Hanson only as much information as necessary. "Little under the weather. Can you talk for a second?"

"Sure. Come on down to my office."

Keller saw that Hanson knew everyone. A nurse said hello as she passed, and a doctor in a white lab coat made a seemingly innocuous comment that caused Hanson to burst into laughter—an inside joke, apparently. They passed the room Holly entered, and Keller saw a young woman supervising perhaps a dozen girls his sister's age as an animated movie played on the TV. They went around the corner and down a tiled hall toward the main part of the hospital. Hanson stopped and unlocked a small office and entered ahead of him. Keller remained on his feet as she went behind her desk and sat. He saw diplomas and citations on the paneled walls and eyed a cork bulletin board loaded with post-it notes and other correspondence.

"Can I close the door?"

"Sure, and take a load off," she said. "I'm good till the staff meeting at 8:30. Give me just a sec to check e-mail."

He nudged the door shut and took the folding chair across from her. Hanson was wearing a lot of perfume, and the scent quickly took over the cramped little room. She looked up a few seconds later and smiled.

"Okay. How can I help you?"

"This may sound strange, but did you watch my sister Friday night, at my parents' house?"

"I did," Hanson said. Her smile seemed to change. "Actually, I'm glad you're here. We all love Melanie, but the director isn't happy about what happened."

Keller felt his heart sink at the thought of management already involved in whatever this was. He said, nothing, though, and tried to keep his face blank as he waited for an explanation.

"Lord knows she's not the only parent who gets here right at six sometimes to pick up their child," Hanson said. "We know where she is, and I understand that when she has a book signing like she did Friday, sometimes things run long."

So the guy from Hollandale might have been there after all? "She said she'd be late?"

"She called at four-thirty and said she had an author in the store, might be a minute after six by the time she got here. No problem at all," Hanson said with her palms turned upward. "She called right at six, and by then it was just Holly and one other girl. But instead of saying she was on her way, she asked if there was anyone who could babysit."

"So it did run long."

"She didn't say. Just said it was really important that she get someone to sit. Right then the other girl's mom got there. So I figured I'd offer my help for a few minutes."

"That's what Mom needed?" Keller asked. "Help for just a few minutes?"

"That's what I gathered, even when she asked if I could take Holly home—"

"Mom asked *you* to take Holly home?"

"Yes," Hanson said without missing a beat. "Gave me the

alarm code and said where to find the spare key and that she'd meet me." Her smile became bittersweet, like this was a considerable imposition despite the polite face she was trying to put on it. "See, it was Doug's birthday."

Keller had forgotten about him and sat up straighter. "Your husband, I take it?"

"Correct. We'd made plans to eat with another couple in Tupelo. Reservations weren't till seven-thirty, so I figured we'd have time." Hanson shook her head no. "Melanie didn't get in until ten—"

He wondered what his mother could have done all night, especially early in the evening. If she and Nancy linked up in the hospital parking lot, it wouldn't have been until 8:30 or thereafter.

"—and I must admit I'm concerned, Keller. She was drunk. Not asleep on her feet, but we could smell it on her."

He rubbed his temples in an honest show of despair. He wasn't surprised after the screwdriver his mother mixed in his presence Saturday night and the odd titter he heard when she called Friday night at ten-thirty—she did sound like she'd had a couple of drinks. But he couldn't admit all that to Hanson if she'd already talked to her boss. Keller didn't like the sound of *that* and wondered if Hanson was being truthful about his mother asking this woman to take Holly home. He started to speak, but she stepped on his words.

"Doug and I talked three times between six and seven, and he finally called our friends and cancelled. I told him to bring pizza, since I was stuck with a hungry eight-year-old."

"Look, I'm really sorry about all this. I'll write you a check right now…"

Hanson waved this away. "Don't worry about that, and please let me finish. I tried to call her at seven, eight and nine. She answered at seven and said she was on her way, did the same thing at eight. Now, the fire truck and ambulance came down the street about 8:45. We all went outside, and I got scared. I assumed police cars at first, like your mom was in an accident. But they stopped down the street, and we went back inside and kept waiting."

"Let me ask you something," Keller said carefully. "I have a telescope—"

Hanson nodded in recognition.

"—did you guys look through it?"

"Yes. We were in the den watching *Cars*. Holly had to go to the bathroom, and I told her to go change for bed, even though she wouldn't have to go to sleep until her mommy got home. Five minutes passed and she hadn't come back, so we went to look for her. She was up in your room, setting up the telescope, the most adorable little grin on her face. It's really hard to get mad at her."

Keller felt his heart beat faster and tried to sound casual. "You guys look through it with her?"

"She insisted. Sweet thing was so proud of herself."

"She go back up there later?"

The question was out before he could get it back. The *last* thing Keller wanted was for Hanson to put together that the telescope was pointed where the death of Sherry Rutledge had occurred—a death Jeannie Hanson certainly knew about by now. If Hanson had already made the connection, though, she wasn't saying.

"That sounds right," she said. "Because Doug was irritated by then. We'll see our friends this weekend. But he wanted to go home—his birthday and all—yet he felt he needed to hang around with me until your mother or father got home."

Nothing like a good guilt trip. "I'm really sorry about all this. Dad's in Chicago right now—"

"Never clear where he was. But somewhere in there,

Doug asked me to come out in the living room and wanted to know how long before we called the cops." Hanson sighed. "I told him to be patient. But I'm pretty sure Holly went back up there and looked again. Fact, I know she did."

Keller nodded. He was at the limit of what he felt he could ask this woman. Now it was time to get in touch with the family lawyer and lay out the story and ask for guidance on how to proceed. He started to get to his feet and thank Hanson, but her face clouded over. She motioned him back down.

"I'm not finished," she said. "Your mother used some foul language when she got home, most of it toward my husband. Granted, it wasn't his place to give Melanie the third degree. But what she did was totally inappropriate with your father away, as well as quite dangerous."

"Ma'am, I understand, and I apologize. I know Mom will, too."

"Now, I do like Melanie," Hanson said, continuing right over him. "We exercise together and have what I consider a casual friendship, and the director will probably forgive an isolated incident. But it troubles me that she's not here this morning—"

"Mrs. Hanson—"

"—and while you seem like a nice young man, Keller, I sense you're covering for her and that it isn't the first time. Be honest, you sound more interested in the condition of your telescope than how your mother acted in front of Holly. And I find that shocking." Hanson leaned forward and tented her fingers. Her eyes were blazing now. "If Melanie has a problem, please tell me. I can probably help."

Keller and Caitlyn had watched Lifetime movies where social workers seemed almost gleeful at ripping kids away from their parents at the first sign of household unrest. In some cases, they almost seemed to stir up trouble if none existed. Hardly a teenager, Hanson was a mature adult who was probably certified to work with kids, and had the nerve, apparently, to jump into situations uninvited because she thought she knew what was best for everyone. It sounded like Holly's stay here was on thin ice, and if his mother really was ill and Holly wasn't allowed to stay, *he'd* be the daycare while his father ran the clothing store, at least until they found somewhere else for her to go. He'd have no choice but to withdraw from summer school and try to get some of his money back.

"I appreciate your concern," he said. His temper was short, and he paused for an instant to measure his tone. "But frankly, I don't agree with the way you handled this. If you and Mom are friends, you could have given her a chance to explain before you got your supervisor involved."

Hanson's eyes flashed. She didn't like that a bit, Keller saw. She probably got all bent out of shape if anyone questioned her about anything. "Excuse me," she said, "but you brought Holly this morning, not Melanie."

"Then have this conversation with me *before* going to your boss."

"Keller, we are under the strictest of guidelines—"

"Guidelines which include a pickup list. I'm on it, and so is my dad."

"You just said he was in Chicago."

"You didn't know that till I told you. You didn't try him Friday night, nor did you try me."

"That doesn't change the fact that Melanie—"

Keller stood. "You should have gone down the call list," he said, "instead of volunteering to babysit at our house on a night you and your husband had plans."

Hanson sniffed and looked at her computer screen. "Well, you can certainly take it up with the director if you want."

Now she was insulted. She was the professional, by golly,

and he was a snotty college kid who had the gall to question her judgment. She would march right down the hall as soon as he was gone and give the director an earful, Keller just knew, along with her expert opinion that something dreadfully wrong was afoot at the Bryan household, something they needed to look into right away. Keller took a deep breath. He absolutely had to be on good terms with this woman for the time being.

"Look, my mother's with her parents right now," he said. He came up with the lie on the fly and judged it as convincing as anything else he could think of. "She's going through some things, and I thought it best to watch Holly until Dad's back."

Hanson looked up. "This your idea or Melanie's?"

"And I'm truly sorry you're upset at me. That was not my goal."

"You're quite good at evading questions, Keller. But I'm a trained, professional social worker with a Masters degree and over a decade of experience in dealing with—"

"I'm sure you're as qualified as they come." Now he was out of patience and knew he needed to leave before he blew his stack. "I'm just asking you to give my father time to get home and talk to you guys before you throw us out of here. Can you do me that courtesy, please?"

Hanson gave him a long, cool look. She was letting him know she wouldn't forget this. And that regardless of how things turned out with Melanie, Keller knew, Holly's days here were most likely numbered. He was almost certain of that.

"Okay," she said. "But keep me posted. And write down your cell number in case I need you, since you're the point person until I hear otherwise."

THIRTY FOUR

Nancy watched the ragged Camaro putter into City Park. The driver, a redhead, was wearing sunglasses and tooled along until she reached the last softball field. She parked there and cut the noisy engine. Nancy looked around and got to her feet as she swung her purse over her shoulder. The BMW was fifty yards away in the other direction. She would be a good little hike from it while in the Camaro. But this wouldn't take long, and nobody was here. She'd done this many times before, even in broad daylight, and gotten away unscathed each time. Today would be no different.

She saw that the windows were down as she reached the Camaro. Vanessa sat there smoking a cigarette like she didn't have a care in the world. Nancy didn't speak until she'd climbed in the passenger side and shut the rusty door. She looked around again before locking eyes with the girl. Vanessa was as tall as Caitlyn but thin to the point of emaciated, with pale skin, a bad complexion and dirty fingernails. Nancy smelled body odor and wrinkled her nose.

"What up, Nancy Drew?" Vanessa said lazily. She was stoned. "Why so early?"

"Stuff to do. Got my stuff?"

"Got my money?"

"In the magic purse," Nancy said. "Talk to me."

"Well, Mama said we need a little extra this time."

"And why would that be?"

"On account of, she don't work for the police no more."

Oh, hell. "Since when?"

"Since last night, when the chief said she was suspended. She and that detective Higgins both." Vanessa sniffed. "Mama may sue Blair, if we don't move to Memphis like she's talking about. Round up a bunch of women who'll say they've been hit on by him."

"Have they?"

"Naw." Vanessa broke into a gap-toothed grin. "What's this about you and Brad Valentine? Something about some pictures on the Internet?"

"Another story for another time. Unless you know how they got there."

"Ain't even seen it. I just know my mama laughed and laughed."

"Vanessa, please focus and tell me what she said about who's been in the police station."

Vanessa took another drag and exhaled smoke out the window. Nancy felt sweat at her temples and under her arms. They were in direct sunlight, and she would be downright uncomfortable in no time flat. "You really think Caitlyn killed your mama?"

"You know from playing ball with her how crazy she is."

"I thought she got well."

"She's my sister. I know what she's capable of. Now tell me who's been through there. I don't have but a minute."

"It'll cost extra. Mama says she got to grease more wheels to get the info."

"Got it," Nancy said. "I'm listening."

"Well, her real daddy came up there last night."

Nancy felt herself jerk. "What did you just say?"

"Girl, my mama said you ain't never *seen* such a big man." Vanessa chuckled again. "Said there ain't no doubt where Caitlyn got her size."

"Don't you play me, Vanessa."

"I ain't playing you!"

"You're serious? Her biological father?"

Vanessa laughed out loud. Nancy smelled her rank breath

and almost gagged. "So your rich daddy that died wasn't her daddy, huh?"

"What's the man's name, please?"

"Earl something."

"Earl *what*, Vanessa?"

"Have to ask my mama. Damn, you ask a lot of questions."

Nancy looked around again to confirm that none of Oakdale's Finest had entered the park. If one of the pigs did slip in, there might be time to skedaddle before he caught sight of the pimped-out ride and came over for a look. She focused on the disheveled redhead. This all sounded on the level, even if Vanessa might not remember the discussion later.

"Okay, who else? Quickly."

"Caitlyn's lawyer," Vanessa mumbled. She looked like she might doze off right here, with her cigarette going. "Ms. Little, from Tupelo."

"Any idea what law firm?"

Vanessa looked blank.

"But her last name is Little?"

"Think so. Yesterday was her second time. Then that long-haired boy come back up in there," Vanessa said. "One they already talked to. This time, Mama heard he was real upset. Like, he was crying as he was leaving."

That all-too-familiar claustrophobic feeling came over Nancy, the usual sign that a panic attack was coming. Suddenly the car seemed to reek of oil and sweat. The cigarette smoke lingering in their faces now seemed three feet thick, and somehow all the oxygen in the atmosphere had dissolved. The thought that Vanessa probably hadn't bathed in a week made her queasy. Steady, she told herself. She'd have her pills in just a minute and would dry-swallow one and start zoning out.

"Eddie Ray Chester?" she asked. "That who we're talking about?"

"Yeah. Sounds like the chief fried up that man till he wasn't fit to eat. Lot of shouting."

"Who else has been there? Priscilla Hall?"

"Naw, didn't mention that name."

"So that's all you got?"

Vanessa grinned. "When you putting me in a TV commercial, girlfriend? I see you in fancy clothes for that rich place downtown 'bout every time I turn on the TV."

Nancy stifled a laugh. The ladies who ran the place would have a cow if this drugged-out, leprosy-riddled girl staggered in there and lobbied for being the talent—the *new* talent, that was.

"Go in there and ask to speak to Mrs. Brumley," she said with a straight face. "They're always looking for the right model. You're certainly tall enough."

"Cool. So how 'bout you pay for that oxycontin and valium you ordered and pay me extra."

"I can do an extra hundred. You just tell your mama to stay in the loop."

"Oh, she'll do that. Hey, Nancy?"

"What?"

"Maybe we won't worry about that extra if you go parking with me. Like right now, girlfriend."

Nancy was digging through the purse for her pocketbook and brushed past her mother's gun as Vanessa made this startling little proposition. She caressed the firearm as a wave of nausea came and went. The last thing the druggie would expect, as disoriented as she was this morning, was a gun in her face. She might not even move. But there was no way to dispose of her at the park even if no one heard the shot. Too bad they weren't at the Crisler cabin out by the lake.

But she could lure Eddie Ray Chester out there again.

The boy had made a great big mistake if he got scared and talked.

THIRTY FIVE

Keller felt his headache increase as he drove downtown after leaving the hospital. It wasn't easy waking Holly and getting her bathed, dressed, fed, and dropped off at daycare so early. And that was without the complication of his father's absence and his mother's condition, whatever it was. He'd hoped last night and again this morning that Melanie would call and sound like herself and thank him for pitching in. She didn't have to explain just yet. He just wanted to know she was safe and sane, but he didn't hear from her. Nor had James Bryan called. His unease increased with each passing hour.

Jeannie Hanson sure hadn't hesitated to involve management at the first sign of trouble. This struck Keller as a political move and ticked him off. But could Hanson have *wanted* to come over because she felt something was wrong with Holly as well as his mother? Keller couldn't imagine what would concern her. He could have easily grabbed Holly on short notice, though. He and Caitlyn would have taken her to supper, and there wouldn't have been a trip to Tupelo to spy on Nancy and Brad. While that wouldn't have prevented his mother from doing whatever she did, at least no one would have looked through the telescope, and his poor little sister, at the very least, wouldn't be part of this mess. Hanson wasn't going away, though, not after he made her mad. And the do-gooder daycare director could cause the Bryan family all kinds of problems if she got Holly kicked out.

He reached the square and found a spot in front of his father's store. It wouldn't open for half an hour, but he knocked on the glass front door nonetheless. If no one came out, he would call the business line and hope to catch a manager in the back. If no one answered, he supposed he would go back home, shower for class, then return on his way to the university. But an older, heavyset man came striding up and greeted him with a wave. He had a key ring in his hand and unlocked the door.

"Keller, come in out of the heat, boy," he said as he pulled open the door and stepped aside. Keller entered and felt a welcome rush of cool, crisp air. "Y'all are back early."

"Excuse me, Mr. Barksdale?"

"Chicago," Barksdale said. "Your dad had tickets for a game at Wrigley Field, talked about Navy Pier and some giant international food fest, which would have been right up my alley." Barksdale grinned as he patted his ample belly. "Thought y'all were gone this week, too, but I obviously didn't hear right."

Keller felt his heart sink. He looked outside and didn't see anyone who would assume the store had opened early. Then he peered at Barksdale. The old man was widowed with grown kids that lived out of state. He was a people person without enough people in his life, James Bryan had said before, and he was knowledgeable about the clothing business and the best salesman James had ever known. But Keller didn't know how well this nice old man kept a secret. He decided to hope for the best.

"We didn't go on vacation," Keller said softly. "I don't know where my father is."

Barksdale gave him an odd look.

"Mom hasn't seen him since last Thursday. Now, he left a note about a trip to Chicago. But Mom said it was a business trip, about some clothing line that was about to cancel. I tried to call him last night, and he didn't answer or call back. And he told you it was a family vacation?"

Barksdale nodded and tried to force a smile that came off miserably. "I'm sure there's an explanation, Keller. Meantime, if there's anything I can do for you or Melanie…"

Keller again went to his poker face. He knew not to say

that his mother was behaving erratically, and that he was his sister's temporary guardian. He was already questioning what he'd told Barksdale about his father.

"Who's gonna be in today?" he asked.

"Larry's managing," Barksdale said. "I ain't cut out to run a store. More like a glorified flunky."

Larry was younger than Barksdale and not as friendly, but he was a CPA by trade and did the books as part of his salary. He was short on people skills and much more likely, Keller felt, to make out-of-school comments than Barksdale.

"Let's keep this between us," Keller said. "I'm sure Dad'll be back in a day or two. I just don't want folks talking. Call me if you hear anything from him, and I'll do the same."

"You bet. Let me get you a card."

Barksdale started away and disappeared into the back. Keller looked out the front of the store. His mother's bookstore was across the street and in the next block. She opened at ten and didn't arrive until 9:30 or later. He would run home and dress, then hit the bookstore on the way to campus and still make it in time for class. Gina Roland, his mother's part-time employee, would be along by then to man the café and chat with folks that strolled in for a bite of brunch. Gina probably wasn't prepared to open by herself, but Keller had a strong hunch that his mother wouldn't be in this morning.

"Here you go," Barksdale said. A business card was in his outstretched hand, and a worried look that he didn't disguise well was on his face. "Cell number on the back. Anything I can do, my friend..."

"Thank you, Mr. Barksdale. Just keep it in the road, and keep this to yourself."

THIRTY SIX

James Bryan was wiped out after spending the last three days hiking in the mountains of Gatlinburg, Tennessee. He didn't have a cabin, and the best hotel room he could find because of the holiday weekend was a fleabag place forty miles from the state park. But money wasn't an issue at this juncture, nor was gasoline. He was taking stock of his life and deciding if he wanted it to continue.

He'd journeyed in this morning and driven high into the mountains for the fourth day in a row. He parked his car, soaked himself in bug spray and sunscreen, and started along the medium-skill hiking trail. Again he reveled in how much cooler it was way up here. He was prepared to walk another twelve or fourteen miles, but today he'd only gone an hour before running out of energy. Now, as he leaned against a support rail and sweat dripped from his temples and nose, he looked down to where steam rose from several hundred feet below. Out ahead of him were beautiful trees of all shapes and sizes, juxtaposed against craggy mountains and brilliant blue sky. Words couldn't begin to do justice to the spectacular view.

He'd opted to reach his destination before making a firm decision about ending his life, but he wasn't able to make up his mind when he began hiking Friday morning. The same had been true each day since. The guard rail he now leaned against had beckoned each day as he thought about the storm cloud that hovered above his marriage. It would be so easy to jump and end it all, he knew. But although not a terribly religious man—he took his family to church each Sunday because he knew he should—James suddenly felt a sense of calm inside him that he hadn't experienced in eons. And with that calm came a clarity so profound he might as well have seen it written in the sky.

He would deal with Nancy Rutledge head on, like a man.

Sure, there would be repercussions. Melanie might leave him, and even if she didn't, their marriage would never be the same. But if one wanted to be honest, the last decade hadn't been nearly as much fun as the first. Although the bookstore had given her a boost, his spouse hadn't wanted a second child and didn't enjoy Holly the way she did Keller when he was little. Melanie was doing what she wanted, she claimed, but he sensed genuine boredom from her. Everything was *okay*, she always said. Their sex, their friends, the vacations, the kids—all of it was merely okay, instead of adding joy to her life. He could see it in her eyes and wasn't sure what he could do to change it. James Bryan was a quiet, unassuming, small-town clothier who enjoyed a good baseball game and round of golf. He wasn't a dynamic TV personality like Leno or Letterman that could keep his wife in stitches. Nor was there a great deal to do in Oakdale.

He'd kept his cell phone off since leaving the Oakdale city limits, and Melanie would be upset about that. But he would call this morning and let her know he was returning tomorrow after several maddening days in the big city. Then, after he unpacked and put the Colt .45 safely away, he would have a heart to heart with his spouse. Melanie might start yelling and screaming and wake up poor Holly and take their daughter to a motel for the night. James was ready to come clean, though, and regardless of what happened with Melanie, he would corner Nancy Rutledge and tell her to *back off.* Nancy would probably put her mother in the middle of it, and Sherry might make all kinds of trouble, too. But that, James knew, was what one got for making a bad choice in a small community where everyone knew everyone else's business. He would deal with it.

He'd lived all his life in Oakdale and couldn't imagine being anywhere else.

THIRTY SEVEN

Keller looked down the street before climbing into his car. There was no point in running the air conditioning since he would shower at home before heading back out to campus. He'd have to leave his cell phone right there in the bathroom in case it rang, he figured. He would hear it in the shower but would have to keep it on silent during the two-hour lecture he would sit through beginning at ten, though. Profs went nuts these days if phones rang in class, and Keller didn't blame them. Students were text-messaging each other every minute as it was.

A woman caught his eye. She was in the next block and across the street.

He knew it would take longer to back his car out, drive a block and hunt for a parking place than to just run over there. He slammed the door, looked both ways and dashed across the street at an angle, his messy, sweaty hair piled underneath his baseball cap and his flip-flops slapping against the asphalt. It definitely wasn't his mother, and as he got closer he saw it was Gina Roland, his mother's very pregnant employee.

He called out her name and waved. Her husband Phil had taught Keller high school algebra, and Phil's daughter was nearly killed last winter by that nutcase cop Gary Quinn. But nobody wanted to talk about that any more: Gina, known to many as the town slut, met Roland in AA, and Roland, who'd lost his wife to cancer, befriended Gina, got her pregnant and married her in a hastily-arranged ceremony early this year. Even James Bryan told Melanie that she might be asking for trouble in hiring someone so notorious. But while short on sophistication, Gina, who also styled hair in Hampton Falls, had proved as hard-working and loyal an employee as Mr. Barksdale. Keller saw Gina shield her eyes from the sun and look in his direction.

"It's me! Keller!"

Gina waved back. Keller slowed to a trot and caught his breath as he covered the last few yards to the bookstore. It was already blazing hot, with puffy clouds welling up in the sky. A few cars were parked in the diagonal spaces along the square, but now that the Oakdale Café had finished serving breakfast and most businesses didn't open until ten, he hadn't attracted anyone's attention by yelling down the street like a madman.

"Hey, sweetie," she drawled. "Come have something cold to drink and let's get out of this sun. Your mama ought to be showing up in a little while."

Keller took off his cap and mopped his brow with the back of his hand. He placed it back on his head as Gina unlocked the door and disabled the security alarm.

"How's Mr. Phil getting along?"

"Just peachy. Said he caught some big catfish this morning," she said. "He'll be down here for coffee after while. Pampering me 'bout to death, Keller." She gave him a warm smile. "But I wouldn't turn his attention down for nothing. Nice to feel so loved."

Keller smiled back. The elite women of Oakdale hated Gina not only because she wasn't one of them, but because she'd landed the most eligible bachelor in recent memory. Leading the gossipy charge, of course, was Sherry Rutledge: Caitlyn was certain that her mother had longed to capture Roland's fancy and was furious at being upstaged by an uneducated hick who'd slept with half the men of Smart County.

Word had spread that Gina lived with Gary Quinn last summer, too.

Quinn was twenty-three when he died, which meant that Gina, whom Keller understood to be forty, had shacked up with a much younger, clearly unstable guy—before marrying a man old enough to be her father. Patrick was among those who expected Gina to fall off the wagon and go wild again before long, even with a brand new baby. Keller, though, was careful not to comment. There were way too many people around here who expected Caitlyn to go off the rails again, too.

"Your mama has plenty of water and diet drinks," Gina said, looking over her shoulder as she waddled toward the back in her green maternity dress. "I cut out caffeine being pregnant and all, so I'll have water. Diet Coke okay, or you want me to make you a cappuccino?"

"First cold thing you get your hands on. Water's fine."

"How's little Holly, besides growing like a weed?" she called out after unlocking the office. Keller couldn't see into the room but thought of his mother and the damn-good-lawyer-turned-author bouncing on the hide-a-bed and tried to push the image from his mind. That wasn't a visual he wanted to dwell on, regardless of whether it was from Melanie's imagination.

"She's great," he said. "Loves soccer and t-ball. Fun watching her grow."

"She'll be a beautiful girl, no two ways 'bout that." He heard Gina rooting around in the fridge before he heard it shut. A second later she closed the office and came toward the front with bottled waters for both of them. "Before you know it, boys will be asking her out." Gina sighed as she presented his water to him. "I've told Melanie more than she cares to hear, but y'all do better than I did."

Keller understood Gina had kids about his age who'd accumulated impressive rap sheets and were incarcerated at present. She claimed to have been the worst parent imaginable.

"You'll be a good mom. Won't be long before Holly's watching your little one."

"I sure hope." Gina unscrewed the top from her water and guzzled half the bottle. "How's Caitlyn? I sure been thinking about her."

"She's hanging in there," Keller said. "I'll tell her you asked."

"You just take good care of her."

Gina was a nice lady and would gab all morning, and it wasn't just because he was the boss's son: Keller was struck by how much Gina wanted to be liked, how she wanted to get to know everyone in this new world of hers as the wife of beloved Phil Roland. But there were things Keller needed to know—or at least ask about—in case his mother showed up early. Gina went behind the counter and sat on the stool, her pregnant belly pressing against the dress. He leaned against the counter.

"So how'd the signing go Friday?" he asked.

"What signing?"

Keller frowned. "The author from the Delta. Lawyer who wrote a legal thriller."

"Stool ain't gonna work for this big fat pregnant girl," Gina muttered. She shoved it aside, grabbed a padded chair with rollers, and sank into it before looking up at him. The cushion made a soft hiss. "Now, then. I was here Friday, darling, and there wasn't no signing."

"Then what the hell was my mother talking about?"

"You mean last Friday, three days ago?"

"Yes, ma'am."

Gina shook her head no. "But she's just tickled James Patterson's coming."

"*The* James Patterson? Here?"

"What I said, Keller! Phil loves him—got every single one of his books—and he just flipped out when I told him." Gina winked at Keller. "Be honest, I think he wants to hear straight from Melanie that Patterson's coming. Don't quite trust his new wife to have all her facts straight."

"I know she had Pat Conroy and Dennis Lehane... when'd this happen?"

"Right after lunch Friday. I'd just got here, and she was prancing about, saying he had stops in Jackson and Memphis, and that his publicist had heard of this store, and she begged and offered to dance a jig and all that, and they had a deal worked out when she got off the phone."

Keller looked away. The Delta boyfriend hadn't signed here Friday, if the man even existed. And Keller refused to believe his mother had booked *James Patterson* to autograph books here anymore than he accepted the earth being flat—it was about as likely as Stephen King coming to town. If Melanie wasn't careful with what she told her customers, it wouldn't take long to destroy her modest but successful book business.

As well as her family.

"What time did you leave Friday, Gina?"

"Closed up at six."

"You, or both of you?"

"Just me. Melanie left 'bout four-fifteen. I know it was before four-thirty."

"She say where she was going?"

"No. I assumed home. It was Friday, kinda slow, and she'd landed her big coup in getting Patterson and thought she'd take a load off, I guess." Gina looked at her watch. "Be honest, I'm a little surprised she ain't here. She said Friday we were gonna start opening at nine, that we were losing out on business by not opening before ten."

Keller stared at her. Then he walked to the door and looked through it. A lone car passed, looking for a place on the other side of the street. He looked back at Gina. She couldn't help a chuckle.

"Got that right," she said. "Ain't nobody coming in here between nine and ten Monday through Friday unless we build some sort of skywalk that would bring café customers directly here."

"And Mom wanted you here now. So you guys could open at nine."

"She didn't say this early, sweetheart, but she likes me here fifteen minutes before my shift, and I finished up errands a little early and came on over."

Keller now saw concern in Gina's eyes. She would tell her husband everything Keller told her, but he didn't have a problem with that. He had great admiration for Phil Roland and would confide just about anything in him. And Gina wouldn't tell anyone else. Nor would Roland. The secrets would be safe here, and Keller just wasn't sure that was the case at the clothing store.

"Is something wrong, baby?"

"Yes." He opened his water, took a long drink, and stood directly across the counter from Gina. "You can tell Phil everything I'm going to say, but *please* do not tell anyone else."

"I promise. Is Melanie all right?"

"No, she's not," he said. A vision of his mother sucking on a cigarette as her boobs exploded from that halter flashed through his mind. He did his best to focus on the woman in front of him. "I think Mom's had some sort of breakdown. Or is having one."

"What do you mean? Where is she?"

"I don't know." He gripped the counter and tried to will away the tears forming in his eyes. "Dad's away on business right now, and Mom called late Friday night to tell me about Sherry and sounded a little odd. I went over there Saturday evening, and we had a big fight—long story. So Caitlyn and I met her and Holly at City Park yesterday morning, and she said all kinds of crazy things. Truth is, I was worried enough to demand that Holly stay with me and my roommate a few days, until Dad gets back from his trip. She got in her van and drove off. We went over there yesterday afternoon to get clothes and things for Holly, and

Caitlyn and I went back last night while my roommate watched Holly. She wasn't there either time. I called yesterday afternoon and got the voice mail. She didn't call back."

"Oh, my lord," Gina whispered. "I tried her cell this morning and got the voice mail. Figured she was at the wellness center. I just wanted to be sure about opening early today."

"I took Holly to daycare myself. I know she didn't exercise this morning. But she definitely left here before four-thirty on Friday?"

"I'm certain of it, honey. And I swear to you there was no signing."

Keller knew he might as well level with this lady. He needed every shred of information he could get. "Has Mom mentioned anything she's unhappy about, even about my dad? Please don't hold back."

"No," Gina whispered. A sad smile was on her face. "Not a thing."

"What did she tell you about Dad's business trip? Or did she?"

"Not a word. Had no idea he was out of town."

Was the note about the trip even real?

Keller rubbed his temples again and took a long swallow of water. He'd been relying on information from his mother, but the all-important note about the trip to Chicago might be fiction as well. Now nothing at all made sense, he thought, as he looked at Gina. She had what looked like a million questions in her eyes.

"I went by the house Thursday morning, and nobody was home," he said. "Came downtown, saw Mom's van out front and stuck my head in here. She said Dad had just left for an emergency meeting in Chicago, something about a clothing line that was about to pull their distribution, and would be back in a few days. All this in a note he'd left for her, okay? But I just talked to Mr. Barksdale. He asked why we were back from vacation so early, because Dad told him we'd be gone all this week. *We*, as in the whole family."

Gina covered her mouth.

"Have you noticed anything odd about Mom lately? Anything at all?"

"Know what was weird: I swear I smelled cigarette smoke on her Friday. I'm real sensitive about it because I used to smoke three packs a day—told Phil I'm more worried about getting re-hooked than drinking again." Gina shook her head as if merely talking about it was difficult. "But I know I smelled smoke on her, and I know she don't smoke."

"She must have had eight or nine cigarettes in the half hour we were at the park, one right after the other. Also made herself a huge drink Saturday night right in front of me and wound up passed out in a lawn chair on the patio. They don't *ever* drink, Gina, at least not in front of us. It was like she was a different person. And she was saying all kinds of crazy stuff Saturday night and Sunday morning."

Gina came out from behind the counter. She looked like she was going to cry, and the last thing he wanted was to upset a pregnant lady who was trying so hard to succeed after hitting rock bottom. He embraced her. She clung back as tightly as Caitlyn.

"Keller, this is scaring me," she whispered. "Is she even coming in today?"

"Call Phil, okay? He'll help with the customers," Keller said gently. "I have class at ten, or I'd stay. If Mom doesn't show up, you open at ten like always. Makes no sense to open at nine."

"All right. I know Phil can be here by ten. And he can stay as long as I need him."

"I'll come straight by after class, meaning I'll get here a little after twelve. We'll put our heads together and decide what to do."

THIRTY EIGHT

Keller sat across from Clint Young, a bearded, graying man who was the Bryan family attorney as well as his former scoutmaster and little league baseball coach. Young had told Keller he was booked all day when he called after class. But when Keller said it was urgent, Young promised ten minutes if he came right then. The law firm was in a remodeled house on a residential street two blocks off the square. Keller had raced to the bookstore to check on Phil and Gina, then barreled over here and slammed to a stop along the curb. He'd just summarized the chaos in his life in two devastating sentences:

"I don't know where either of my parents are, or how to get in touch with them. And Holly may have witnessed the death of Sherry Rutledge."

Young stared for quite a while, long enough for Keller to wonder if his old coach thought his leg was being pulled. Then he reached over and punched a button on his desk phone. He didn't take his eyes off Keller as he instructed his secretary to reschedule his lunch meeting. Then Young leaned back and tented his fingers behind his head.

"Okay, young man," he said. The tension in his voice showed on his face. If nothing else, Young believed him: It sounded to Keller like he now had all the time he needed. "The floor is yours."

Keller talked for thirty minutes and laid everything out in chronological order. He began with the note about his father's business trip that his mother mentioned last Thursday—that brief visit with his mom now seemed a lifetime ago. He described why Caitlyn snooped in Sherry's house and the Friday night stakeout of Brad and Nancy. He covered his shock at his mother's behavior at City Park, the disbelief at seeing the Valentine stunner on

ESPN, and concluded with the stop at the bookstore minutes ago: Gina and Phil, thankfully, had a handle on things. He felt relieved when he finished and knew he'd done the right thing by confiding in a trusted family friend instead of a police chief who was quiet, difficult to read, and ran a leaky department.

"Good grief," Young said. "What a mess."

"Amen to that."

"First, I'm with Caitlyn: Your dad either lost his phone or broke it. Wife and I were talking about how much we rely on the damn things, after surviving just fine without 'em for the first forty years of our lives. But if something has happened to James, and if Melanie is indeed sick and requires serious, long-term care, you and Holly won't be alone. As well-liked as your family is in our little corner of the world, *all* of us will rally around you, son. That's not an empty promise."

Young's voice had thickened, and Keller felt a lump in his throat. He knew the emotion of the last few days would explode forth in a crying jag if he tried to express his gratitude. He needed to cry, to purge some of the anguish that had built up inside him, but to do so would hurt his focus. Protecting his sister was top priority right now, and he quietly thanked Young.

"You're welcome. I'm now going to switch from friend to attorney," Young said. "I picked up on your distrust of Henry Blair. I don't blame Caitlyn for feeling betrayed, and I know you're loyal to her. And Henry sure took his lumps after the Gary Quinn fiasco." Young eased his chair forward and leaned across the desk. "But he's a good man, son. A man I consider a friend. He inherited a police department in awful shape when he came here five years ago, and he's tried to clean it up and faced a ton of resistance within. There are still problems, as this leak indicates. But I assure you that nobody feels worse about Caitlyn's name getting out than Henry. And he *must* know what you just told me about your sister. Right away."

"I understand, sir. But I'm scared to death of Holly having to testify in court if it comes down to that," Keller said. "Caitlyn has her own lawyer, by the way. She wasn't about to call Vincent Cockrell, the man Sherry's always used. I'm sure you know him."

"Tried lots of cases against him over the years."

"Caitlyn said he's ruthless."

Young hesitated. Keller sensed him choosing his words carefully. "Well, he wouldn't be able to represent both Rutledge girls, anyway. Not if Caitlyn might wind up testifying against Nancy."

Keller swallowed hard. He'd spent so much time thinking about Holly on the stand that the possibility of Caitlyn testifying against Nancy hadn't even occurred to him. For that matter, *he* might have to testify against Nancy, too. He saw himself answering Young's questions after his old coach prepped him for testimony. Then he saw Cockrell, in his perfect suit and slicked-back dark hair, trying to paint him as a liar during his heated cross-examination, while Nancy, the girl he thought he loved at age thirteen, looked right through him from her perch at the defense table.

"By the way," Young said, "my wife and I have met Mike Morgan and watch him every morning. Will he even work there anymore? It'll surely get out that the girl in that picture is his wife."

"No idea."

"Well, *everybody* is talking about that. Between the two of us, Brumley's will be informing Nancy that she won't be affiliated with them anymore."

Keller whistled. He hadn't thought about that, either.

"I didn't know Sherry well, and I'm not privy to how real estate is divided up among agents, but I'm told it's pretty cut-throat," Young said. "My wife wondered aloud if Nancy would take over her mother's listings, the way a new sales rep would inherit an account list. And I'm just speculating, but I figure the way people are talking about this, they may let her go, too."

Young's secretary buzzed and announced that the lunch meeting had been rescheduled. While Young was jotting down the new date, Keller thought about what his attorney had just said: Even if Nancy had nothing to do with Sherry's death and wasn't charged with anything, the public humiliation stemming from the pictures on the Internet might leave her unemployed and a laughingstock around town. If she was already unstable, she might really come unglued if—

"Anyway," Young said, bringing him back to the present, "if Nancy were to be arrested on suspicion of murder, and the D.A. files charges, yes, Henry would need your sister's statement."

"Could it be taped?"

"Up to the judge, but there are new laws in Mississippi which require confrontation—by that, I mean putting children on the stand. I'm going to call Henry as soon as we're through. My guess is that he'll want Holly interviewed by his people."

Keller thought of Caitlyn's description of the stuffy, windowless interview room at the police station. "Mr. Clint, won't that scare her to death, bunch of officers in uniform in a smelly, scary place she hasn't been before?"

"I'll ask if it can be done at your house."

"Like that a lot better. I know Holly would be more relaxed."

"I'll see what I can do. Give me your cell number, and I'll call you as soon as I've talked to Henry. I know he'll want to move as fast as possible."

THIRTY NINE

"This is Jeannie Hanson. May I help you?"

"Ms. Hanson, this is Chief Henry Blair with the Oakdale

police department. Can you talk just a moment?"

Hanson had answered her direct line while perusing an e-mail from her supervisor, who thanked her for staying on top of the Melanie and Holly Bryan matter and praised Hanson's commitment to the children at the facility. She closed the note and focused on the voice at the other end of the phone. She'd never met the chief but knew he'd blown his stack on the news yesterday—she had heard several people talking about it. Blair sounded friendly enough today, though.

"Yes, sir. How can I help you?"

"Like to send two of my officers over to ask one of your campers some questions," Blair said. "I know you got a bunch of kids and don't want to disrupt everybody. Won't take but a few minutes."

Hanson raised both eyebrows. She couldn't ever remember the police coming to the daycare. "Uh, sure. When'd you want to do this?"

"Next few minutes, if possible."

"Well, there's a baby playroom that isn't in use at the moment." Hanson pictured the room in her mind. "Has mobiles hanging from the ceilings and wallpaper with bears and cats and stuff. I'll try to have the child ready, if you can tell me who it is."

"Be great. It's Holly Bryan," Blair said. "Dark hair, eight years old."

The plot thickens, Hanson thought, and flashed back to the morning last week when Melanie bit her head off: The vending machine was out of lime-flavored Gatorade, and Melanie acted as if she, Jeannie Hanson, was responsible and should face death by lethal injection. The unexpected tirade had turned heads, but Hanson chalked it up to a bad mood when Melanie was her normal self that evening while picking up her child. But a woman who saw the blow-up claimed to have been in the bookstore the previous week and watched in astonishment as Melanie, with a wild look in her eye, quoted at the top of her lungs from the Book of Revelation to a pair of college-aged girls that had wandered in and sent them scurrying off down the street.

It was possible that Melanie was just going through some things, as her lamebrain son suggested this morning. But the odd sitting request just before the daycare closed Friday evening, followed by Melanie's drunken, profane display when she finally made it home that night, was evidence of a real problem— Hanson was certain of that. And she wasn't going to turn the other cheek, not when a helpless little girl was involved. After all, someone had to step in and protect the kids when the parents were too wrapped up in themselves, or on alcohol and drugs, as Melanie might be. Her son had sure circled the wagons this morning and ticked her off to boot. And now the police wanted to talk to Holly?

Hanson had an idea.

"Sure," she said smoothly to Blair. "Holly's group is on the playground for a few more minutes. When they come in for their snack, I'll bring Holly down to my office until your people are here. Then I'll take everybody down to the playroom and leave Holly with them. They can come get me when they're through."

"Thank you so much," Blair said. "I'm sending Officers Pete Clark and Amanda Owings right now. They'll be in street clothes, so don't worry about the kids staring at a bunch of uniforms, holsters, and guns. Be real low-key."

"Very good, Chief Blair. We'll help any way we can."

Hanson hung up, came out of her office and walked down the carpeted hall to the baby playroom. It smelled of disinfectant, but so did every other room inhabited by infants. Nobody was in there, and she strode to the monitor on the far counter and switched it on. There were two walkie-talkies in a charger alongside. She took one and started out of the room. She hadn't bothered to ask about watching the interview in person because she knew Blair would tell her it was police business.

But she would listen through the walkie-talkie and take notes on her computer.

FORTY

Clint Young called Keller with instructions to meet two plainclothes officers from the Oakdale police department at the daycare at 3:30. The last thing he wanted was further interaction with Jeannie Hanson, but Chief Blair felt this was the quickest way to interview Holly while keeping her in her daily routine. The logic, Young said, was hard to knock.

Keller arrived early and parked near the entrance to the daycare area, hoping to recognize the officers and introduce himself so he could enter with them. The muscle-bound Clark was easy to spot in his Chicago Cubs replica jersey, faded jeans, sunglasses, and buzz-cut hair. Owings was in a plaid sun dress. She had brown hair, looked Hanson's age, and wore a wedding ring. They found Hanson and Holly waiting for them at the sign-in desk. Hanson gave the officers warm smiles and hand-shakes while ignoring Keller. She led them to a foul-smelling playroom and let them know she would be in her office if they needed anything. She'd just walked out and closed the door.

"You have fun out on the playground?" Keller asked Holly. He felt tense even without Hanson in the room but hoped to put his sister at ease. He was in a chair made for someone Holly's size and sat next to her. Hanson had given her a glass of red Kool-Aid and a handful of animal crackers. Holly had already gulped down most of the drink and was now inspecting the crackers.

"Yeah, but it's too hot out there."

"It sure is, Holly," Owings said. "You can call me Miss

Amanda and this nice man Mr. Pete, okay?"

"Yes, ma'am," she said. Holly turned to Clark. "Hi, Mr. Pete."

Keller had figured the guy to be a typical macho cop with a chip on his shoulder, but Clark seemed friendly and looked relaxed around Holly. He might have a niece or nephew her age and maybe kids of his own, even though he wasn't wearing a ring. Based on the way Owings bantered with Holly, Keller figured her for a mom. The officers were also in kid chairs and sat six feet away. Keller saw that Clark's small steno pad and a pen were hidden from Holly beneath his hip. He guessed Owings would do most of the talking, while Clark would take notes and maybe chip in a question or two.

"Hey, sweetie," Clark replied. "You like camp?"

"Oh, yes!" Holly punctuated her response with a loud slurp of Kool-Aid. "Know what I like best? Swimming! It's so fun, 'cause we play this game called—"

"Now, Holly, Mr. Pete and Miss Amanda don't have a lot of time," Keller said. "So let's be quiet and see what they want to talk about, okay?"

Owings caught Keller's eye and winked, seeming to convey that there was no hurry. "Do you like to play with dolls, Holly?" she asked.

"Sometimes."

"Like to watch movies?"

"Oh, yes! *Cars* is my favorite! Right, Keller?"

"That's right," Keller said.

"Keller is my brother. He's a lot older than me," Holly added, directing the comment to both officers. They smiled, as did Keller.

"I've seen *Cars*," Clark said. "And you saw it Friday night, right?"

"I've seen it a million times. Right, Keller?"

Keller shifted his weight so he could stretch his legs before his foot went to sleep. He saw Owings fiddling with something that she, too, was shielding from Holly. He peered at it and realized it was a mini-cassette recorder. Before they'd entered the building, Clark asked Keller to sign a form which allowed the discussion to be taped. Clint Young told him beforehand that this would take place.

"Yep," Keller said. "And you saw it Friday night when Miss Jeannie and Mr. Doug came over."

"Yeah, 'cause they hadn't seen it." Holly was now separating the animal crackers into two groups, like they were going to face off in some sort of contest. Keller couldn't help but imagine a similar struggle for control of his sister if one or both of their parents didn't return soon: Hanson would lead the charge to take her away. He wondered if Hanson was standing outside with her ear pressed to the door.

"Did they like it?" Owings asked.

"I think so."

"Well, I don't know about you, darling, but I can't watch a movie straight through without having to take a break." Owings paused. Keller watched as Clark eyed Holly. Maybe he was trying to get a feel for her personality—and whether or not she was likely to lie. "What about you, Holly?"

"Yeah. Sometimes I get bored."

"Sometimes I have to go to the bathroom," Owings said.

"Yeah, me, too."

Keller wasn't sure why he felt pressure to move this forward, but he did. "Did you have to go during the movie, Holly?" he asked gently.

"Yeah, once."

Nobody said anything for a moment. Keller looked at Owings, and she smiled and shrugged. It looked like he was welcome to chime in if he wanted to coax his sister. He smiled back and said nothing, not wanting to overstep his bounds. Another second passed before Owings continued.

"Did you do anything else before going back to watch the movie, Holly?"

Holly looked up. Confusion was on her face. "What do you mean?"

"Did you walk around the house, or play with any toys?"

Holly looked at her animal crackers. Keller wondered if she didn't understand the question, but recognition suddenly lit up her face. She looked at Owings. "I looked through Keller's telescope! It's so cool!" Then her smile faded as she turned to Keller. "I'm not supposed to play with it without asking. I'm sorry."

Keller smiled. "That's okay."

"But you enjoy playing with it, Holly?" Owings asked.

"Yeah, because you can see a long way."

"And what did you see when you looked through it?"

Keller felt his heartbeat quicken and noticed the tension in the room. Clark, though clearly trying to look casual for Holly's benefit, was now watching her the way he might eye a rabid dog that backed him into a corner. Owings shifted her weight.

"The pool," Holly said.

"What pool, honey?"

"Miss Sherry's pool."

"Was anyone out there?"

"Uh-huh."

Keller felt beads of sweat at his temples despite the cool air blowing through the room. He almost spoke but didn't. Owings looked like she knew what she was doing, and he didn't want to disturb the connection she'd made with Holly, especially with the crucial part of the exchange at hand.

"Can you tell me who you saw?"

Holly drained her Kool-Aid and looked disappointed there wasn't more. Keller saw Clark glance around, as if looking for a pitcher. Then he became still.

"Can you tell me, sweetie?" Owings repeated.

"Miss Sherry and Miss Nancy."

"Sherry Rutledge and her daughter Nancy, right?"

"And Caitlyn," Holly said.

Keller felt himself jerk. He saw Clark do the same thing from the corner of his eye. If Owings was surprised by this, though, she didn't show it.

"Was Caitlyn there, Holly?"

"No. But Miss Caitlyn is Miss Sherry's other daughter. She's a basketball player." Holly grinned. "And she's Keller's girlfriend."

Owings smiled. Keller felt so much relief surge through him he half expected to wet his pants.

"But you saw Miss Sherry, and you saw Miss Nancy. And you *didn't* see Miss Caitlyn. Is that right, Holly?"

"It was so funny," Holly said suddenly, startling Keller with her high-pitched little giggle. "See, Miss Nancy pushed Miss Sherry in the pool, and I told Keller it was just like when I swim up here! There's always one lifeguard up in the chair, and another in the pool, and they let us push each other in and everybody splashes water all over the place. Hey, sometimes I go swimming at Miss Sherry's pool. It's so fun."

Owings smiled again. Keller thought she looked amazingly cool and figured the woman would make a good hostage negotiator, if the need for that in these parts ever arose. "Do you remember what Miss Nancy was wearing?"

"A dress," Holly said.

"Do you remember what color?"

Keller felt his heart pound as the seconds passed. If this was a march toward the end zone, they were right at the goal line—Holly was that close. But the incident was Friday night, and this was Monday afternoon. Had she already forgotten?

"Black," Holly said triumphantly. "Can I have some more Kool-Aid?"

"In just a minute, baby," Owings replied. "What does Miss Nancy look like?"

"She's on TV."

"What does she do on TV?"

"She's in commercials for dresses," Holly said.

Keller wondered if Brumley's had supplied the funeral garb Nancy and Sherry wore to Jackson last Friday. If that was the case, now that he thought of it, a Brumley's dress really was on the Internet for the world to see. That, he reasoned, was a big reason for the snooty old woman who owned the store to kick Nancy's little butt to the curb. If Mr. Young's information was accurate, that was. He couldn't wait to share it with Caitlyn.

"Can you tell me what she looks like?" Owings said. "Miss Nancy, I'm talking about."

"Her hair is black."

"Is she tall?"

"Taller than me."

"I suppose so. Is she as tall as her sister?"

"No, silly!" Holly said. Owings grinned, and Keller almost laughed when he saw Clark stifle a chuckle. "Miss Caitlyn is *very* tall. Miss Nancy is a lot shorter."

"What color is Miss Caitlyn's hair?"

"It's blond. Like Mr. Pete's," Holly said, pointing to Clark. "But hers is curly. And goes down her back."

"Did you see anything else through the telescope, Holly, after Miss Sherry went into the pool?"

"Well, Miss Sherry must be a good swimmer, because she stayed down there under the water."

The cheerful response hit Keller hard. Holly was so

young and trusting and had been thrust, through a remarkable confluence of bizarre events, into possibly determining whether an adult might be charged with murder. Although he knew this fiasco wasn't his fault, he berated himself nonetheless for not checking on his mother during the day on Friday. He could have volunteered to take Holly for the evening, and none of this crap would have ever happened.

"Did you see her get out, sweetie?"

"No, 'cause I heard Miss Jeannie calling for me and went back to watch *Cars*."

"Okay, but did you see Miss Nancy after Miss Sherry went in the water?"

"Yes."

"What was she doing? Did she go in the water, too?"

"No. But maybe she went to get her bathing suit so she could swim, too."

It certainly sounded like this was the truth: There'd been absolutely no variation in any of the answers Holly gave to these strangers. Keller inhaled the ripe air of the nursery in hopes of loosening the knot in his chest. Owings and Clark pried themselves from the kid chairs and stood. Maybe this was finally over. It couldn't have taken fifteen minutes but seemed like hours.

"Maybe so," Owings said to Holly with a big smile. "How 'bout some more Kool-Aid?"

FORTY ONE

Jeannie Hanson strode into her office and slammed the door. She went behind her desk, plopped into her chair, and exhaled sharply enough to rattle the stack of papers in front of her. The police were gone. The walkie-talkie was charging and the baby monitor had been turned off. Keller Bryan had just signed his sister out for the day, so they were gone, too. Nothing was said in the playroom about Melanie during the interview with Holly, so Hanson assumed that the cops had no idea the girl's mother wasn't playing with a full deck and might be missing. She definitely planned to follow up, even if it meant going behind Keller's back to do so.

But the little girl had witnessed a murder.

On my watch.

Something was wrong with Melanie. There was no doubt about it, not after the behavior Hanson had seen and heard about in recent days. There was also Keller's evasiveness this morning. But as much as Hanson hated to admit it, the boy was exactly right that she didn't follow protocol. Her director would have insisted that she go down the pickup list before taking action that was beyond the facility's responsibility and liability, such as driving a child home. In her defense, Holly's dad was on a business trip, but it sounded like Keller was available. And if he'd picked up his sister at six o'clock Friday evening, Doug and Jeannie Hanson would have celebrated his birthday with their friends in Tupelo and she wouldn't be part of this…this cluster.

She closed her eyes and tried to think. It was just her and Holly that first hour. They watched blooper videos on Animal Planet while she updated her husband every few minutes and finally asked him to bring pizza. Holly insisted on showing them her bedroom after they ate, Hanson recalled, and she'd also taken them into what turned out to be Keller's old room and set up his telescope. They all looked through it, but Doug, by then, was losing patience. They went back to the den because Hanson wanted them on the ground floor when Melanie arrived. But Holly made a second trip upstairs, that one under the pretense of a bathroom break after they started the movie. Hanson remembered standing at the foot of the stairs and calling out her name. Holly came trotting into sight a few seconds later.

After apparently witnessing a homicide.

As implausible as this whole scenario was, Hanson felt deep in her bones that it was accurate. The fire truck and ambulance which rolled by at 8:45 were headed to the Rutledge abode, which was down the hill from the Bryans. Hanson, when she looked through the telescope, saw what turned out to be the Rutledge pool from Keller's bedroom window, although nobody was out there at the time. The emergency vehicles, though, had to have been called when daylight remained in the Friday night sky. No wonder Keller tap-danced like mad this morning! Holly had told him what she saw through the telescope, and plans were probably underway for her to tell the police. Hanson raised an eyebrow at something else that was said in the interview. It sent a shiver down her spine.

Keller was dating Caitlyn Rutledge. And the police, she'd heard, had already talked to Caitlyn.

Like everyone in Oakdale, Hanson was stunned by Sherry's death. She was friendly with Sherry and Nancy and saw them at luncheons and parties. Everybody was talking about the Internet photos, though, and the good Rutledge name had taken a hit—Nancy and Brad had *really* messed up this time. That was small potatoes compared to Sherry perhaps being murdered, though. And while Hanson was well aware of Caitlyn's basketball exploits, she didn't know the younger girl personally. All she had to go on was what people had talked about for years: Caitlyn, though quite the athlete, wasn't stable. There were rumors of a suicide attempt and a stay at the state hospital, and Sherry never denied any of it. It was almost eerie, now that Hanson thought about it, how swiftly Caitlyn's lawyer accused the Oakdale PD of a leak. Was that part of a master plan to hide the fact that Caitlyn did it?

And would Keller have pressured his little sister to lie about who pushed Sherry to her death?

Hanson wouldn't put it past him. Poor Holly sounded

confused, like she'd been coached and couldn't remember what to say. Hanson would read her notes to Doug and get his take on whether those cops—especially that woman—were asking some incredibly leading questions of Holly, or if it was just her imagination. But what went down at the Rutledge pool would certainly impact Doug: As Oakdale's only home inspector, he'd worked extensively with Sherry and Nancy in recent years. Some unsavory things would be buried with Sherry, and Doug disliked Nancy and had long felt she was up to no good. He might breathe a sigh of relief if both were no longer involved in local real estate. Yet Hanson found herself almost hoping Caitlyn would be charged with and convicted of the crime.

She picked up her phone and dialed a cell number from memory. It went directly to voice mail.

"Hi, it's Vince Cockrell. I'm in court all week, but I'll be checking messages often. If this is urgent, please call my secretary and have me paged. Thank you."

"Hey Vince, it's your favorite and most beautiful daughter-in-law," Jeannie Hanson Cockrell said. "We have to talk right now. Unless something changed I didn't hear about, you were Sherry Rutledge's attorney, right? I'm assuming you'd also represent Nancy, and, well…we absolutely *must* talk right away. Call me the second you get this."

FORTY TWO

"Come in," Keller called out loudly in response to the knock on the townhouse door. However noble his intentions were toward his sister, he wished he could drug her at the moment. She was watching *Cars* and turned to shush him because she couldn't hear the dialogue. Keller fought back the urge to snap at her—or stop the movie—as Caitlyn entered. She had an economics textbook in one hand and her purse slung over her shoulder. She patted Holly's shoulder as she walked by.

"Miss Caitlyn, can you take me home? Keller won't, and I'm *so* bored."

Caitlyn gave Keller a pained look. Keller put his index finger to his temple and pulled the trigger of an imaginary gun.

"Not right now, sweetie," she said. "But maybe I can watch the movie with you while I study. How about that?"

"Well...can we watch the special features?"

"Sure can. You watch for just a minute, and your brother and I are gonna go in the kitchen and talk, okay? Then we'll watch."

Holly nodded. Keller stood and followed Caitlyn into the kitchen. She put her book and purse on the counter and looked around. Dirty dishes were in the sink, and Keller still smelled hamburger from the tacos he'd made them an hour ago.

"You look like you need a hug, baby doll," she said.

Keller embraced her and rested his head against her shoulder with a grunt.

"How'd the interview go?"

"Fine. Didn't take but a few minutes," he said under his breath. "Holly told the cops exactly what she told me. Sounds like it really happened."

"I'd give anything to know what Nancy and Mother fought about, assuming they got into it," Caitlyn said. "Autopsy sure won't tell us that."

"Patrick and I had a big fight."

Caitlyn pulled back. "Great. About Holly?"

"Yep. Wanted the place to himself because his date's in a dorm and her roommate's there. And while we were arguing, of course, I missed Dad's call because my damn cell was on silent. Never turned it back on after class."

"Where is he?"

"Gatlinburg, of all places," Keller said. "Promised we'd

talk when he gets home, but he admitted there wasn't a trip to Chicago after all. Said he needed to clear his head."

"Has he tried to call your mother, or did he say?"

At the moment Keller wanted to leave everything behind and run off with Caitlyn to the mountains or somewhere. He was tempted, if he didn't hear from his mother tonight, to call his grandparents tomorrow and be honest about what was happening. They were old, excitable people, but they needed to know their youngest daughter was in trouble. If James Bryan was finally coming home, though, *he* would resume control of Holly and would be a far better choice to update his in-laws. Keller had hit an emotional wall this evening and figured he'd do well to get through tomorrow in one piece.

"Dad called from a pay phone," he said. "Mentioned this real pretty place overlooking a waterfall where he's been doing a lot of thinking. Problem is, he'd just finished a hike and was all sweaty when he tried to call earlier today. Cell slipped out of his hands and went down the embankment."

Caitlyn looked like she was going to be sick. "Meaning he didn't get any of your messages. Meaning he assumes everything's fine, and there's no way to call him, is there?"

"No. It was hard to hear, but it sounds like he tried to call Mom, too. Couldn't tell if he talked to her. But he said he's leaving in the morning, which probably puts him here tomorrow night."

Caitlyn hugged him again. She smelled nice, and her embrace felt so good. He wanted to make love to her, but not with Holly here. She spoke, perhaps reading his thoughts.

"Hang in there, baby. One more night. And Patrick will apologize—he'll really feel like a chump when he finds out your dad's back tomorrow night."

"I'm not sure I want to know why Dad had to go clear his head, though. I'm really wondering if something happened between him and Nancy. And might still be happening."

FORTY THREE

Chief Blair didn't like District Attorney Neal Cramer and had no doubt it showed on his face in front of the younger, neatly-groomed, self-important politician. After all, Blair reasoned, *he'd* stepped up to the plate after Quinn killed those nice old folks and admitted an error in judgment by pushing for the low bond that allowed his former cop back on the street. He thought the D.A. would do the same, since Cramer could have overridden him and thrown the book at Quinn. Cramer, though, who never met a camera he didn't like, did a lot of public hand-wringing but tacitly blamed the Oakdale police chief for the gaffe which led to the shootings. And Blair knew if he backed the huckster into a corner about it, Cramer would look him in the eye and tell him it was simply politics.

Blair was behind his desk, with Cramer and Pete Clark in the chairs across from him. Everyone agreed that Nancy Rutledge should be arrested on suspicion of murder. When it would take place was the topic of discussion.

"We have the little girl," Cramer said, addressing both of them. "We have the neighbor, Eddie Ray Chester, who puts Sherry and *one* of the Rutledge daughters poolside. We have the biological father, who'll testify exactly when he saw Caitlyn arrive and leave." Cramer paused. "He struck you guys as pretty solid, right?"

Both men nodded firmly.

"Give me your gut on Chester taking the stand."

Blair nodded at Clark. Clark turned to the D.A. "Like I told the chief last night, he ain't real bright. But I think he's sincere. Knows he messed up and feels horrible about it. The jury would see that, and I think they'd sympathize with him."

"So do I, Neal," Blair said. "Vince Cockrell may tear him apart, but if it comes down to who a jury believes between him and Nancy Rutledge, my money's on Chester."

Cramer picked at a fingernail. "How much of a flight risk is she?"

"We were just talking about that," Blair said. "Anyone's guess with the funeral. Visitation's tomorrow night, service Wednesday at eleven. What I understand, Caitlyn and Sherry were estranged, and Caitlyn and Nancy are like oil and water. I wouldn't be surprised if Caitlyn didn't even come. I think Nancy will, though."

"My brother married into a family like that, has horror stories about holidays." Cramer smiled to himself. "Anyway, Vince'll want us to wait until after the service before you arrest her, out of respect to the family and well-wishers."

Blair sighed. That was a reasonable request, given Sherry Rutledge's standing in the community. His wife had commented that First Baptist Church would be overflowing with mourners and floral arrangements. But if something went wrong—such as Nancy fleeing for the baseball player in Atlanta—Cramer would tell the media that the idiots at the Oakdale police department had screwed up again. And the mayor might just fire him, as dependent as he was on the Sherry Rutledge crowd for support.

"Think he'd ask her to surrender voluntarily?" Blair asked. "If we wait till after the burial?"

Cramer nodded firmly. "Probably offer to bring her down here himself."

"We arrest her right this minute, though, she doesn't get out of our sight."

"You know she'll post bond, Henry. She'll be back on the street within the hour."

Blair didn't want to mention the name *Quinn* aloud ever again during this lifetime. "You really think that judge will grant bond after…?"

"Depends on how persuasive Vince is," Cramer said. "But based on the evidence you have, I'll file a murder charge. I'm ready to play hardball, especially with the Chester testimony tying everything together."

Blair started to solicit Clark's input but stopped. He didn't want his young officer—or the D.A., for that matter—inferring that he had any doubts about what he was doing. And the public could kiss his butt if they thought he was being mean-spirited by arresting this snake before her mother was laid to rest. After all, Nancy had bribed a neighbor into lying about Caitlyn's role and might have pulled it off had that behemoth from Ripley not been Johnny-on-the-spot.

"Screw Vince Cockrell," Blair said as he turned to Clark. "Go bring her in."

FORTY FOUR

Eddie Ray Chester listened to the crickets in the humid evening air as he sipped his bottle of Budweiser. What would life be like as an insect? Sure, the odds that you'd get exterminated by the bug man or eaten by a cat were pretty good. And you wouldn't live long, that was for sure. But as far as Eddie Ray knew, if one cricket knocked up another, there were simply more crickets. The male didn't have to fret over whether the female he'd impregnated would be a good mother, or how the heck he'd put food on their table. For that matter, he could stay out with the boys and spend all night raising hell in the pines along Golden Drive if he wanted.

The newlyweds were back, having pocketed six grand playing the slots. But it was clear from the strain on his mother's face as she steered her new husband into the house tonight that Webber was a drunk. She'd fallen head over heels all over again

on the cruise—the way Eddie Ray would with Nancy if she'd
just give him a chance—and Monica's swelled heart had blotted
out all rational thought during those glorious days and nights on
the water. Reality was probably setting in about now. It was an
I-told-you-so moment, but he felt awful for her.

Daphne, meanwhile, appeared to have little interest in the
Mommy thing after all. They'd bickered today when she asked
about using Nancy's money to party in Tunica, and when he said
once and for all that the funds weren't for such a purpose, Daphne
announced she was going out with the girls tonight and not to
bother her for any reason. She was no more interested in settling
down and being a responsible parent than she was in joining the
circus. The best thing for the baby was adoption. But Daphne, he
thought angrily, wasn't about to carry a child to term only to give
it up. She would get an abortion faster than Eddie Ray could snap
his fingers and go jump right in the sack with someone else until
she got pregnant again. The thought made him sick to his stomach.

He took another swig and flung droplets of condensation
from the outside of the bottle. He'd hopefully removed the noose
from Caitlyn's neck after admitting the bribe to the cops. Nancy
might kill him if she found out, though. If she wanted her money
back, he'd be glad to give it to her. But she would demand more
than just the money, like his scalp as well. Now that he'd cleared
his conscience, it was time to think about protecting himself.

Hell, tape her. Get a confession and go to the cops.

He sat up straight in the cheap lawn chair. That wasn't a
half bad idea, if he could pull it off. He didn't have access to the
fancy surveillance equipment the pros used on *Law & Order*. But
he had a very old hand-held tape recorder someone from the
trailer park gave him years ago. It recorded and played cassettes,
and he saw himself riding with Nancy in the Grand Am, the
recorder under the seat, and Nancy casually admitting she'd
killed her mother. The thought of taping her on the sly made

him antsy. But it seemed like the only way to hold her off.

Now he felt hope. He might redeem himself with the cops, who could make real trouble over that ten grand—what he was thinking when he blurted *that* to Blair? If he lucked into a taped confession from Nancy and turned it over to the chief along with the cash, though, maybe they'd call it even and leave him alone in the future. And after the dust settled, he'd look up Caitlyn and admit the truth and beg her forgiveness. Then he would walk the straight and narrow. Even if it meant living alone and busting his butt to get by.

He got up to look for the tape recorder.

FORTY FIVE

Officer Pete Clark rolled slowly along Pleasant Acres Drive and gazed at the fancy homes in the fading sunlight. *Lifestyles of the Rich and Famous* could be filmed out here, with the two- and three-story houses on multi-acre plots of land and fancy cars and SUV's in every garage. Clark rented a two-bedroom home outside town that didn't even have central air conditioning. Like every other cop on the force, he lived hand-to-mouth. Try as he might, it was difficult not to feel resentment when he was out here. Not so much toward the adults, but at the snotty teens that raced around in Escalades and Hummers purchased for them by their rich parents. A few weeks of living the way he did would give those kids some badly-needed perspective about life.

The home owned by Nancy Rutledge Morgan and her TV star husband came into view. It was set back from the road and fronted by a semi-circular driveway, with a pair of white columns that bracketed the front door and supported the second-floor balcony. The house had beautiful landscaping and looked spectacular against the pink sky and the forest of pines out back.

The garage, which opened on the side of the house, was closed. Clark was a mile away when Blair had called. He could tell from his boss's icy tone that Blair wasn't happy about the directive *not* to bring Nancy in for questioning after all—now the D.A. wanted to wait until after the burial to make the arrest.

Politics. It made Clark sick.

He turned into the Morgan driveway and lingered a moment, peering at the house and wondering if Nancy was really the monster she appeared to be. Then he left.

FORTY SIX

Nancy bent at the waist amid the wreckage of her living room and tried to catch her breath. Shards of Waterford crystal and bone china littered the buffed hardwood floor and reflected the fading sunlight through the open curtains. She'd destroyed every framed picture, painting, and design on the walls before turning her attention to the bookcases—she'd ripped pages from books and catalogs and hurled them across the room, then grabbed a handy coffee cup and blasted away at the plasma TV and stereo components. While doing this she'd screamed herself hoarse. Only now did she notice the small cuts on her hands and arms that she acquired during the rampage.

"Nancy, they're going to arrest you. She saw you do it."

Vince Cockrell had just left. He didn't say where he got his information, but Holly Bryan was supposedly in her brother's bedroom Friday night and saw her push Sherry into the pool through Keller's *telescope*! It sounded like a bad joke. Vince was dead serious, though, and said an arrest was likely. He even told her to consider a plea of temporary insanity if the D.A., as Vince suspected, was serious about going for the jugular. Vince normally boasted about his skills in court, but this time he acted like he didn't have a chance at an acquittal and scampered away as if the cops were after him instead of her. She heard a car pull into the driveway and stepped around the rubble to the front door. She looked through the peephole, expecting Cockrell again.

It was an Oakdale police cruiser.

Her heart began to pound. She thought of the gun in her purse, but shooting a cop wasn't an option. She would face certain arrest and spend her life in prison, if she wasn't executed as quickly as the state of Mississippi could make it happen. She could race through the house and out the back door, but where would she run? The woods? For how long? Would they get a warrant if she didn't answer the door? She felt the noise swirling in her head as she stared at the idling car.

It backed out of the driveway and disappeared down the street.

Nancy stepped back from the door and exhaled. Her central nervous system cried out for another pill, and she stepped around the glass and went to the kitchen to fetch her purse from the granite counter. She dug out the stash of valium and dry-swallowed one of the small, white tablets. The sheer act of doing so had nearly the calming effect on her that the narcotic would in the next few minutes. And destroying the living room had been an unintended act of finality, she realized.

Get out of here NOW!

Maybe that's what Vince was trying to tell her without actually saying so. The information he'd just shared, of course, was a serious ethical breach that could result in his disbarment. Yet she could see Vince playing dumb when a judge wanted to know where the accused was. She saw herself chopping off the thick, luxurious black hair she'd fussed over for so many years and dyeing what was left an awful shade of red. She could wear reading glasses and no makeup. She could pork up in no time flat if she quit exercising, guzzled Red Bull, and ate three balanced junk-food meals a day. She could wear cheap hoop earrings and hideous print dresses bought at discount stores and start completely over, maybe clear across the country, as a totally new person. The hell with the people around town—like the jerks at the funeral home—who were staring at her like she possessed a rare and highly communicable disease.

The hell with the funeral, for that matter.

Sherry was *dead*. Nancy would never have to worry about pleasing her mother again, and that's what her whole life to this point seemed to have been about: making sure everything always looked and went just right so Sherry Rutledge got her props. But this, Nancy knew, was now about her own survival. A freakin' police car had lingered in the driveway for an excruciatingly long moment before changing course, and it would be back. She had no doubt of that. She also had no doubt that Caitlyn could handle everything at the funeral home, if she cared to do so. Caitlyn, for that matter, sure was cocky Saturday afternoon at her little pig sty of a home. Now that Nancy thought about it, not only did the pictures hit the Internet the following day, Keller Bryan, whom she'd loved from afar for years, had steered his little sis to the cops this afternoon! If the ugly bitch and her turncoat boyfriend had plotted to throw her under the bus, she would shoot both of them dead.

But there wasn't time to do that now. She had to get out of town.

She ran upstairs to pack clothes and grab her laptop. She'd thought over the years about writing suspense thrillers and developing a serial protagonist like the Stephanie Plum character in those Janet Evanovich books everyone read, only darker. Sherry, of course, said *no* to that happy fantasy, insisting that no daughter of hers would be a weird, creative type with purple hair and a nose ring. Her maternal roadblock had finally been removed, Nancy thought, as she crested the stairs, but the world's most inept police department might provide one of their own—and soon. She'd have plenty of time to indulge her creative fantasies once she'd escaped.

Her cell rang. It was in her purse, and she went flying back downstairs and into the kitchen. She yanked it out and looked at the screen.

Eddie Ray Chester.

She scowled. The boy had *stones* to call after selling her out, if that's what he'd done. Was this a trap? Vanessa, the daughter of the mole inside the PD, made it sound like he'd gotten scared and talked, and maybe Blair dangled an arrest over his head if he didn't cooperate. But Nancy was willing to bet everything in her home—before she trashed it—that Remedial Eddie Ray was too stupid to pull anything off involving a wire, or whatever else Blair and his bunch might have up their sleeves. Besides, whether he'd gone to the cops or not, Eddie Ray had a thing for her. She could still probably get him to do just about whatever she wanted.

A scenario began to unfold in her head as she answered her phone.

FORTY SEVEN

Melanie Bryan opened her eyes and looked around. A loud thump had startled her to consciousness and pulled her from a dream that exploded into nothingness as she tried to make sense of it. The sun was setting, she saw. She realized she was sitting in the minivan, which was parked in the garage of their home on Peachtree. When had she arrived? And where on earth had she been?

She started to turn her head and look behind her, but a searing pain in her neck put a stop to that. Now that she was fully awake, she realized her whole body ached. She could only remember bits and pieces: a smoke-filled little bar, the unmistakable scent of sex emanating from the sheets of a cheap roadside motel, the smell of smoke that she knew wasn't from over-the-counter cigarettes. And lots of tattooed men, with long hair, dirty fingernails—

What had just made that noise? Or had she really heard one?

Her purse was next to her on the front seat. The keys, she discovered, were in the ignition. She started to crank up and go, but where? She looked gingerly to her right, not wanting to hurt her neck, and saw that the other side of the garage was empty. Where was James? And was her neck broken? Was that why it hurt so much? She reached out and opened the door, finding that she could move a little at a time without pain that made her want to scream. She swung her feet and prepared to climb out. She found that although there were various aches along her arms and legs, only her neck really throbbed, and only when she turned it a certain way. She sure wouldn't do that again.

She felt the slate garage floor beneath her feet and looked down. Where were her shoes? She was in a string top and blue jean shorts. She smelled smoke on herself and thought about lighting up, but her stomach gurgled—maybe a cig wasn't such a good idea. She wobbled toward the door that led inside the house. She tried to find the house key but dropped the ring of keys when her hand trembled. She swore to herself, then leaned over and picked them up. Now her back hurt. What had happened to her? She couldn't remember which key unlocked the house but tried the door anyway, hoping it was unlocked. It was, and she walked in.

The alarm that sounded nearly caused her to pee on herself.

She whirled around. This set her neck on fire, and she yelped at the pain. She found the security system and started punching numbers, but the damn thing continued to blare as if sounding the end of the world. She dropped the keys and her purse and ran to the center of the living room, ready to start breaking things if that's what it took to stop the ear-splitting tone. It didn't go off. She walked back over and punched more numbers, then beat on the system. The plastic cover popped off and landed next to her purse, but the alarm still rang. Finally it went off.

"Anybody here?" she heard herself say in a woozy voice. "James?"

Nothing. Where was everybody? Where were the kids? The last light of day streamed through the open living room curtains and provided a measure of illumination. She looked around the room, taking in the bookcases and TV. Then she headed for the stairs. The carpet felt good against her bare feet, and she clung to the banister as she eased her way up to the second floor. She called out her husband's name again and wasn't surprised when he didn't answer. His truck wasn't here, but that didn't mean he wasn't in their bedroom, going at it hammer and tongs with Nancy Rutledge. If they were—

The master bedroom was empty, the bed neatly made. She padded back down the hallway and looked in Holly's room. Nobody in there, either, and the teddy bear was gone. Something flashed across her internal radar screen, a snippet of her and Keller and Holly and Caitlyn at the park. That's probably where they were. She went into Keller's room and looked around. She was so proud of him, all grown up and becoming just as much of a man as James. But she hated that damned telescope. It had always been a problem and needed to go. She walked over and looked through it and saw a swimming pool several houses down. The Rutledges place.

She was seized with anger that came from nowhere, rage that shoved away the fierce pain of her injured neck. She reached past the telescope to the window and tried to pull it open. The window wouldn't move, so she hoisted the telescope. It seemed to weigh a ton, and it took a second to get a good grip. She flung it against the window, breaking out the glass panes, and the telescope fell and lodged between the desk and the wooden sill. Dimly aware of blood dripping from cuts on her right hand and arm, she picked up the telescope and used it as a battering ram, knocking out the remainder of the glass. One final thrust took care of the screen, and a whiff of warm, humid air hit her in the face. She took a deep breath and heaved the telescope out the window, cackling to herself as it exploded into a gazillion pieces on the patio below.

Now the phone was ringing.

The heck with whoever was calling. What she needed was a nice, hot bath. Maybe some bubbles, too, and some wine. But that would take time and trouble to set up, and she didn't feel like thinking—she did too much of that in the classroom each day. The Rutledges had a pool, though. If she could walk her happy butt down there, she could get right in and swim until her heart was content. They wouldn't mind. Gosh, Nancy had watched Keller for years, and Caitlyn had practically grown up here. Melanie eased back down the stairs, stumbling on the bottom step but regaining her balance before she fell. She retraced her steps and passed the busted security pad, where her keys and purse lay below. She didn't need to take anything with her. And the phone had stopped ringing. It was probably a telemarketer. They called at all hours every damn day of the week.

She stepped outside, pulled the door closed and walked slowly across the driveway to the sidewalk. Everything seemed blurry but she started down the hill nonetheless. She heard voices in a nearby yard and thought of the park again. Hopefully Keller and Holly and Caitlyn were having fun. Maybe James was there, too. After she swam, she'd go join them. They were probably grilling hamburgers or watching softball or something. An old man she didn't recognize was walking his dog and coming toward her. He was really looking her up and down, which she found rude. She bared her teeth at him, trying to mimic the dog, and he immediately went across the street and dragged the canine along with him. Melanie kept on, putting one foot in front of the other and trying to keep her balance. At one point she looked up and realized she was in front of Jack and Sherry's house. The garage was closed and no cars were in the driveway. But they'd been neighbors for years. It would be perfectly alright if she swam.

She strolled through the yard, stepping on pine needles and hearing the crickets and birds and taking in the pink sky. It was so peaceful out here. There just wasn't enough room in their own yard for a pool with all the trees, but at least one was here. Nobody was in it, so she had it all to herself. And the best way to relax in the water, she knew, was to ditch her clothes. She stepped onto the cement and gazed at the water. It didn't look all that blue, actually. Maybe the pool hadn't been cleaned in a while. But she'd come back tomorrow or sometime and do that for the Rutledges. Because that's what good neighbors did for each other.

She slipped off the top and felt the gentle breeze on her breasts, which felt as bruised as her arms and legs. The shorts were hard to remove—she would have to lose a little tummy and backside before she put them on again. She got the fly unbuttoned and peeled them off, letting them drop at her feet next to the halter. She frowned when she realized she was naked. Where were her panties? But she could worry about that later. Right now, the only thing that mattered was how cool and relaxing the water was going to feel. Probably do her poor neck a lot of good.

She walked to the shallow end and saw the three steps that were built into the pool. She touched her toe to the water and found it cool but not cold. She held onto the silver railing that was built into the cement and started down into the water. It felt soothing as she immersed herself. She stood in the shallow end, the water covering her waist, and felt the breeze once more. Then she walked several feet toward the deep end until the water was up to her neck. She ducked her head and got her hair wet, then lifted her head back out and shook it. Big mistake: pain shot through her head from the base of her skull. Maybe the best thing would be to head back to the steps and have a seat right there.

She thought she heard whispered voices but ignored them. They wouldn't bother her if she didn't bother them. And she wasn't planning on bothering anybody while in this pool. She couldn't remember the last time she felt so relaxed. The song "Hotel California" was stuck in her head, and she opened her mouth and began to sing.

FORTY EIGHT

Nancy eased the BMW along the rutted road to the fishing camp. She'd never been out here at night and was uneasy about who might be lurking in the woods. Lights were on in the first cabin she passed, a smattering of them on in structures across the lake. Her laptop was in the trunk and her mother's loaded gun was in her purse. The weapon might prove problematic if Eddie Ray was wired and the police were nearby and stopped her. He said he wanted to talk, and she was gambling that he wasn't bright or calm enough to help with their surveillance. For that matter, the dimwitted bulbs at the Oakdale police department might not have anything more high-tech than their police radios.

She reached the Crisler cabin and saw the Grand Am. Eddie Ray had backed in, like he was prepared to tear out of here. She pulled in next to him and let down her window as he lowered his. The air was thick and humid, and there didn't appear to be a breeze at all.

"Hey, girl," he said. "Come get in and let's go riding."

"No. Get out, and let's go inside."

She could see him in the dome light coming from his car. A funny look crossed his face. She wondered if he'd been instructed to take her somewhere, but that didn't make sense: If he really was wearing a wire and the cops were in the woods, it seemed that they would pick up a conversation more clearly in the cabin because she and Eddie Ray would be stationary. But she was the first to admit that she knew nothing about police work.

"You sure? Just got my air serviced. Cool as an igloo in here."

"Cool in there, too," Nancy said as she pointed at the cabin. "I don't have long, so let's go."

She cut the engine. She'd left only two feet of space between the driver's side doors, and it took a moment to climb out. She locked the car and dropped the keys in her purse, which she slung over her shoulder. She wasn't wearing makeup or perfume and had no plans of getting drunk and seducing him. She stepped around the BMW, walked to the cabin, and retrieved the key from her shorts. She unlocked the door, leaned in, and felt for the light switch on the wall until she found it. She flicked it on, which lit up the room and sent shadowy light out toward the cars. She turned back to Eddie Ray, who looked like he was doing something in the floorboard of the Grand Am.

"You coming or not?"

He got out and shut his door. He strode to the cabin and walked inside. She entered behind him, then closed the door and appraised him. He was in a skin-tight muscle shirt and had on a ton of cologne. He sure wasn't wearing a wire. But had the police told him to dress and act like he was going to get laid, once they discussed whatever pressing business he wouldn't reveal over the phone? His surprise call had prompted her quick little brain, and she'd dreamed up what she thought was a rock-solid way to escape this little hellhole of a hometown without anyone ever knowing where she went. But it would have to be done carefully.

"Sit down." She pointed to the couch. "What's on your mind?"

He looked flustered but sat where he had last time. She adjusted the air conditioning and took the other end of the filthy couch. This put four feet between them, and she set the purse on her other side. She took in the various scents: his cologne, the cigarette smoke on her clothes, the stale air of the cabin, and perhaps a whiff of sex from their encounter here a few days ago. Eddie Ray, though learning-disabled and about as bright as a box of rocks, was admittedly handsome in a roughneck way and had a nice body. He was also well-endowed and no kid in the sack. But she couldn't lose her focus.

"I'm waiting," she said.

"Sure we can't ride? Car runs like the wind, air's nice and cold, put on some good music—"

"What were you playing with in the floorboard?" This was a risk, but it would force him to show his cards. "You didn't go to the cops a third time, did you?"

Panic crossed his face. He looked all around, as if the mounted deer heads or some unseen figure would suddenly materialize and save him. She sensed he was operating on his own and slid toward him.

"You played me," she whispered after grabbing his testicles. She tightened her grip and took an instant of pleasure at the complete control she was in—his eyes had bugged out, and he looked to be in so much pain he couldn't draw a breath. "I don't like being played, especially when the freaking police are involved."

Eddie Ray tried to speak and couldn't get anything out.

His face was turning purple.

"If you want to make it out of here alive, you do exactly as I say. Got that, Eddie Ray Chester?"

He nodded. She let him go and shoved him backward. He wheezed and tried to catch his breath. He turned away, and she wondered if he would be sick. She would also barf if he tossed his cookies in this foul-smelling little room. But he turned to her and wiped his forehead with the back of his hand.

"You can have your money back," he rasped. "It's out in the car, every bit of it."

"I know you went back to the cops. Why? Caitlyn threaten you?"

He coughed again. "Naw, I ain't seen her. The cops came and got me. Brought me down there and started in on my story. Someone done seen your sister arrive at the house that night and leave, police chief said, without going up that sidewalk. He knew I'd lied, and I got scared. Don't know what to say, other than I'm sorry. You can have your money back, Nancy."

That, she had to admit, was feasible, if Caitlyn's biological father had shown up and told the cops he was right there on Peachtree Street Friday night. Gosh, it was a good thing she'd met with Vanessa Flagg one last time.

"What'd you tell them?"

"Everything." Eddie Ray turned away and sniffed back what sounded like tears. "I should have just stayed in my own yard that morning. All my life I've minded my own business, even though everyone else in the world don't. And the one time I stick my nose where it don't belong—"

"Turn around."

He did and looked as if he felt horrible for letting her down. He would probably beg her to shoot him if he saw the gun. Her gut told her that if the *cabin* was somehow wired, the sniveling boy next to her would be too nervous not to let it slip.

If she was skipping town tonight, she could say whatever she wanted and probably get him to do anything she asked, as long as he felt he was in danger. And poor Eddie Ray just wasn't smart enough to see through the lines of bull she was about to spread before him.

"Look, it's done," she said. "You help me—*really* help me this time—and we'll forget it."

He grimaced again, still in pain from the Power Grab, and nodded.

"First, think back to when your daddy died. Now, that contractor your mother sued was definitely negligent. My mother knew of him through the real estate business and said he built shoddy houses and wasn't surprised when someone died on site. And your mother sure deserved the settlement that wound up bringing y'all to our part of town. But the jury tampering got hushed up."

"Hold on, now. What tampering you talking about?"

This was downright evil, she knew. But this fool had gone back to the cops and turned on her, and not only that, he had the stones to call her up and request a meeting. Why, she didn't know yet. But he was desperate to get her into his car. Had the cops installed some sort of GPS and were monitoring his travels and passengers? She thought it possible but unlikely. The easiest thing to do, it seemed to Nancy, was simply arrest her. But if that cop had stopped in her driveway without coming to the door, maybe they didn't have their ducks in a row yet.

"Let's just say someone got bought off," she said. "In a big way."

"But Nancy, Mother didn't—"

"Look, the contractor got what was coming to him. Everyone was on your side, but money changed hands in that jury. There were a couple of people who wanted to *make sure* the contractor got run out of business, and that's not the way the system is supposed to work."

Eddie Ray put his fingers together and cracked his knuckles. He looked like he wanted a cigarette. She'd never seen anyone so gullible and did her best not to laugh.

"I realize that," he said. "But what'll happen to my mother? You're saying the contractor wants his money back that he had to give her?"

"That could happen," Nancy said. She looked him in the eye. "If word of the tampering got out, the contractor's lawyer would ask for a new trial. And in all likelihood, the contractor would sue your mother to get his money back, until he was forced to pay it back a second time—assuming he was found guilty at that second trial. And a second trial, given that it would have a different jury, well, there might be a different conclusion. You follow me?"

"Kind of..."

"Put it this way: Long as you don't cross me, none of that will ever happen."

Eddie Ray looked more than relieved. It was like he'd been diagnosed with lung cancer, then informed a second later that someone else had it, not him.

"I *swear*," he murmured. "My mother is the most important person to me in the world, Nancy, and I'm fit to be tied because of what her jerk of a husband's already putting her through, revealing his self to be nothing but a damn drunk! He and Mother went to Memphis for the weekend, and it sounds like his face was in a bottle the whole time, even coming back home tonight."

This didn't surprise Nancy, based on what she'd heard over the years. She gave him a sad smile. "That's too bad. And what about Daphne? You sure that baby's yours? And are you sure she isn't angling for some of that contractor's settlement? Money does bad things to people."

Eddie Ray lowered his head. "Been asking myself that. Tried to tell her to watch her eating and not smoke and drink and stuff while expecting, and all she wants to do is party. What she's doing right this minute with the girls, I expect. We had a big fight, and I just know she'll get an abortion. Makes me just sick. But I can't do nothing to stop it."

"She can't get an abortion in jail."

"Huh? What's she going to jail for?"

"Attempted kidnapping."

"Kidnapping *who*?" Eddie Ray sat straight up. "What are you talking about?"

"A little girl," Nancy said. She held up her hand when he tried to interrupt. "We'll come back to that. Right now I need Daphne's license plate and social security number. She have any credit cards?"

"Way too poor for that." Eddie Ray laughed uneasily. "She got a checking account, but ain't nothing in it. She and her mother use food stamps and such."

"Where is Daphne, right now?"

"Probably with all those girls over at the trailer park. But how—"

Nancy stood and pulled Eddie Ray to his feet. She poked a finger into his chest. "Okay, we'll ride in your car. But first, look me in the eye and tell me what you were doing in your floorboard before you came in here. And before you answer, remember what I said about walking out of here alive."

A second passed before he answered. "Really rather not say, okay? But I *promise* you I ain't talking to them cops again. And I swear Officer Clark came to my door last night and asked me down there. I didn't go blab to them, honest I didn't."

She gave him a long look. Then she grabbed the purse. "Long as you understand I can make life miserable for your mama, as well as you, if you cross me. And I'd sure hate to have to do that."

"I'll do whatever you want, girl."

"Then let's head to the trailer park."

FORTY NINE

Scott Perry sat at his computer desk and stared at the screen of notes he'd just typed up. The audio of his phone conversation with Mike Morgan was passable, even though Mike was on his cell. And although Mike hadn't specifically designated that his comments were off the record, Scott knew that's what his friend assumed. The word *friend* was stretching it, though. He and Mike had anchored together whenever the meteorologist worked a weekend or filled in on a weeknight. Once, while Scott's girlfriend Tina was in town, he'd taken her out to the Morgan's huge place in Oakdale for dinner. Mike was loose and funny and relaxed, but Nancy was aloof and seemed uptight. Tina hadn't liked her a bit and didn't care to see them again, so no further plans were made. He and Mike were friendly acquaintances, to put a finer point on it.

Would that justify screwing him? Or was that overstating it?

Scott had approached the call as a friendly chat instead of an interview, although he'd set up the phone recorder with sound bites in mind. Mike was somber but composed, and he said right away that he was through in Tupelo: One of his hometown Jackson stations had an immediate opening for a weekend meteorologist that could handle general reporting assignments three days a week. A decent offer, Mike said, was on the table. He was halfway through a five-year deal in Tupelo and didn't expect management to let him out of his contract without a fight. But the Jackson station was with a large broadcast group, Scott knew, and Mike agreed that they would offer some sort of buyout and eventually get their way. The Internet photos weren't discussed. Even Scott Perry, who never met a tough question he didn't like, just didn't have the stomach to ask his now-former colleague for a comment.

But Mike's mother's will had come up, and that made for a *hell* of a news story.

Scott's jaw had fallen as Mike described what Nancy tried to do in order to steal nearly half a million dollars from the estate. He thought back to the night he and Tina were at the Morgans showplace of a home and wondered what in God's name Nancy wanted that she didn't already have. She struck him that night as hard to get to know, and while Tina used the word *smug*, Scott sensed that Nancy was a very guarded and insecure person. As to his mother's illness, Mike didn't mention it until the week of her death. Scott understood that completely, as it was a family matter. But perhaps Nancy, certainly in the know about the late Mrs. Morgan's condition, had plotted against Mike for some time.

Mike was restrained on the phone but assured Scott that both he and his brother had experienced, powerful attorneys that would make mincemeat of the Oakdale lawyer who would represent Nancy when this nonsense went to court. And Mike did plan to sue. But Scott didn't sense that Mike would talk on camera, even if he raced to Jackson with Billy-Bob right this minute. Mike's lawyer would almost certainly prohibit his client from discussing the situation, anyway. But Scott *really* wanted to build a story around it. Mike would garner a ton of sympathy in this area: He was already well-liked by viewers, and anyone who thought of him as the poor sap whose cheating wife had been caught with a boob hanging from her dress would see him in a whole new light.

Scott drummed his fingers on the computer table. The funeral of Nancy's mother Sherry would be Wednesday, he'd learned, but it sounded like Mike's lawyer was planning to move forward as early as tomorrow. Would *Nancy* talk to him on camera if he and Billy-Bob showed up at her home unannounced? She'd probably slam the door in their faces. He would have to listen to the tape again, but he remembered the name Cockrell and was pretty sure Mike was referring to Nancy's lawyer—he could run down the law firm the guy worked for in minutes. They could certainly get a loud NO COMMENT from him. And maybe more, since sometimes these country lawyers and small-town politicians just couldn't help running their mouths when a camera was aimed at them.

He tried to imagine what Mike might say or do if Scott took this presumed off-the-record chat and ran with it. Although Mike was a big-time air talent in Scott's estimation, he had family and friends in Jackson and might want to make the place home after what he'd gone through. Scott, for his part, knew that whether he made it to the top of the broadcast mountain or not, he'd likely work all over the country on his way up and might never see Mike Morgan again, let alone work with him.

He thought about his news director. Zack Bowen would demand that Scott air it: His rationale would be that if Mike screwed the station by bolting in the middle of his contract—family tragedy or not—the butthole deserved any public humiliation he got. That was hard to argue with, too. People burned bridges when they bailed out mid-contract, and what went around came around in this business. If Mike worked in Jackson several years and wanted to move to a bigger market, the Tupelo station he left high and dry would be the first thing any news director mentioned.

Mike was a nice guy, and Scott would do his best to protect him. But this was a potentially huge, multi-faceted story, what with the mother's death and the initial suspicion of Caitlyn, the basketball star. Something told Scott that he was pawing at the edges of a good-old-boy network in little Oakdale that would rival what went on in much larger cities, a web that might ensnare some very powerful area residents. And unearthing blockbuster stories and loading a resume tape with network-quality packages was why he, a native of Dallas, was toiling away in Mississippi.

He would get right on this in the morning.

FIFTY

"Is Mom under arrest?" Keller whispered.

Clint Young had called a few minutes ago and said that Melanie was resting comfortably at Smart County Hospital after being sedated. Chief Blair wanted to talk to him, Young said, and Keller and the family attorney were now sitting across from Blair in what Keller assumed was the place Caitlyn was deposited Saturday night while waiting for Tina Littlefield. Blair, who'd trained his red face and green eyes on Keller after exchanging a glance with Young, looked surprised. Then his face softened. He looked for an instant like a dad who had some bad news for his kids. And Keller was determined not to break down in front of these men. He would do that in front of Caitlyn, who was watching Holly and would get her to bed. But he just wasn't going to pieces in front of Blair and Young.

"No, son," Blair said. "But they want to keep her at the hospital overnight for observation. Which means you'll need to sign some more paperwork."

"Keller, I'll take you over there after we're through," Young said.

"Thank you. By the way, Dad called," Keller said, addressing both men. "Said he's been at Gatlinburg a few days, needed some time off. Now, I didn't get to talk to him—my cell got left on silent. He was calling from a pay phone and left a message, said his own phone slipped out of his hands and went down the side of a mountain. I don't have a way to contact him."

The men exchanged another look. Keller figured that both felt James Bryan was just as irresponsible—if not certifiable—as his mother. He shrugged, trying to convey that he, too, didn't know what to make of the odd-sounding explanation or the trip itself.

"But he's leaving in the morning," Keller said. "Ought to be here by supper."

"Good. Your mother will really need his help," Blair said. The chief paused and tented his fingers in front of him. "Y'all have a security system at your house on Peachtree, don't you?"

"Yes, sir. I set it when Caitlyn and I left last night."

"One of my officers answered a call there about an hour ago. It was prompted by the security company, meaning the alarm went off. They called the house first, didn't get an answer, then went down the list of people to call in an emergency."

Keller frowned. Maybe his parents never thought to add him to the contact list. But there was probably no need. Mr. Barksdale had a key to the house and knew the alarm code. So did Phil and Gina Roland.

"Someone broke in?"

"We don't think so. Your mother's minivan was in the garage. My officer said the door going to the kitchen was closed but unlocked. He found your mother's purse and keys on the floor just inside the doorway." Blair paused. "The keypad cover was next to it. As if—and this is only a guess—Melanie went inside and couldn't recall the password. Got a little frustrated, maybe."

Keller imagined his mother staggering into their home, her mind gone, and trying to rip the keypad off the wall when she couldn't shut off the security system. While James Bryan had successfully managed the clothing store since taking it over after his father's death, he needed a CPA to run the financial end of things. But Melanie, though not a math major, had a natural affinity for numbers and did the accounting at the bookstore by herself. Forgetting how to tie her shoes seemed more likely than being unable to remember the security code.

"Now, the downstairs seemed totally undisturbed," Blair continued. "But there was some damage to one of the upstairs bedrooms. Yours, I'm thinking, Keller. Window overlooking the south side of the street had been busted out, screen and all."

"*What?*"

"Four different calls came in from the neighborhood, as well as the one from the security company. One had to do with a crash on the patio a minute or two after the alarm shut off on its own. Officer looked out there with his flashlight after determining no one was in the house. Our best guess is that your telescope was thrown through the window and landed on the patio. Officer said pieces of glass and metal were strewn in all directions."

Keller said nothing as his mind played a painfully vivid slide show of his mother barging into his bedroom and hurling the telescope out the window. She seemed to be in her own little world yesterday at the park but was lucid enough to have gotten Holly dressed and fed. Like Blair, all he could do was guess. But if Melanie's mind wasn't working properly, rational and irrational thought processes might commingle and lead to incomprehensible behavior, memory failure, and God only knew what else.

"Question, Henry," Young said, "and you tell me if it's something you're obligated not to answer. But I'm wondering if Nancy was in there, looking for Holly. Figured she'd destroy that telescope and ruin what evidence she could, if she couldn't find the girl."

This hadn't occurred to Keller. His eyes shot to Young, then to Blair. The red-faced man now had a hard look in his eye. For an instant Keller thought Blair was mad at Young for asking such a thing with him sitting there. But he realized Blair was mulling over what he wanted to say.

"I thought about that, Clint. Aren't but a few pieces of that telescope big enough to take prints from, but we'll do what we can," Blair said. "I made sure we got prints from Melanie at the hospital, once she was sedated, and I'm thinking we'll have a match if we have decent fragments from the patio to work with." There was a long pause before Blair continued. Keller watched, wishing he could hear what was going on in Blair's mind as the chief considered what to add. "The D.A. and I are mindful that Nancy and Caitlyn just lost their mother. There's some hesitation on his part to act before Sherry is laid to rest, and I can understand that. But in light of what just happened, I'm ready to move."

"Could they have both been in the house?" Keller asked Blair. "Mom and Nancy, I mean."

"I wouldn't rule anything out." The chief turned to Young. "We've definitely got enough to go to the judge and get a warrant for her arrest. I'll tell Cramer that I'm all for Nancy going to her mother's funeral, long as she has an escort. We'll get that moving once we're done here."

"That's an excellent idea," Young said.

Blair turned back to Keller. "But I do think your mother was in the house. It's our assumption that she walked down to the Rutledges and decided to go for a swim—without any clothes. There was quite a little crowd, unfortunately, by the time my officer got there and called for backup."

Keller's face fell. He couldn't control his reaction any more than he could put out of his mind the reaction of the neighbors. Anyone who saw the display—and there was apparently daylight when this happened—would make sure everyone else knew. He allowed himself an instant of self-pity as he imagined the stares he would get from families on the street. He'd known most of them all his life, and they would never look at him the same way again after the free show they got from his crazy mama. Then he thought of Holly and Jeannie Hanson. Hanson wouldn't be able to tell her boss about this latest development fast enough. The bookstore popped into his head next, but he couldn't figure everything out at once. He took a deep breath and gazed at the police chief and waited for him to continue.

"My officer said Melanie was groggy but conscious when he arrived. She was sort of lounging on the steps inside the pool, her head resting on the top step."

"Was she hurt?"

"Yes," Blair said. "It was close to dark by then, but he could tell she was pretty bruised up. Backup arrived, and an ambulance was called. She was very calm, Keller, until they asked her to get out of the water. She wouldn't, and it took four people to get her out while she swam around and kicked and clawed and bit at them."

Keller turned away from the men. He squeezed his eyes shut and bit his lip.

"I know this is rough, son, and I'm sorry." Blair paused. "An EMT gave her a shot right there at poolside to knock her out. They covered her in blankets and took her to the hospital. As of a few minutes ago, she was sound asleep. I imagine that's exactly what she needs right now."

His mother had snapped, and like Caitlyn said, people didn't just bounce right back from that kind of thing. As he'd told Caitlyn tonight, he was deeply grateful for his stable childhood: The older he got, the more he realized how blessed he was in that regard. But Holly, only eight and in dire need of a loving, devoted mother, wouldn't be as fortunate. He and Caitlyn would take care of her the best they could, if it came down to it. For that matter, if something happened to Caitlyn, he would raise his little sister himself. No matter what it took, he would find a way.

But Keller sure hoped his dad made it back tomorrow night as promised, and was of sound mind.

"What did the doctor say?" he asked.

"All I talked to was the EMT's," Blair said. "They both think she was beaten and raped, and might have a concussion. Like I said, they want to keep her overnight, and I'm certain the doctor will request a full psychological examination. My people talked to her after requesting the ambulance, before she got all excited. They said she wasn't making much sense: kept referring to not only Sherry as if she was still alive, but Jack as well."

Keller felt a comforting hand on his shoulder and knew it belonged to Young. He imagined his mother in a hospital gown, breathing deeply and lying motionless as her heartbeat and other vital signs were monitored by a bank of equipment a few feet away. He thought about their discussion at the park yesterday, which followed on the heels of the shouting match the night before. There was just no getting through to her—several times Sunday morning he wasn't sure she knew she was sitting across from her son. He'd told her he loved her and urged her to open up, but Caitlyn was right that the Melanie Bryan they knew and loved wasn't the woman that smoked, drank, and swore in front of him. He didn't want to imagine where she'd been and what she'd done the last day and a half. But at least she was resting. And the Oakdale medical community knew what it was doing. She was in good hands.

"Clint, why don't you take Keller over to the hospital to sign that paperwork," Blair said softly. "Then take him to be with his sister."

Keller turned to face Young. "Can I go see Mom?"

"It sounds like she's on pretty heavy sedatives right now," Young replied with a fatherly smile. "Go see her tomorrow night with your dad. If James doesn't get back, I'll take you up there myself."

Blair got to his feet and stuck out his hand. "You're a brave young man, son. Your mother's safe and will be given the best of care, don't think twice about that. And you have my solemn promise that we will do everything in our power to keep your sister safe."

FIFTY ONE

Eddie Ray had no idea how he would steal Daphne's car tag and driver's license. Nancy was no help, completely ignoring him when he asked for suggestions during the ten-minute drive to the trailer park. He reached his old stomping grounds and entered the wide grassy expanse with the rutted dirt lanes between the trailers. Some had been maintained relatively well, while a strong gust might topple a number of them. Lights were on in most, and clumps of people were outside. He saw several folks cooking out as he steered toward Daphne's trailer and heard booming music coming from several places.

"Hey, I know," he said. "What if I tell her the three of us need to go riding, talk over a little business? For that matter, we're home free if we can get her drunk—you can get in her purse, and when we bring her back here, I'll grab the plate off her car."

Nancy said nothing. It sounded like this was his problem, and it made him both angry and fearful after her threats. He was about to repeat his plan when he pulled in next to Daphne's little car and spotted his girlfriend on the tailgate of a pickup maybe fifty yards away.

"I'll be damned," Eddie Ray said.

Nancy didn't reply to this, either, but she followed his eyes and sat up straighter. Another girl was sitting next to Daphne. Several young-looking guys were standing there, all drinking beer, and one of them leaned in for a kiss. Eddie Ray, knowing Nancy was watching, felt a wave of shame wash over him when Daphne pulled the boy onto her lap and let him feel her up. He sighed as he cut the engine, thinking that the boy couldn't be more than fifteen.

"Damn, that TV's loud," Nancy said. "Coming from in there?"

"Probably her mother," Eddie Ray muttered. He slid out of the car and kept his eyes averted. If nothing else, the boy playing with Daphne's boobs would keep her and everyone else from noticing the Grand Am. "Be right back."

He kept his eyes downcast as he walked up to the trailer. He pulled open the flimsy screen door and stepped into the foul-smelling little place and looked around. There was Patricia in the easy chair with a bottle between her knees. The lights were off, but the TV was indeed wide open. Patricia's eyes, he saw, were closed—the sick woman was probably passed out. He didn't see Daphne's purse and crept down the hall to her bedroom. The lights were off back here, too, but Eddie Ray gambled that Daphne was too drunk or preoccupied enough to notice the sudden illumination in the back of her home. He flipped on the overhead bulb and looked around the small, messy room. It had the same stale smell as the rest of the trailer.

The purse was on the dresser.

Daphne didn't wear a fanny pack, so Eddie Ray was confident he'd find her pocketbook. He did, and a second later he had the driver's license. He latched the pocketbook and returned it to the purse, then set the purse back on the dresser. He switched off the light, thinking he'd been in there no more than half a minute, and came back down the hall. Patricia hadn't moved, and Eddie Ray eased out the door and down to the ground. Nancy leaned across the front seat and handed her BMW plate through the open window as he reached the Grand Am. He took it and went around behind Daphne's car. He hadn't thought about a wrench until now and wondered if Patricia even had one as he pried the rusted bolts with his thumb and index finger. But he loosened them all and was able to replace Daphne's tag with the much more expensive Beamer plate. He looked across the way before getting back in the Grand Am and saw Daphne with another boy on her lap. She deserved everything she got, as far as he was concerned.

"Your first visit to a trailer park?" he said to Nancy as he pulled onto the blacktop road that led back to the four-lane. Nancy was looking out the window, her big purse on her lap. Daphne's car tag and license were already in there.

"Yep. You said you lived here?"

"Just a few steps from where they were all sitting, actually."

"And that was her mother watching CSI? I could hear the dialogue."

"Ain't all there, sorry to say. Passed out, probably wouldn't have noticed if I'd shot bottle rockets in there," Eddie Ray said. "You made out pretty good, girl: got yourself a tag that don't expire till next spring, while Daphne better not run into a road-block 'cause she's got no license and a tag that probably costs a fortune, not to mention expires end of this month."

"How old were those kids?"

"I don't know, Nancy. Ain't lived there in a few years."

"How old's Daphne?"

"Twenty-one."

"Cradle robber."

"Real funny," Eddie Ray said. "Least she's legal. Think she saw you?"

"I don't think so. Pretty wrapped up in what she was doing." Nancy paused to light a cigarette and let down her window partway to release the smoke. "Look, I know you like her. But you're beating your head against a wall trying to make a girl like Daphne grow up and fly right. From what it sounds like, your mother's trying to do the same with Arnold Webber. And some people, Eddie Ray, just can't be saved. I'm not talking about in a spiritual way, either."

Eddie Ray turned onto the four-lane as he mulled this over. They would pass Wal-Mart and Pizza Hut and Sonic and McDonald's and a flock of convenience stores in the next mile before the highway narrowed again to two lanes. He wondered if Nancy was saying this from personal experience—maybe it came from dealing with Caitlyn, Sherry and other family members. Maybe men she'd been involved with, too. She sure was smart, no doubt about that. He figured he learned something just about every time she opened that pretty mouth of hers.

"I know," he said. His eyes shot to his speedometer as a police cruiser passed in the other direction. "Other girls out there, for sure. But if she's pregnant and I'm the daddy—"

"You sure she's even pregnant? Some girls not only lie about that, they lie about the miscarriage they didn't have," she said. "You know Daphne better than I do, but it's possible."

"Sure is."

"If you really want to know what I think, I see a girl who got real excited about having money for the first time in her life. She changed her tune real fast when Arnold Webber followed your mother home from that cruise, didn't she?"

Eddie Ray sighed. "That sorta puts everything in black and white, don't it?"

Nancy reached up and flipped on the dome light. Eddie Ray blinked and focused on the road as it narrowed to two lanes—now they were two miles from the cabin. He saw her hold the license up to the light. "She looks like Britney Spears."

"I can see that," Eddie Ray said. He wasn't about to admit how hot *he* thought Britney Spears was, and the huge turn-on Daphne's similar looks were in the beginning. "Got that blond hair, wears them big sunglasses and tank tops and jean shorts.

Sure don't have her bank account, though."

"The state of Mississippi doesn't take kindly to folks driving with three-year-old licenses," Nancy said as she threw her cigarette butt out the window.

Eddie Ray waited until an oncoming car whizzed past before squinting at the driver's license. Sure enough, Daphne hadn't renewed it in three years. He laughed when it occurred to him that she would have gotten a ticket for that, too. And Daphne weighed 145, not 120 like it said—

"Watch the damn road! And your turn is coming up."

He looked up and steered them away from the shoulder and back into their lane. He turned off the dome light and hit his blinker before slowing. The moon had gone behind a cloud, so it was even darker than usual out here. He could see specks of light across the lake but nothing on this side. He could get used to coming out here whether Nancy was with him or not. Be a great place to fish, that was for sure, and peaceful as could be with the trees and wildlife. Even if none of the other folks who frequented the camp ever spoke to him, well, he was used to that from living on Golden Drive. He'd still have his buddies at the sports bar. He turned in next to the BMW and saw Nancy shake another cigarette from her pack. She lit up and inhaled, holding the smoke in her lungs the way he and Daphne did when smoking pot.

"Want one?" she asked as she sent smoke out the window.

"Don't smoke unless I'm having a beer."

"I used to be like that. Then I started for real once we moved back up here."

"Your husband seems like a nice fella. Watch him on TV a lot."

"Let's not talk about him."

Eddie Ray berated himself. He'd just said something stupid, the same dumb way he offered to return Nancy's money in front of Blair. Was it nerves or just his nature? He'd gotten comfortable venting about Daphne in front of Nancy, since Nancy said a whole bunch of judgmental things about her. And he'd simply said he enjoyed watching her husband do the weather. Then something occurred to him: maybe Nancy *liked* him a little. A tiny bit, but enough for her to be uncomfortable talking about the husband she was cheating on. Maybe she would leave the TV star for him one day. Maybe pigs would fly, too, but he could dream.

"You think about your daddy much?" she asked.

This was a sore subject. But though he wasn't sure he could trust Nancy, it felt so natural to open up to her. Maybe one day she'd feel that way about him.

"I don't miss him. Never seemed happy unless he was laughing at someone else's suffering," Eddie Ray said. The question took him back to his early teens, when he became aware of how much his mother tried to please her husband. Blake Chester was a relatively stable man but just never seemed to enjoy life. "Now, my mama's real upbeat. I'm more like her. I feel bad for you, Nancy, both your parents being gone." He paused. "I ain't half as smart as you, but I'm pretty good at listening, if you ever need a shoulder."

"That's sweet," she said softly. She leaned over and kissed his cheek, which made him feel like a million dollars. Then she inhaled deeply from her cigarette and tossed the butt out the window. "Let's go in. Business to discuss."

He followed her to the cabin and started to give her cute little bottom a swat but thought better of it. She unlocked the door, felt along the inside wall, and turned on the overhead light. She stood to the side and let him pass, then came in behind him and closed the door. The air conditioning was still on, and it felt great in here even with the bad smell. He heard her lock the door and turned. She set the purse next to the couch and walked up to him, her gorgeous blue eyes never leaving his.

"I meant what I said about being a good listener," he mumbled.

This was designed to heighten any romantic notion she had. She didn't say anything, but she put her little hands on his pectoral muscles and squeezed. Electricity zipped through him. He leaned down to kiss her and expected her to back away, but she took his face in her hands and pressed her mouth to his. A voice in his head reminded him that they were here to discuss a *kidnapping*, so what was she doing? But the same hormonal fog from Saturday now had him in its grip and wouldn't let go. She pulled back, took his hand, and led him to the couch.

"Stretch out," she said. "And close your eyes."

He did. He was aware of the painful pressure in his groin but knew sweet relief was on the way. Could this actually be the business she wanted to discuss? Hell, would she want to spend the night with him? Not out here, of course, but maybe in a hotel room somewhere?

"Don't peek."

"I won't," he said.

He heard her rustle in the purse. Then he felt her climb onto him and settle on his waist. She was sitting almost directly atop his manhood, and in seconds those firm, full breasts would be in his face. Man, he could get used to this. If Nancy really did like him and Daphne turned out not to be pregnant, he'd get rid of Daphne the way he'd hurl a live grenade. The fifteen-year-olds could have her.

"You can look now."

Nancy's eyes, which Eddie Ray saw first, were just as cold as the barrel of the handgun which was two feet from him and aimed between his eyes.

FIFTY TWO

Keller didn't know where Patrick was and didn't care. Holly was asleep on an air mattress with her teddy bear and looked peaceful. He'd told Caitlyn before that he envied the way kids slept. One day they would say that about their own children, he knew. They hadn't discussed marriage or even joked about it, but Keller had no doubt they'd walk down the aisle. At the moment they were holding hands on the couch where he would hopefully spend just one more night. He'd described the meeting with Young and Blair and the paperwork he signed that allowed the psychological workup of his mother. Caitlyn's eyes suddenly bulged.

"Oh, my God," she said quietly. "I just put something really obvious together: Jeannie Hanson is married to Doug Cockrell, the home inspector. *They* watched Holly on Friday night."

Keller felt himself deflate. "You're right. The nameplate on her desk says Jeannie Hanson and so does her little badge. But I knew that and should have caught it, too."

"Well, this changes everything. That woman's a big social climber—married into the Cockrell family and kissed up to Mother the way Mother kissed up to Mrs. Brumley and that bunch, and she fawns over Nancy for good measure. But it's more than that. I know I'm right about Mother and Doug screwing Angie out of that fifteen grand on the appraisal."

"If *Nancy* had played college tennis and *her* coach bought a house, nobody would have been screwed on an appraisal," Keller said bitterly. "Wouldn't dream of doing that to the princess."

"Of course not. And you can't tell me Jeannie's in the dark about what her husband's up to. She knows all about what happened to Angie—she knows Angie's my coach—and she knows you and I are together. And you, love of my life, are the enemy through guilt by association. But hear me out: Vince—Doug's dad, of course—was Mother's attorney and would certainly represent Nancy. And you guys think Nancy may have been in your house tonight?"

"Possibly. Blair said he wouldn't rule it out."

Caitlyn whistled. "Is it possible Jeannie could have told Vince that the police took a statement from Holly, and Vince told Nancy, and Nancy really went looking for Holly?"

Keller looked at the sleeping child on the floor and turned to Caitlyn. "I'd kill Nancy with my bare hands."

"Well, she's safe with us and we know your mom's at the hospital. They're probably arresting Nancy at this very moment."

"But now I'm wondering if Dad's caught up in some stuff. Why else lie to his employees?"

"That bothers me, too, but I refuse to believe he's crooked. Give him a chance to explain."

Keller nodded. "At least he's coming home. One more day of taking Holly to daycare and dealing with Jeannie. She better not start with me tomorrow."

"Just remember something: the woman is a glorified diaper-changer," Caitlyn said as her voice took on a hard edge. "You nailed it about her overstepping her bounds Friday night by not calling you before taking Holly home. If she even looks at you the wrong way in the morning, call Clint Young with her standing there. We won't be bullied by these people, damn it."

FIFTY THREE

"I was beginning to think I could trust you," Nancy said slowly. "But I guess I was wrong."

Eddie Ray didn't dare speak, let alone move a muscle.

"You never answered about your floorboard, so I looked

while you were in that hideous trailer and saw your tape recorder." A mean smile colored Nancy's angelic face. "How stupid do you think I am, you blithering idiot? Especially after you sold me out to Henry Blair!"

Eddie Ray had never felt more foolish and ashamed in his life. He now had no doubt he was going to die in the next minute. She climbed off him and stood a foot away, the gun aimed between his eyes. He felt his erection wilt.

"I wouldn't have turned it in," he said. "I didn't even turn it on, just couldn't. I know you won't believe this, but I've always loved you and could never do anything to hurt you."

"I won't even dignify that with a response. The tape is in my purse, as is the money. Next time, moron, try a bank instead of your floorboard."

"Nancy, I was going to give it back. I told you that."

"Sit up."

"I'll do anything you want, I swear. Just please don't hurt my mama."

"Sit, up, damn you!"

He pulled himself up and kept his eye on her. She sat at the other end of the couch and pulled the purse to her. She placed the gun on the floor, keeping it within easy reach, and rubbed her temples. Now it looked like she was in some discomfort. After several seconds she exhaled and faced him.

"Here's the plan: You'll tell Daphne that y'all are about to come into some *real* money," she said. "When you and I are done, you go get her and take her to Wal-Mart for a pair of hospital scrubs. Light green."

"Okay…"

"Know where the hospital is?"

"I hand out towels in the wellness center, remember?"

"Then you know the daycare is on the backside of the facility—"

Eddie Ray felt his chest tighten. This was the kidnap info, and there was no getting out of it now.

"—you listening to me? Hospital's on the left side of the road, and you'll take the last driveway. Go straight back to the daycare area, which has gray double-doors. That's where you drop Daphne off." Nancy lapsed into a coughing fit. He thought she was about to vomit, but she gave her head a firm shake and faced him. "You'll wait in the car. Now listen to this part real carefully, Eddie Ray: Daphne needs to walk from there all the way to the front of the hospital. Out on the *sidewalk*, I'm talking about. Then she goes in and starts for the daycare, which she can find because signs are everywhere. With me so far?"

Eddie Ray nodded. He could easily picture Daphne in the green scrubs, her blond hair bouncing back and forth as she waltzed through the main entrance of Smart County Hospital. If she looked like she had somewhere to go, instead of glancing about the way she would in front of a skyscraper, she just might look convincing. But who the heck was she—*they*—going to kidnap, and why?

"This must happen at exactly 8:35," Nancy said. "You need to write that down?"

"Naw, I can remember."

"That's because the hospital staff has a meeting every morning at 8:30, managers only. Meaning the daycare workers themselves are in charge from then until nine, which is when the meeting usually ends. And Daphne will walk through the hospital, wearing her scrubs and looking like a nurse. Understand?"

"Won't she need a badge?"

"Not if she keeps moving. Just tell her not to stop for coffee."

Eddie Ray almost smiled. He said nothing.

"She'll come down a long hall and reach those double-doors where you dropped her off. The reason she'll walk all that way is simple: We don't want anyone seeing her in the kid area until that moment." Nancy paused. Her eyes were really intense now. "Picture yourself outside in your car, looking at those double-doors. The hallway inside runs east and west from your vantage point, and you'll see Daphne come into view from the east—your right—because she's gone all the way through the hospital. The fire alarm is right there, on the wall opposite the doors."

"She's gonna break the glass and pull it, like they do on TV."

"Nothing to break," Nancy said. "Tell her to make sure the coast is clear, pull up the little piece of plastic, and yank that lever. All hell will break loose, but the daycare director will be in a meeting halfway across the hospital. What you'll have is a bunch of scared teenage girls and old women who watch the kids, and a stampede toward the double-doors. I know because I've seen it happen."

"What, you did this before?"

Nancy coughed again. "Kidnapped someone? No. But I worked there two summers in high school. Same management, top to bottom, same exact way of doing things right down to the little routine the kids are in each day. You can make book on it."

"And Daphne's going to grab this kid you want?"

"Yes. But you're dead if your car is sitting there in the doorway, where it would be if you were driving a taxi and about to pick up a fare, understand? Those doors are going to burst open, and kids and adults will come running out in all directions. It won't take long before the workers have their act together—they'll be doing head counts. That's why it's important that you and Daphne agree on where *you'll* be when she comes out with the girl, so y'all can escape in that little window of confusion. There'll be plenty of places to park. But you want to be close to the double-doors, yet far enough away so that once Daphne gets the girl in the car, you have a clean way out."

"All right, I got all that. Who's the girl?"

"Holly Bryan."

Eddie Ray stared. He wouldn't have been more surprised if he'd been told to kidnap Britney Spears. He knew that Mr. Bryan ran the nice clothing store on the square, and that his wife had opened the bookstore a while back after teaching English for years. He didn't know them very well, but they were a heck of a lot nicer than most of the neighbors. He sensed that this had something to do with Caitlyn—Caitlyn dated Keller Bryan— although it might be for some other reason.

"You may think I killed my mother," Nancy said mildly. She'd turned her powerful gaze directly on him. "But although I can't prove it, Caitlyn did. And although Caitlyn has some powerful people behind her, I do, too. I have it on good authority that Holly Bryan saw Caitlyn push my mother in the pool that night, a few minutes before I got there. And that Caitlyn got hold of that information."

"But how in heavens would—"

"Y'all just bring Holly to me, and I'll get her out of town. To somewhere safe, so Caitlyn can't get her." Nancy rubbed her temples again and lowered her voice. "Because that little girl could put Caitlyn away a long time. Maybe for good. And Caitlyn doesn't want that, as you can imagine."

"But Nancy, she wouldn't hurt her! That's her boyfriend's little sister!"

Nancy's eyes flashed. "I tried to tell you Caitlyn isn't stable."

"I know, but—"

"So let me tell you again: She isn't stable, and she lost it Friday night. She thinks she's smarter than the cops, and she'll say anything to anyone and hurt whoever she needs to. Why? Because she thinks she can get away with it. She'll do something awful to that little girl—like throw her off a bridge—to save herself from arrest and prison. Then she'll cry her eyes out in front of Keller and his parents and jump right back in the sack with him and continue her sham of a life."

"All right, but if you know this hospital so well, wouldn't it be easier if—"

Nancy aimed a finger at him. He stopped his thought mid-sentence, the way he would if she whacked him on the wrist with a ruler. She took a long look at the gun before turning back to him. Eddie Ray understood exactly what she was getting at.

"You're right about one thing," she snarled. "You *should* have stayed in your yard Saturday morning and minded your own damn business. But you went marching over there hoping I'd spread my legs for you."

He reddened and looked away in shame.

"Goes without saying that Oakdale High will never name an academic scholarship in your honor," she continued, her voice radiating the contempt he knew she had for him down deep, "but you seem like a pretty nice guy. Thing is, Eddie Ray, you screwed me, and I'm not talking about our little romp on this couch. Then you were going to do it again, with that idiotic plan to tape-record our conversation and turn it over to the bubble-headed police chief. So you've dug yourself a pretty deep hole. And if you want to get back in my good graces, you'll do exactly as I say."

Eddie Ray felt hot tears in his eyes. "Okay. Just don't hurt my mother. Tell me where to bring Holly, and please don't do nothing to her, either."

"You have my cell number. Go north on 505, past Hampton Falls, and out to the interstate. Start north and call me. I'll be up that way, most likely meet you at the parking area five miles south of the Hernando exit. Holly knows me and won't be scared. Fact, just keep saying you're taking her to Miss Nancy, and Miss Nancy's taking her toy-shopping and then to McDonald's. It'll be fine."

Eddie Ray nodded. He knew he was in *way* over his head. But Nancy wouldn't hesitate to kill him and might really put a hurting on his mother if he didn't follow orders. And he understood why Nancy didn't trust him—she sounded almost hurt that he betrayed her. He still wanted to apologize even though she was throwing around threats like a mob boss.

"Oh, and your woman will need this," she said.

She dug into the purse and pulled out a designer pocket-book. It was about the size of the one Daphne owned but probably ten times as expensive, Eddie Ray guessed. She reached inside and grabbed a wallet-sized photo and handed it over. He wasn't surprised to see a picture of Holly Bryan. She was dark-haired and adorable. It made his heart ache to think of putting the sweet little thing in danger.

"Tell Daphne that Holly will be in the last classroom on the right, on the carpeted side of the hallway," Nancy said. "She'll make that long trek around the outside, enter through the front, and walk through the hospital until she reaches the double-doors. Then she'll set off the fire alarm. And tell her to start walking on that carpet toward the classroom—last one on the right, hear? That's where Holly will be coming from, and there won't be more than a dozen or so kids in that room."

"She grabs her then?"

"No. Have Daphne follow Holly outside and stay close to her," Nancy said. "Just make sure Daphne knows to *look* like she belongs there, like she's trying to help. Best-case scenario is Holly walking out the double-doors on her own, in the general direction of your car. But the second Holly looks like she's going to one of the teachers—or away from you, Eddie Ray—Daphne grabs her and whispers that she's taking her to Miss Nancy and toy shopping and McDonald's. We want Holly quiet, not yelling her little head off. And she absolutely can't get away from you guys. Got it?"

"Got it," Eddie Ray said.

"Let's recap: At what exact time does Daphne pull the fire alarm?"

"Uh, 8:35."

"What do you do once she and Holly are in your car?"

"Drive like a bat out of—"

"Drive *discreetly*, Eddie Ray," Nancy growled.

"Drive discreetly out to the four-lane, then start north to the interstate. Call you once we're headed north. We'll most likely meet you at the rest area south of Hernando."

"Very good. Now, once you drop her with me, take the back roads home. You do this right and you'll be way out ahead of the cops and won't have sheriff's people looking for you."

"All right, I guess," Eddie Ray said. "Then what?"

"Once I leave Holly with the folks who'll watch her, I'll come back to town. That's it."

She put the gun in her purse and slung it over her shoulder. He stood as well, realizing the meeting was over. He didn't know who'd drowned Sherry and why, nor did he care at this point. He would probably have nightmares about the kidnapping going wrong, or what Nancy might do to the little girl once Holly was in her clutches. But he'd interfered, as she pointed out, for the stupidest of reasons: sex. He'd fantasized about Nancy Rutledge most of his life and should have known that sleeping with her would come at a heavy price. And it had. It was the gift that might keep on giving for who knew how long. Nancy stepped up to him as if she heard his thoughts. Her eyes were like lasers.

"No mistakes," she said. "Sure hate for your mother to go broke. Or suffocate."

FIFTY FOUR

It had begun to rain, and Nancy toasted the dreary night with a can of Red Bull as she headed west on I-40 toward Little Rock. Daphne Kendall's license plate was affixed to the BMW, and the slut's three-year-old driver's license—the outdated model which prominently featured Daphne's social security number—was safely with Nancy's own license and credit cards. She'd stopped in Germantown, the area of Memphis she knew best, and bought supplies for the first leg of her journey. Not wanting anyone to recognize her, she wore sunglasses into the store and piled her hair under a Ralph Lauren ball cap. She planned to shave it and buy a bright red wig. Her huge purse, a gag gift she won at a party, was on the floorboard and contained the money she'd initially given to Eddie Ray. Her mother's gun was also in there.

Sherry's safe was in the trunk, next to the laptop.

She discovered it one night after her mother passed out following an especially heavy bender. It was in the closet of her bedroom and had been left open, amazingly. Nancy didn't touch it but made a note of what she saw inside, and the safe was the first thing she went for after Sherry sank to the bottom of the pool. She'd moved it to the BMW after confirming that the key which opened it sat right there in the lock. Only then did she call 911 and race across to Priscilla Hall's house.

Over $70,000 in cash was inside the safe.

So there would be no need to make multiple ATM withdrawals and leave a paper trail, since she had plenty of money to get started as she reinvented herself in a different part of the country. She would drive into the wee hours before finding a hotel for the night. And she would gleefully guzzle Red Bull and stuff herself with fast food, since she no longer had to watch her figure to fit into the formal gowns for the Brumley's ads that made Sherry Rutledge so proud. Now that she was leaving Oakdale for good, Nancy felt free from all vestiges of her mother, who was hopefully toasting to a nice golden brown on Satan's personal rotisserie unit.

The kidnapping of Holly Bryan was a ruse, as learning-disabled, love-struck Eddie Ray Chester would find out in the morning. She had no intention of harming the sweet young thing and in fact had a soft spot for her. Perhaps it was because she remembered all too well the signature look in her father's eye when *she* was only eight. But the rest of the family, Melanie included, could go to hell. Hopefully the e-mail she sent Melanie would screw up the happy household. And Caitlyn would pay with her life if she and Keller had set her up. Nancy didn't know how or when, but time was on her side. She would be back to Oakdale someday—incognito—to extract her revenge.

And take Keller with her.

In the meantime, the perfect alias had formed in her mind: Chesapeake. It was hardly a Southern name, but she'd also thought of a nickname and a middle name. She would be Chessie Rhea Edwards, which sounded plenty trailer-park Southern. That name and her new look and social security number would go on her driver's license, which she would manufacture herself.

It was the least she could do to honor dimwitted classmate Eddie Ray Chester.

FIFTY FIVE

Eddie Ray looked at the clock on the Grand Am dashboard as he idled forty feet from the gray double-doors of the Smart County Hospital daycare. It was 8:31. He cracked his knuckles and inhaled deeply from the cigarette he'd swiped from Daphne's pack. He wondered again what he was doing by trusting Daphne to pull off such a heist. There was still time to get out of Dodge, since she hadn't made her appearance and pulled the fire alarm. But Nancy would almost certainly go after an unsuspecting Monica Chester if he didn't deliver Holly Bryan a few minutes from now. There didn't seem to be another option, since Chief Blair was liable to arrest *him* if he crawled back to the police station and reported more threats from Nancy.

Daphne was with the same kids and totally inebriated when he arrived at the trailer park for the second time last night. She was disoriented when she awoke next to him in his mother's guest room and didn't remember a thing about last night, but he'd wrestled her into the shower and got some coffee down her throat while his mother and stepfather snored in the back bedroom. It took a while before she was alert enough to comprehend what Nancy wanted them to do, but she came on board when Eddie Ray lied about the small fortune Nancy would turn over to them at the rest stop. Daphne would blow her stack when she realized they weren't getting paid, but he'd decided to issue an ultimatum right then and there: If he was the father of her kid, Daphne was going to take care of herself, by God. If he wasn't the daddy— or if she'd lied about being pregnant—she would find another way back to Oakdale.

They'd gone to Wal-Mart and found her a set of cheap, clingy scrubs and headed to the hospital. Daphne, who hadn't noticed that her driver's license was missing, put on makeup and chewed gum so her breath wouldn't set off the fire alarm by itself. Then she started for the front of the hospital.

He checked the time again: 8:33.

It was interesting that at no time today had she mentioned the baby. Was it all a lie like Nancy said, a little trick to get her hot little hands on Monica's money? For that reason he hadn't felt a shred of guilt lying to her this morning, while he felt horrible when Nancy busted him last night over the tape recorder.

Nancy even vowed to harm his mother if this got screwed up. Yet he wished he could take her away somewhere, like to the Bahamas. He'd sure picked the wrong girl to fall for.

He heard a sound behind him and looked in his rear-view mirror. An ancient-looking man was driving a great big car and looking for a parking place. The geezer would probably spend ten minutes trying to save ten steps of walking. Eddie Ray looked at the dashboard clock again. Now it was 8:34. He took one more nervous drag and stubbed the cigarette in the ashtray rather than lowering the window and tossing the butt into the parking lot. The last thing he needed was a security guard walking up and giving him the business about littering.

There she was.

He sat up straight and felt his heart race. Daphne was inside the doors and standing completely still. What was she doing? He saw a woman pass her and head off in the other direction, back toward the hospital. As Nancy had promised, there was good parking on this side, and he had a clear view of Daphne and saw her look over her shoulder. The woman was almost certainly an employee and would remember Daphne's face. Maybe she asked Daphne who she was. Was Daphne about to come outside and tell him she couldn't go through with it?

But he saw her reach for something he couldn't see. An instant later an alarm sounded which jolted him all the way out here, inside his car with the windows rolled up and the air conditioning blowing for all it was worth. She'd just set off the fire alarm, and he saw her start off down the hall toward the room with Holly Bryan. He felt sweat at his temples and on his palms, even though the car's interior was cool and comfortable. So many things could go wrong as they abducted the little girl, and God only knew what might happen to Holly in Nancy's hands.

He still had time to escape, he knew.

And he was going to the police after all.

FIFTY SIX

"There you are," Jeannie Hanson said. "Need a quick word with you before the meeting, which I'm already late for."

Keller recognized the voice and grimaced before looking up. Hanson had mentioned the daily meeting at 8:30 when they talked in her office yesterday, so he'd made sure to bring Holly *after* 8:30 this morning. He'd even entered through a side entrance of the hospital to make sure he and Hanson didn't cross paths, and Holly grinned and waved at a whole host of smiling doctors and nurses they passed in the antiseptic-smelling hallways. The villain was nowhere to be seen when they reached the sign-in book on the dais next to the double-doors, and Keller scribbled his name, hustled Holly into the last room on the right, and was exiting the room when he saw Hanson.

Was she late for the staff meeting because she was waiting for him?

This was Vince Cockrell's daughter-in-law, after all, as well as the wife of a home inspector that Caitlyn was certain had done dirty business with Sherry and Nancy. He and Hanson were *not* on the same side, regardless of the concern she continued to mouth about his mother and Holly. He did his best to keep his voice light, but he knew the dislike and mistrust he felt for this woman was visible on his face despite his attempt at a smile.

"Morning," he said. "What can I do for you?"

Hanson walked over to him and lowered her voice. "I understand your mother was hospitalized last night. Can I ask why?"

Keller felt his chest tighten. Never mind how Hanson had gotten the information or exactly what she knew. His mother's situation was *none of her business* as long as his sister behaved while here. He thought of Caitlyn's suggestion to call Clint

Young and was tempted to do it. Holly had no idea that Mommy was in this very facility, and Keller would be damned if this nosy woman made her aware of it without permission from him or their dad.

"I'd rather not get into it, ma'am."

"I see," Hanson said. Now she looked displeased. "When is your father arriving?"

"I promised to put him in touch with you when he gets here, and I will."

"I take it you don't know. And in that case, it would definitely be in Holly's best interests—"

"You listen to me," Keller said. He closed the distance between them to two feet. "You back off right now or you're going to get yourself sued."

Hanson's eyes popped. She looked like she'd been slapped.

"I'm serious, lady. If you don't get off my back, I'll withdraw my sister right this minute. Then our attorney will pay the director of the entire *hospital* a visit and demand that they justify your totally inappropriate conduct Friday night."

"Excuse me, young man, but your mother asked me—"

"She did *not*," Keller said as a trio of male nurses in blue scrubs came into view. He knew they would sprint this way in a heartbeat at the first sign of an altercation but aimed a finger at the haughty woman nonetheless. "After all your noise about rules and regulations, you broke a bunch of them by taking my sister home yourself. And you did it so you and your husband could snoop through our house."

Hanson gasped and turned a brilliant shade of red. Then her eyes narrowed, and she looked as fierce as Nancy had at the duplex Saturday afternoon. "Young man, you will *regret* saying that—"

"If Holly doesn't behave up here, Mrs. Hanson, you let

me know. Otherwise, stay the hell out of our business, or you'll be doing well to wash dishes in the hospital cafeteria."

Keller almost couldn't hide a triumphant grin. He could tell that the male nurses had stopped and were listening, and Hanson, who seemed insistent on having the last word, was apparently so angry she couldn't manage a response. He couldn't have scripted a more effective comeback if he'd had an hour to rehearse—

The fire alarm went off.

Keller felt himself jerk at the furious blast of sound. It momentarily froze his decision-making capacities, but his nemesis turned, undaunted by the clamor, and darted around the corner. This shook him from his brief trance. Hanson was certainly headed to get the kids out of the building—or to safety if there was a fire or bomb threat—but Keller, even in this most extraordinary of circumstances, wasn't about to take the chance that Hanson might grab Holly and stash her somewhere before attending to whatever had happened. He went sprinting after her.

This wasn't going to become one of those Lifetime social worker moments.

FIFTY SEVEN

Eddie Ray started to floor the Grand Am but jammed on the brakes just as quickly. The old fool in search of a parking place eased past right then, and Eddie Ray would have plowed smack into the man's car if he'd moved. So he was still in his spot, even though his bladder was now pounding at the prospect of disaster. He thought about the advice his daddy gave him long ago about bullies: Stand your ground and fight them off, or let them walk on you and live your life looking over your shoulder. Blake Chester was proven right over the years, and throwing a punch—even when it led to a butt-whooping—let it be known to those around Eddie Ray Chester that he wasn't to be messed with.

Problem was, Eddie Ray was being bullied by a woman.

Nancy Rutledge had money, power, and carried a gun, too. Worse, he had feelings for her and had made some awful choices because of it. But what if he stood up to her? There were law offices around town, those little buildings with three or four names on them. It might take barging right in there and asking some dumb questions, but for crying out loud, this woman had already asked him to lie to the police and was now strong-arming him into kidnapping an innocent little girl! He didn't know how the legal system worked, but there had to be one of those pony-tailed types that could help him, maybe be alongside when he went back to Chief Blair. The chief might not be so hostile if he returned with a lawyer. That gave Eddie Ray some hope, especially when the old man's car finally started to clear his line of sight.

The double-doors burst open then, and the alarm was even more ear-splitting. He could only imagine what it sounded like inside the building. As Nancy promised, adults and kids began streaming out...and there was Daphne holding Holly Bryan's hand. She'd done it! For a brief instant Eddie Ray pictured them handing Holly over to Nancy at the interstate rest stop after all. Then a stroke of genius hit him and actually brought a smile to his face: They would tell the little girl they were taking her to see Miss Nancy—

And drive to the police station instead!

He and Daphne would bring Holly inside and ask for Chief Blair—or Officer Clark if Blair wasn't there—and explain what was happening. That would sure fake Nancy out, since she was half an hour north of town.

But he saw the panicked look on Daphne's face in the same moment he realized his girlfriend was leading Holly *away* from the Grand Am. What was Daphne doing? He couldn't exactly honk at her, and now he really felt scared because kids and adults were everywhere—it might be hard to get out of here with everyone milling around in a panic. Suddenly a guy in blue scrubs came running out and grabbed Daphne's arm. He spun her like a rag doll and got right in her face.

Had he seen her set the fire alarm, and for that matter, had he seen her take Holly?

This freed the little girl, who covered her ears and looked all around. Eddie Ray felt waves of guilt that nearly paralyzed him. He'd followed Nancy's instructions and sent Daphne to kidnap the poor child, and now Holly was standing amid a sea of kids and could easily get hurt. It occurred to him to leap out of the Grand Am and run over to her, as if saving her from *Daphne*.

Then he saw Keller Bryan.

The boy looked like a handsome young superhero sent to save the day as he dashed to his sister and scooped her into his arms. He turned and spoke to the man in blue scrubs while aiming his index finger at Daphne's chin. Daphne didn't even try to argue and simply looked at her shoes.

They were busted.

Eddie Ray threw the Grand Am into gear and stomped on the gas, knowing he couldn't sit here and wait to get arrested after Daphne rolled on him. And as he did, he noticed one more horrible sight.

The old man in the huge car, who perhaps didn't hear the alarm and might not even see all the adults and kids, was *backing* his car toward Eddie Ray, like he somehow knew Eddie Ray was about to bolt and planned to claim that very parking space. There was nowhere to go but directly into his car.

And no chance at all to stop.

FIFTY EIGHT

Scott Perry was flipping through his reporter's notebook when his cell phone rang. He grabbed it from his belt and punched a button. "Scott Perry."

"It's Zack. Where are you guys?"

"Leaving Mike and Nancy's neighborhood," Perry said as his photographer pulled onto the highway. "Nobody came to the door, garage is closed. We'll see if she's at the real estate office, although I doubt it with visitation today—probably at the funeral home. By the way, the attorney is Vincent Cockrell. Has a law firm couple of miles from here. Thought we'd run by there now."

"That's fine, Scott, but I need you to run to Smart County Hospital, since you're already in Oakdale," the news director said. "Report of a fire alarm on the scanner and a big car crash in the parking lot. May be nothing at all, but it sounds like chaos over there. See what's up, then get right back on that will."

"You got it," Scott said. "We'll keep you posted."

FIFTY NINE

Keller and his father were standing in the kitchen of the home on Peachtree Street after he'd situated Holly in front of *Cars*. James had several days of beard growth on his face as well as a dark look in his eye. Keller could tell that his pop knew something was bad wrong: His wife's purse and keys and the security system keypad cover were still on the floor, right where she left them before apparently traipsing down to Sherry's house to swim. It wasn't lost on Keller that he and his mother had faced off in this very spot three short nights ago. He could see the patio through the window and the pines beyond, and while everything looked the same, he sensed that a chapter of his life had ended.

His childhood was over.

"Talk to me, son," James said. "What happened while I was gone?"

Keller had grown up thinking that his parents were totally infallible, the way all kids did, he figured. Over time he'd learned that not only did adults make mistakes, they made some hideous choices. But his father was a good man. And he looked and sounded sane. Keller, as he'd promised Caitlyn, would let him speak before passing judgment.

"You first, Dad," he said. "You left Mom a note saying you went to Chicago on business, but you told Mr. Barksdale you took us there for a week-long vacation. So why don't you tell me what this trip to Gatlinburg was really about."

James Bryan nodded. Something told Keller that his dad was about to admit to an affair. He braced himself.

"I did something I shouldn't have six years ago," James said quietly.

"You cheated on Mom?"

"Yes," he said with a sigh. "Now, before I get into this, is Melanie out for a walk or down the street visiting? When I talk to her I'd like it to be one-on-one."

"We'll come back to her. Go ahead."

James frowned. He clearly wanted to ask questions but thought better of it and nodded again. "It was one time, with one person. Six years ago, not last month or anything. Nothing's going on now, and nothing with this person has happened since or will ever again."

"Does Mom know?"

"I don't think so. But this person convinced me she was intent on breaking up our marriage. She finally gave me an ultimatum last week, right before the holiday." James paused. "And I did a very cowardly thing: I ran."

"You took your gun with you. Unless Mom has it."

"It's in the truck." James didn't say anything for a long moment. Keller felt him gearing up to spill his guts. "It took me a few days, but I'm ready to come clean and confront this person," he said as he made eye contact again. "I know you're going to be very upset, as will Melanie. All I can do is ask your forgiveness. And I understand, son, that you—and your mother—may not be willing to give it."

Keller felt his heart thudding in his chest. Here it came.

"It was Nancy Rutledge."

Keller reached behind him and gripped the kitchen counter when his knees weakened. It was *true*, just like his mother said at the park, even though Melanie Bryan was clearly out of her mind and might not have been aware that her son was sitting across from her that morning. Keller realized he might not ever know if Nancy had discussed anything with his mother in the last few days, but he was willing to bet everything he owned that she did.

"It was the day Nancy left for Jackson," James continued. "She came by the store, said she was leaving town. Asked if I'd go out to the cemetery with her. Said she hadn't been able to make herself go yet and knew she needed to before she left. Understand that *nothing,* to that point, had ever been said or hinted at, Keller. I swear to God I never for an instant imagined what might happen—"

"I loved her," Keller whispered. He felt anger building in him like strong winds ahead of a storm front and clung to the knowledge that Holly, who might be without her mother for a long period of time depending on what the doctors said, didn't need to see her brother and father at war. "It doesn't matter if I was just thirteen, Dad. You *knew* how I felt about her. Remember what I saw through my telescope right before Jack died? Nancy, sobbing in that tree house, as she held a razor blade to her wrist.

Remember me crying my eyes out in front of you? Or have you just conveniently tried to forget?"

James Bryan sighed. It was a long, slow sound that radiated deep sadness and utter exhaustion.

"Of course I remember," he said. "I'm sorry, son."

"*Anybody* but her."

Keller thought of his mother as this popped out of his mouth. She'd said basically the same thing at City Park on Sunday morning, as if she was somehow trying to make the point that James had hurt her *and* Keller by having a fling with Nancy. If there was any point in trying to dissect what came from Melanie's mouth over the weekend, of course.

"I'm truly sorry, Keller. I don't know what else to say."

"You could have walked away."

James looked for an instant like he was going to argue. Keller knew he'd hit a nerve and imagined his father insisting, as Caitlyn surmised, that Nancy may have blackmailed him into it—she might have threatened to go to Melanie, Sherry, and everyone else regardless of what happened at the cemetery. And while that was sure possible, Keller didn't want to hear it. He would do his best to forgive his dad, but right now everything James Bryan had ever taught him about honesty and courage seemed pretty flimsy based on his own actions once push came to shove that day.

"Yes I could," James said. "And I didn't. I accept full responsibility for what happened, and all I can do is apologize. I've spent the last six years living in fear that this would come back to haunt me. Dreading it, honestly. But I'm going to lay all my cards on the table with your mother. Then I'll sit down with Nancy. In fact, I may talk to Sherry, too, because—"

"Sherry's dead," Keller said. "Drowned in their pool Friday night."

His father's mouth fell open. He looked like his knees

might buckle, too.

"Not only that, it looks like Nancy's going to be arrested. She pushed her in."

"*What?*"

"As best we can tell, this was around 8:30 Friday night. Caitlyn and I had gone to Tupelo for supper," he said. Now certainly wasn't the time to get into the Nancy-and-Brad stuff. "*You* were gone. Mom, I found out late that night, had gone out—where, we have no idea. Jeannie Hanson Cockrell, the daycare director, brought Holly home and was watching her till Mom got in. Doug was here, too. Holly showed them my telescope and let them look through it. And Holly went back up to my room later, on her own, looked through it again, and managed to see Nancy shove Sherry in the pool."

"Oh, my God."

"Holly told me, I told Clint Young, Clint Young told Chief Blair, and two plainclothes police officers came to the daycare yesterday and took a statement from her. I was there."

James bent at the waist and covered his mouth. He looked like he was going to be sick and seemed to be in great pain when he straightened up and stood at full height. But he steeled himself and refocused his gaze on his son.

"Good lord," he said softly. "Now please tell me what's going on with your mother."

"She's hospitalized. I'd rather let the doctor explain."

"Son, tell me what's going on with her before we go."

Keller didn't want to get into this with his father because he didn't know where to start, let alone how to put a succinct diagnosis on Melanie Bryan's behavior. He looked away.

"Is she physically hurt?" James asked impatiently.

"She was admitted to the hospital with a concussion. They think she was beaten and raped." Keller turned to his father and stared as he said this, hoping to convey that none of this would have taken place if James Bryan, head of household, was here like he was supposed to have been. "And something else happened. Might be a nervous breakdown, I don't know. But she was completely out of her head Saturday night, and I'm not sure she knew who I was at City Park Sunday morning. So I took Holly with me. We didn't see Mom again, and she didn't answer when I called her cell a bunch of times. The police found her last night." Keller paused. There was so much acid gurgling in his stomach he thought he might be sick. "Caitlyn asked if there was any history of mental illness or medication on either side of the family. I told her there wasn't, as far as I knew. If you know different…"

A cornered look appeared on James Bryan's face. Keller felt his heart sink.

"Oh, no. What did you guys not tell me, Dad?"

James rubbed his forehead with his hand. If he'd thought about ending his life in the mountains of Tennessee, Keller thought, he probably looked a lot like he did now. But Keller didn't feel a bit of sympathy for him.

"Your mother has been on anti-depressants since college. There was a suicide attempt back then, before we met," he said quietly. "We almost didn't get married. We were days from the wedding when she disappeared after an argument with her parents. They felt I needed to know her history, and she said it was in the past and wasn't my business. When we found her, they told me everything with Melanie sitting right there. She was furious and initially said the wedding was off."

"For God's sake! Why on earth would she not want—?"

"She's very sensitive about it, son. It's a deeply personal thing." He held up a hand when Keller tried to interrupt. "You asked once if she was going to die. Remember that, before we opened the bookstore? That was right before we went to the doctor and he put her on a new medication. As far as I know, there've been no more flare-ups since then."

"Well, there was a great big flare-up, as you call it, this weekend. She was talking crazy and smoking one cigarette after another and guzzled a ton of vodka!"

James looked like he'd been punched in the stomach. "Please don't tell me she was drinking. She knows she's not supposed to. Mixing alcohol with what she takes—"

"Mom passed out in a lawn chair on the patio Saturday night. I stayed here and read to Holly in her room for two hours so Holly wouldn't see her like that. Then when she was asleep, I went out there and scooped Mom into my arms and carried her up the stairs to bed when I couldn't wake her up."

"That much alcohol could kill her!"

"How the hell was I supposed to know?"

"Daddy," Holly called out immediately from the den. "Keller used a bad word!"

"I'm sorry, Holly," Keller replied to her, gearing down his voice as much as he could. "I won't do it again. Watch the movie, okay, sweetie?"

"This is getting boring, Keller."

"Just a few more minutes, okay? Dad and I are almost done." He turned back to his father. "I don't believe what I'm hearing. Mom has been on medication for twenty years and I wasn't supposed to know? That's just great! What, you guys just *hoped* nothing would happen while you were on the road three or four times a year for a week at a time? You just *hoped* nothing would happen once I moved out and it was just her and Holly?"

"Your mother felt very strongly about it, and I didn't feel it was my place to override her."

"What a copout." Keller stepped close to his father. His heart was pounding and his adrenaline flowed at the prospect of punching his dad's lights out. "I don't know who I'm angrier at," he said in a fierce whisper. "Caitlyn, who the police actually thought *killed* Sherry initially, sat in our dining room that night in high school and spelled out to you guys exactly what she takes and why. And Mom held her hand and looked her in the eye and told her how brave she was and didn't say a bloody thing about her own medication. What a freaking damn coward."

"Now, look, son—"

"Oh, you're no better. Congratulations on finally getting your courage up to tell the truth—about six years too late! While you were sorting your feelings and communing with nature 500 miles away and completely unavailable by cell phone, I was signing a power of attorney to assume guardianship of Holly because I wasn't sure I'd ever see you and Mom again! Hope you enjoyed your little hiking trip."

James bit his lip and looked at the floor. Keller backed away and took a deep breath, trying to settle his stomach and calm himself down.

"I'm not going to the hospital with you," he said hoarsely. "You can do that by yourself. I'll stay here and watch Holly."

"I understand," James whispered. Keller sensed that his old man was deeply wounded by what he'd said and could use a hug in the worst way. But he started for the den and spoke over his shoulder.

"Stay as long as you want," he said. "But I'm gone the second you get back, and don't call me for any reason for a good, long while. I'll get in touch when I'm ready to talk. I'm sure you can relate to that."

SIXTY– A YEAR LATER

Keller and Caitlyn were at Stan Earle's house, a sprawling old place with a basketball goal mounted on the roof of their driveway for his oldest son, who was six-four. That was no surprise because Earle was the size of Paul Bunyan. The big man was athletic, too. Keller's jaw fell when he dunked the ball after his youngest daughter pestered him. The couple's four kids ranged from ten to sixteen, and all were enamored with their celebrity half-sister. Keller felt his eyes water when they asked Caitlyn to autograph newspaper clippings and university basketball programs. As always, she was happy to do it.

The one uncomfortable moment of this initial visit had come when Earle's wife asked Caitlyn where she went to church. When Caitlyn explained that she was Catholic and was Keller's sponsor as he converted as well, the woman's eyes clouded over. But Stan Earle absolutely frosted her with a glare—he looked like he would drop-kick his spouse all the way to Oakdale if Caitlyn walked out because of religious intolerance. Keller had told Caitlyn moments ago that the glare was just as genetic as the size Earle passed along.

Caitlyn looked relaxed, though. Earle did, too, when he brought glasses of sweet tea to the picnic table under the oak and said to yell if they needed anything. Keller sensed that Earle knew his daughter and her fiancé wanted to compare notes, and that Caitlyn needed a few minutes to decompress before continuing the visit. That was a good sign, as was the fact that Earle and his family appeared to be decent, honest folks. Ripley was half an hour away and about the size of Oakdale, and it sounded like Earle had built up a nice windshield repair clientele and carpentry business despite his lack of formal education. The kids sure were polite.

"We can stay as long as you want," Keller said. "Or if you want to go, we'll tell them we're having supper with Dad and Holly and need to get on over there."

"I'm okay so far." Caitlyn smiled across the table at him. She was tanned and lovely in the navy and white dress he'd purchased for her twentieth birthday. "Thanks for coming. I know you're bored to death. But I couldn't have done this without you."

"I've enjoyed it," Keller said. "Holly and his youngest would have a big old time together, if you want to come back at some point."

"I could handle that. Maybe before school starts." Caitlyn smiled and waved at the little girl, who was watching them from forty feet away. She was quite the talker, and Keller figured Earle had told her to give them some space, that the two guests would come back and play in a few minutes if she let them catch their breath. "He's been nice. Said he's glad we came, and I don't think there'll be any pressure about anything."

"Good," Keller said. "I didn't think he'd smother you after all this time. Although he'd send that turnaround-jumper of yours into about the eighth row."

Caitlyn laughed. Then her smile faded. "We talked about your mom. His mother has Alzheimer's and is in a facility near Jackson. He and his wife sat down with the kids a couple of years ago and said their grandma wasn't going to get well. Gave them the choice of not going any more if they didn't want to, so they could remember her the way she was. Told him I thought that was very humane."

Keller nodded and thought of his mother. She was in a coma when James Bryan reached the hospital the night he returned from Gatlinburg. She hadn't awakened since. She was legally drunk when admitted the night before, Melanie's doctors told him, and had taken enough Xanax to kill herself. James and Keller were in agreement that she hadn't planned to commit suicide—a breakdown of some kind was taking place, and she clearly wasn't thinking straight when she drank and popped pills that weekend. Keller confided to Caitlyn that it remained easy to blame his father for not being there to help his spouse at the first sign of trouble. James, though, was living in his own private hell. Keller could see that each time he was around him. He'd never shared his suspicion with James that *Nancy* may have had something to do with his mother's coma, but he would always wonder if Nancy had met with Melanie that awful holiday weekend and slipped her something. They might never know: Nancy, who vanished without a trace, was wanted for Sherry's murder. Keller figured she'd left the country.

"And I was waiting for the right moment to tell you this," Caitlyn continued. "Angie's really leaning on me to leave school early and go pro. She thinks I could start for any team in the league at this point, and she doesn't want me getting hurt and my stock dropping. I admit she has a point…"

Keller smiled when Caitlyn trailed off. "If you're burned out, I sure don't blame you. You've spent as much time on drills and games the last seven or eight years as any tennis pro that ever hit the proverbial wall."

"It isn't that," she said softly. Keller mopped his brow with his tea glass and let the droplets of condensation fall across his face. It was no less humid in Ripley than in Oakdale, but there was a measure of shade under the oak and a gentle breeze blew. It was quiet, too: the Earles lived on a dirt road with the nearest neighbors a quarter mile away. "I'm just not sure I want to go pro at all. I love playing SEC ball and going to school here and being with you and your dad and Holly. But I absolutely do *not* want to move to New York or Los Angeles or even Houston. It's not a fear of being able to compete at the pro level—I know I can hold my own against those girls. It's a fear of…well, you know. Being away from home and cracking up."

"Caitlyn, if it feels right to go directly into coaching after you graduate, do it and don't look back. The hell with everybody who doesn't understand."

"Thank you, baby. I love you."

"I mean that. You could coach here in Ripley or some-where, and I could learn windshield repair from Stan Earle," he said, gesturing toward the house with a grin. "Or work full-time for Phil and Gina instead of part-time. Phil's making noises about retiring soon."

Caitlyn gave him that wonderful smile. "I can see you owning that store, you up there each day and your dad across the street running the clothing store. And me, maybe, coaching hoops at Oakdale High. Boys *and* girls," she said with a wink. "That'd be fun."

"You'd start winning championships like Bud Crisler did. Oh, speaking of the store, Phil called. He and Gina just finalized an event for October with some children's author from Colorado who's made a big splash. Has a goofy name: Chesapeake Rhea Edwards, I think. Her publicist told Phil she just couldn't wait to come to Oakdale. I'm sure they say that to everyone, but Phil's real excited."

"Good for him."

Keller sipped his sweet tea. "Mom always said the store was nothing special without author appearances and unique books, and we've got plenty of time to prepare. Told Phil I'd do whatever I could to help, including handing out flyers to everyone in this part of the state."

"I will, too," Caitlyn said. "Even come up there to work that day if need be. In an unofficial capacity, of course, so Angie and I will continue to have clean hands with the NCAA."